TILL THE END OF TOM

Till the End of Tom

AN AMANDA PEPPER MYSTERY

Gillian Roberts

 BALLANTINE BOOKS · NEW YORK

A Ballantine Book
Published by The Random House Publishing Group

www.ballantinebooks.com

Library of Congress Cataloging-in-Publication Data is available from the publisher upon request.

ISBN 0-345-45492-8

Manufactured in the United States of America

9 8 7 6 5 4 3 2 1

First Edition: December 2004

Book design by Julie Schroeder

This book is dedicated to the two people who have consistently made my life of crime a delight: Jean Naggar and Joe Blades, whose official titles are agent and editor, but who are so much more than that.

Acknowledgments

Many, many thanks to:

—punsters Suzanne Proulx and Owen Edwards, for dreaming up the title for this book and for appearing in it as well;

—Jo Keroes, Louise Ure, and Marilyn Wallace, the trio of wonderful writers and friends who read *Tom* in its various stages and provided invaluable feedback; and

—Shirley Wetzel, whose review of *Claire and Present Danger* inspired part of this book's plot.

TILL THE END OF TOM

One

My mind was on Steinbeck; my foot was on a hand. I screamed.

No one responded, most definitely not the man on the floor.

I had wanted to escape the headmaster's annual interminable address to the student body. Neither his ideas nor his words had changed or improved over the years I'd heard them, and when I reached the limits of my endurance, I fabricated an excuse.

Put more precisely, I lied. "An emergency," I'd whispered as I made my way out of the auditorium.

A new wise saying: Be careful what you fabricate, because I turned the corner and there he lay, a certifiable emergency, crumpled and inert at the foot of the wide marble stairs, a thin halo of blood around his head.

He was face-up, looking surprised, as well he might be, given his position and the fact that his right cheek was indented, as if it had buckled.

My mind finally activated. I pulled out my cell phone to dial for help, although the man seemed well beyond any.

I saw movement out of the side of my eye, and turned quickly, fearing another shock, but it was only Mrs. Wiggins, the school's most recent—and again unsuccessful—attempt to find a competent secretary. She tiptoed out of the office, not exactly racing to my rescue. In fact, she approached so slowly that she was close to moving backward. She stopped altogether when she was a few feet from me.

I reached the 911 operator. "This is Amanda Pepper," I said, "a teacher at Philly Prep." I gave our address and the situation and ended the call.

Mrs. Wiggins remained as immobile as the man at the bottom of the stairs. "What—what—" she said, shaking her head as if to negate the evidence of her eyes. "What—"

"Please—go to the auditorium. Tell Dr. Havermeyer to keep everybody there. Explain what's happened."

"Who—do you know who that is?" Her voice was a hoarse whisper.

"Better hurry. The assembly's nearly over."

She shook her head again. Maybe she had a degenerative disease. "I'm not supposed to leave the office." She sounded the way a rabbit would, if it could talk. "I'm not even sure I should be out here, because what if the phone—"

"Mrs. Wiggins, this is an emergency." You had to spell things out for this woman, basic, primitive things, and although our recent rapid turnover of school secretaries was not a good situation, I couldn't help but hope it would continue, and that the Wiggins era was nearing its end. "I think this man's dead," I said as patiently as I could manage. "A lot of people are about to burst in here—police, paramedics, I don't know who all else. The last thing anybody wants would be several hundred adolescents converging on this spot."

"Police? But—why? Is this a crime? Do you—did you see something? Somebody?"

"They have to be called for accidents, too." I waited. So did she. "Go, Mrs. Wiggins. Hurry!" Even Havermeyer's seemingly endless drone, "Musings on the Possibilities of Life During and After High School," ultimately concluded. "Hurry!" I said. "Do you want the students to see this?"

"Well, maybe you could—I could stay, and you could go tell—"

"Mrs. Wiggins! You're his secretary." I didn't care if that made sense. I had gone AWOL from assembly and didn't want to underline that fact. Besides, she was such a nervous, distracted creature that if I left her as sentry, she'd amble around the poor man and inadvertently ruin any evidence there might be.

She blinked, nodded, and moved toward the auditorium.

I searched for a pulse without disturbing the body. I wasn't sure what I'd found, possibly only my own fingertips' pulse, but he was still warm. I fumbled in my purse for a mirror to hold to his mouth. Meanwhile, I studied him, trying to figure out who he was and why he was at Philly Prep, let alone on the floor in this condition.

He was—or had been—an attractive enough middle-aged man. He had dark hair with the slightest threading of gray and regular strong features. He looked to be in his forties or early fifties, and seemed surprised to be found in such an undignified and awkward position, one leg bent to the side, the other heel still on the bottom step, his arms flung wide as if, coming down that expanse of staircase on his back, he'd tried to brace himself and failed. But the hands that failed had been well tended. No calluses that I could see, and the nails were buffed and clean.

His suit, rumpled and twisted as it was, nonetheless spoke of expensive fabric and expert tailoring, and his feet were shod in beautifully polished Italian-looking soft black leather.

How had he gotten in without attracting notice? It didn't say much for school security, but aside from that, why would a man like this go upstairs? Everyone was obliged to be in the auditorium, so no one would have made an appointment with him for that hour. Maybe he was a parent who hadn't been informed of the assembly or who misunderstood the time of an appointment with a teacher or counselor.

I could understand Mrs. Wiggins looking horrified by the man's fall, but not her questions about who he was. She should have recognized him because he should have stopped at the office as the large sign by the front door requested. He looked like a man who followed the rules—at least, the easy ones.

Before I could find my mirror, the painful whine of a siren interrupted my search and speculations, and I gladly relinquished all further inquiries to the police and paramedics.

"Alive," a paramedic said, and though they were already working at warp speed they upped the tempo, even while the officer in charge directed the forensic people to photograph the man and the area. Then he went over to stare down at the man as he was put on a gurney.

"I did it." Mrs. Wiggins's whisper startled me. "I did as you said. Dr. Havermeyer wasn't happy about the situation, but he understood. You were right. He's holding the assembly awhile longer." She turned, frowning.

"Who is he?" I asked her.

"You're asking me? Why?" Her eyes were coffee colored with, at the moment, the white showing all around them. "How could—why would you say such a—why would I?—what do you mean?"

She looked as if she might faint, but I didn't take it to mean much because she looked like that a lot. Mrs. Wiggins was not a woman who delighted in surprise or change. I wondered, not for the first time, what Mr. Wiggins was like. "You're the school secretary," I said. "And visitors have to sign in. He's a visitor, right?"

She paled. I watched her lips half-form syllables, then go slack again, so that only airy wordlessness emerged. There goes another job, she had to be thinking. Correctly, I hoped. We had metal scanners at the doorway, but did we need an actual guard at all hours? Even if the man had burst into the school and refused to make the slight right turn into the office to identify himself, Mrs. Wiggins would have seen him pass. The person at the desk could see the base of the staircase. If he'd refused to comply with the request to register, she could have—should have—called the police.

Unless, of course, Mrs. Wiggins—she had never offered a first name, and the more I knew her, the more I doubted that anyone had ever been on a first-name basis with her, including Mr. Wiggins—unless Mrs. Wiggins hadn't been at her desk when this man entered.

"Please," she said. "I—I can't lose this job. I've had hard times. I—don't tell, please?" Her shapeless body compressed, grew wider and closer to the ground in a near-cringe, as if she expected me to hit her.

Or as if too many people already had hit her.

The "hard times" registered, but still, asking me to "not tell" sounded like we were in playschool. We were here as guardians of the students' safety, and it was painfully obvious she'd failed to even say "yoo-hoo" to the stranger. "What is it I shouldn't say? Who is it I shouldn't tell? Why didn't you sign him in?"

She looked pathetic, colorless, timid, and terrified, and I knew I should consider what evil forces had forged this pitiable creature. However, compassion sometimes seems too much of a psychic effort.

I wanted an answer. And maybe the right to get angry about that answer because whatever its cause, her failure to stop the visitor—not precisely a world-shaking or difficult job—had potentially endangered the school.

"I just . . . I must . . . I wasn't feeling well, and I had to . . . you know . . . he must have come in while I was . . . *you* know. In the ladies'? You won't tell, will you?"

There was no possible response except a sigh and a headshake. I wouldn't tell—but I wouldn't have to. The police and the headmaster would ask her the hard questions directly.

So I stood at the side, listening—I hoped discreetly—even after the man had been rushed away and the crowd had thinned.

I listened as the forensics guy walked up and down the staircase, taking pictures and making notes. The remaining officer did, in fact, ask Mrs. Wiggins what time the man had entered, and what he'd said his purpose was.

The secretary looked ever more pitiable. Rashlike patches erupted on her cheeks. Her shoulders grew rounder, her stance more like a whipped dog's. She stammered, blushed, and shook her head. "I am so sorry," she whispered. I saw the glint of moisture on her lashes.

To my disgust, I felt a frisson of compassion. She looked devastated. Normally, there's a student assistant to cover for her if she has to leave for a moment. And normally, Dr. Havermeyer's nearby as well. But during the Annual Address, the pitiable school secretary had been flying solo, and if nature had called loudly enough . . .

She wrung her hands, and she used every euphemism known to mankind for needing to use the ladies' room.

The police didn't seem overly concerned. Events appeared to be unfortunate, but not criminal, an apparent accident, and not an illogical one, as the staircase was not only made of marble, but long—actually two flights in one. Very showy, and perfectly designed as a grand family entryway when the school had begun its life as a pretentious private home. Built for the family's servants back then, and the choice of most of the students and faculty these days, an ordinary, wooden normal-scale back staircase served the everyday needs of the building.

"And you found the victim?" the officer asked me. He identified himself as Owen Edwards. I knew I wasn't supposed to have such thoughts at a time like this, but it nonetheless registered that he had TV-cop looks, not real-life cop looks. That I noticed this proves how shallow and frivolous I am, but in truth, his chiseled features made the situation feel even more surreal. I had to control the urge to scan for hidden cameras.

Maybe I let my noticing go on for too long, but he started to look familiar. "Haven't we met before?" I asked before I could censor myself.

Really wrong thing to say. He backed up as if he expected me to foam at the mouth.

I explained that I was engaged to C. K. Mackenzie, who'd retired from the force earlier in the year and who was now a full-time grad student in criminology, and that I'd been introduced to Officer Edwards at some police-associated function not that long ago. The iron-jawed mask relaxed into an actual smile. He took the time to make mild and unoriginal fun of a guy who'd been a homicide detective for years finally deciding to find out about crime, and I nodded and acted as if nobody else had ever made that joke, and then we both returned to our assigned roles.

I explained about literally stumbling over the man. "I don't recognize him," I said. "Doesn't mean he couldn't be somebody's parent, but I've never seen him at a conference or open house here."

"No students named Severin?"

"Not in any of my classes." I looked over at Mrs. Wiggins. She would have access to the complete student list.

Her face was as blank as one with the normal complement of features can be.

"Mrs. Wiggins. Do you recognize the name Severin?" I asked.

"Why?" She looked at me, then at Owen Edwards, stymied, then back at me.

I tried to speak gently. Maybe she had a learning disability. "The student list—could you check it out for that last name? Maybe the list of applicants, too, if there is a list this early in the year."

She slowly turned toward the office.

"She looks in shock," Owen Edwards said. "Might want to keep an eye on her."

"I'm afraid that's her normal expression and level of responsiveness. So the man's name is Severin?"

"Tomas Severin," he said. "Ring any bells?"

A gasp from behind me. The name had rung for someone, though it had not tolled for me.

I shouldn't have been surprised by the gasper's identity. Maurice Havermeyer, master of Important People's Names, had broken free of his assembly. "Not one of *the* Severins!" He sounded as if he were having trouble catching his breath. Then he looked at me. "Singing," he said.

"Excuse me?" The singing Severins? A show business family?

"I have the students singing the beloved classics."

"Ah. Of course." As if I was worried about which activity he'd selected to keep them confined. As if I might challenge his pedagogical choice. As if the students cared at this point—they were not only free of Havermeyer and his lecture, but they weren't being asked to return to their classrooms, either. It didn't get much better than that.

"That should amuse them," he added.

Actually, it did get better than that, once you factored in Havermeyer's musical taste. Given that music—who liked which group, which track, what type—was a near obsession among teens, a way of judging and ranking each other, an index of where one belonged on the social scale, and given that Havermeyer's "beloved classics" were songs from operettas no one had staged in half a century, I was no longer sure anybody was at all amused.

"Is he—was he—" the headmaster asked.

"He was alive," the officer said. "Unconscious, but he still had a pulse. Possibly comatose. Can happen like that with sudden acceleration of the head."

It sounded as if Severin's head had bolted and raced downstairs on its own.

"He seems to have gone down headfirst," Edwards said. "Back of head on the stairs. That's a pretty sudden stop at the bottom."

"But . . ." I didn't finish my question about how his cheek had come to be dented. Edwards wouldn't have known its cause or said if he had.

Maurice Havermeyer shook his head. "Terrible if—tell me, did he have an *h*?"

"Excuse me, sir?"

"Did he have an *h* in his Tomas? On his driver's license?"

Owen Edwards regarded Maurice Havermeyer silently before he double-checked his notes. "No *h*."

The headmaster sighed loudly, as if the lack of an *h* verified his worst fears. "It's *the* Tomas Severin, then," he said. "Ever since the first one came over without the *h,* they've kept the original spelling."

"Sir?"

"The first Tomas Severin arrived on these shores shortly before the Revolution. They are a most . . . one of Philadelphia's finest families." He came close to choking over the words. If there was one thing Maurice Havermeyer knew, it was who had money and position in the City of Brotherly, but not Egalitarian, Love. There was speculation that Who's Who in Philly had been the subject of his dissertation for his offshore doctorate.

"Very low profile," he continued. "They don't parade their name around because they don't have to. A behind-the-scenes kind of dynasty. Started with manufacturing things people need, but don't notice. Nails, bolts . . . The company had their name for a long time, then it was S.M.F., as in Severin Metal Foundries. They were also S.C.I.—as in Severin Construction International. They were Alta—that means high, you know—Publications . . ." He sighed and shook his head and his skin looked as if it had mummified since he entered the front hall.

"Why *were*?" I asked. "Why past tense?"

"In the eighties, Tomas Severin got involved with the Internet and online marketing quite profitably, and in the late nineties, right before the bubble burst, he sold the entire shebang. Some foreign country owns everything now. He, of course, made a new fortune."

Officer Edwards was visibly impressed by my headmaster's knowledge. Of course, he had no way of knowing that the lore of rich folk was all the man stored in his brain. Except, of course, for nonstop speculation as to how any of this information might affect him. Now, I could almost read the thoughts lurching from one to another of his synapses, all of them lugging the same dire message.

One of *the* Severins had been badly hurt. He might not live. Therefore, the school staircase was in for a Big-time Lawsuit. And then—I could almost hear him pulling the thought through the narrow corridor of "How does this affect me?" until he reached the stuff of Havermeyerian nightmares: The school would close down. After all, what parent would keep a child in a school this unsafe? My headmaster's face gave in to gravity, every part of it sagging, even his eyebrows.

Lost. *Lost.* The words nearly keened themselves, and ghostly echoes bounced off the marble staircase. Lost, lost. The man, the prestige, the child, the tuition, the endowment, the school.

WHEN THE OFFICER and technicians were all gone, and classes were about to resume—not a prospect I relished—I returned to the auditorium. The music teacher, Veronica Wenda, a woman who always looked shocked at where her melodic dreams had led her, gamely poised her two hands in the position of a conductor, and said, "And next, 'Tea for Two,' which was such a hit in *No, No, Nanette.*"

The students were beyond hooting and hissing. They were nearly as comatose as Mr. Severin had been. Lunch followed by Havermeyer followed by Operetta's Greatest Hits combined with Indian summer had just about done them in.

I caught Veronica's attention and whispered that it would be all right for students to return to their scheduled classes now. She nearly wept with relief.

After several more minutes of predictable delaying tactics and honest questions such as which class were they to go to, I shepherded my flock out and up to my classroom. The odds were heavily stacked against accomplishing anything resembling teaching, but if we could simply keep the peace until the day ended, I'd consider it a win.

My thoughts about Steinbeck, so dramatically interrupted by Tomas Severin, had concerned *East of Eden,* which the seniors had been reading and enjoying, despite their usual objections to long books. We'd had a fine and thoughtful discussion based on a quote from the novel:

> ". . . I am certain that underneath their topmost layers of frailty men want to be good and want to be loved. Indeed, most of their vices are attempted short cuts to love. When a man comes to die, no matter what his talents and influence and genius, if he dies unloved his life must be a failure to him and his dying a cold horror."

I thought of that quote now, and the animated and heated debate we'd had about the meaning of evil, of what shaped a man and determined his kindness or malevolence. I'd been thinking about those words when I stumbled over Tomas Severin. Now, the words and idea belonged to him, and I considered the rest of the quote, which suggests that a person should choose his course of action so that his dying "brings no pleasure to the world."

May it be so, I said of the stranger.

We had moved on in class to another discussion based on the inequities between the Cain and Abel-like sons, and I'd assigned a nature-nurture essay, due today.

The official question had been whether people were born programmed to be the "good son," whether who you became was a matter of luck and life events, or whether roles were assigned within the family and then became the person's personality. Or, of course, all of the above.

I'd have thought they would try to use the morning's events as an excuse to talk about anything but the assignment. I would have understood. But the Steinbeck novel had hit a lot of hot buttons, which shouldn't have surprised me given that we were a school designed for young adults who couldn't function satisfactorily in the larger school system. These were kids who'd been in trouble in some way, hadn't performed as desired, children who were not fulfilling their parents' dreams and ambitions. They were more than ready to air their not very buried sense of being treated unfairly, or of being assigned—or thinking they were—the role as the family goof-off or worse, the bad child. I wondered if they ever had a chance to talk about this at home. Maybe their papers would speak for them—if their parents read their work.

We talked through the remainder of the period, I collected their papers, and the day was done.

I didn't see it until then, until I went to the window for a literal breather before I set out for my second job at the PI firm. That's when I spotted a Styrofoam cup, the sort used for take-out coffee, on the sill.

An innocuous object, yes. Except that there was no logical reason for that cup to be in my classroom.

I had unlocked my office door that morning onto a room free of any take-out cups. I hadn't brought any in with me, nor had any student broken the rules and come to class with food or drink.

That brought us to the point where we all trooped downstairs—every single teacher and student—for the god-awful assembly.

And then the return to the classroom, en masse, and not a one of us carrying coffee that time, either.

And yet, there it was on my windowsill.

Only one person I knew of had been upstairs while I was not, and he was in the hospital now, fighting for his life.

I looked at the cup, afraid to lift it, although Styrofoam didn't seem the sort of material that would hold fingerprints. There wasn't much left inside—an inch or so. I bent over and sniffed. Not coffee. It had a faintly flowery scent, and it was pale. Herbal tea.

Tomas Severin, drinking tea in my classroom. I imagined him coming upstairs, checking his watch as no one was here, then coming into my room because it was the closest to the staircase. I pictured him looking out my window at the square.

Biding his time, or on the lookout for someone?

And then—something interrupted him and made him forget his tea, leave it behind.

A lot of information from a take-out cup except how a man got from drinking from it to lying, near death, at the bottom of the stairs and why he was here in the first place.

Two

I started out for the offices of Ozzie Bright, PI, walking slowly, as if weights were attached to my feet. I considered driving, but it was only a few blocks away and parking was next to impossible. Of the two difficulties—moving my body or being unable to get rid of my car—moving was less infuriating, so I trudged on.

"Loooong day," I said when I entered the upstairs offices. Ozzie nodded agreement, as if I'd been commenting about his day, not mine. He was one of the least communicative of men, and, surprisingly for an investigator, one of the least curious. Naturally, he didn't ask for clarification.

Happily, Mackenzie was still there. We're both moonlighting here, theoretically a team, working together. However, since my after-school free hours are mostly the hours he's in grad school, we wind up working together—separately. I was glad today was an exception so that I could tell him what had happened.

He listened dutifully, showing his first real interest when he heard that Owen Edwards had been one of the officers. He asked about him, said he'd give him a call, and then he listened some more.

"Fell down backward—headfirst," I said, touching the back of my skull as illustration.

One of Mackenzie's eyebrows raised.

"What?"

"Odd way to fall. I mean you can't have been starting down the stairs and tripped, and you can't have simply not been paying attention—or it isn't likely."

"His cheek was—something had happened to it." I hated remembering how crumpled he'd looked on that side of his face. "You think he could have rolled? Bruised the back and front of his head? It's a huge staircase."

"Guess anything's possible, but to break a cheekbone would take pretty serious direct force, wouldn't you think?"

"A separate injury? Before the fall?"

He winked, and smiled and said, "That isn't my job anymore." Then he got up and poured himself Ozzie-coffee, a brew unto itself. He held up his cup and mimed an offer to pour me some, but I'd rather lick highway tar, not that I could tell one from the other.

"He was in my room. Do you think he came to see me?"

"Why do you say that?" Mackenzie resettled at his desk. It was a mess of clipped stacks of paper and one loose sheet he'd been working on when I interrupted.

"There was a Styrofoam cup on my windowsill, a take-out cup with what smelled like herbal tea in it. Hibiscus, maybe—a flowery smell. Nobody else could have put it there."

"Really?"

"Why the surprise? We were in assembly, nobody was upstairs and—"

"Didn't mean that. Meant two things: the position in which he fell, and the broken cheekbone. A fatal injury—"

"He's unconscious, not dead."

Mackenzie nodded. "An' we're hopin' he pulls out of it completely and soon. But my experience is that an immediate coma like that . . ." He shrugged again. "Something's seriously hurt in there." His focus or attention drifted into a private space elsewhere.

"And?"

"He looked to be normally fit?"

I thought about the well-tailored suit, the carefully polished soft leather shoes, and tried to remember the body within them. "Trim. Looked like he consciously stayed in shape, yes."

"What would it take for somebody to rush him when he's at the top of that staircase? Why wasn't he more alert? Why couldn't he fend the person off—or move to a safer place?"

"Especially when nobody's there."

McKenzie raised one eyebrow again. "Maybe."

"And the take-out tea? You think the man was drugged?"

"Manda, this is pure speculation. Impure speculation, in fact. And not my job or yours. He'll wake up and say what happened. Meanwhile, I've got actual work to do. The kind that pays bills."

"The cleaning people," I said. "That cup."

"You didn't throw it out?"

I shook my head. "My wastebasket's mesh, and it would have leaked. I was too lazy to go dump the tea somewhere. I knew the cleaning people would take care of it."

He tilted his head. "Maybe you want to call the school? Just in case it's relevant. Tell them not to—"

"The janitors don't answer the phones. I'd get the message machine." I checked the time. "Havermeyer and Mrs. Wiggins are gone by now, too."

Mackenzie wasn't interested. He muttered something that sounded suspiciously like, "That isn't what I do these days." His new mantra.

"See you later," I said without further explanation. "I hope

I'm in time." I'd think of the race back to school as much-needed aerobic exercise.

He knew precisely where I was going and why, and while he didn't wave me on or encourage me, he didn't try to stop me, either. I took it as a definite maybe and left the office before Ozzie with his slow reaction time could even ask why.

I half wished somebody would have cried halt before I bolted through the streets, my briefcase flapping across my side, knowing with each step, with each startled and annoyed pedestrian who moved aside for me, that I was in pursuit of a quarter-filled Styrofoam cup of cold tea.

At least the weather was with me, the air almost warm, but managing as well to have an edgy whisper of winter lurking around the corner. It felt the way crisp new-crop apples taste, sharp and winey-delicious, and each breeze suggested that I enjoy it while I could, because its days were numbered.

Enjoyment did not mean galloping clumsily the way I was. It did not mean sweating and gasping for breath at the back door of the school, the door for which I, along with the rest of the faculty, had a key, and it did not include racing to the front staircase and up it, gasping.

I nearly crashed into Ms. Liddy Moffat, custodian. Ms. Moffat takes her role of caretaker—of the school and of the earth— seriously, and seriously takes care, with a proprietary concern for both. Ms. Moffat also has core convictions about waste, meaning what is allowed to be discarded and what is not. She is fond of reclaiming objects she declares "misplaced." The fourth morning of my first year at Philly Prep I'd found a note on my desk. It said: *Rejected. Too nice to be trash. Somebody else could read it. Sincerely, Ms. Liddy Moffat.* The note sat atop a Xeroxed copy of a poem by Wordsworth. "Waste not, want not," she wrote another time. Those words sat underneath a mostly-used-up lipstick tube someone had chucked. "Anybody in this school ever hear about recycling?" read a series of messages accompanying empty cola cans.

I have nothing but admiration and respect for Ms. Liddy

Moffat, a woman who loves her work and excels at it. At the moment, however, I dreaded her efficiency and eagle eye. Even she didn't save Styrofoam cups.

"Whoa!" she shouted, "Nobody allowed in this school after—" she squinted, stepped back, and said, "Miss Pepper! Sorry. I thought you—"

"Ms. Moffat," I said, catching my breath. "Have you cleaned there yet?" I gestured to the right, to my room.

She sucked in her bottom lip and looked down at her feet, shod in red high-top sneakers. "Meant to, but I'm behind schedule. That chemistry lab, whew! No offense, but some kids are pigs. Not to mention the mess from this afternoon."

"The man's fall?"

She nodded. "Scuff marks and blood! Look at that! Just look at that!"

To my relief, she was pointing not at blood, but at scuff marks, souvenirs of Tom Severin's finely polished shoes, on the landing, just in front of her red sneakers. "How does a man make marks in a place like that?" she asked, rhetorically. She seemed equally appalled by the mess and its unrecyclable nature.

"So you haven't gotten to my room yet—that's great! I left something."

"You shouldn't have worried. You know I never throw things out by accident. I'm a careful—"

"Anybody would throw this out. Even you."

"Real trash and you want it back?"

Explaining why I coveted a Styrofoam cup with the remnants of somebody's tea would take too much time and ultimately not sound that much saner, so I smiled my gratitude and knew I'd given her "this-place-is-crazy" material to discuss with the rest of the maintenance crew.

The cup was still on the windowsill. I contemplated it, wondering what I should do next and how stupid I was going to feel when it turned out to contain nothing more than cold tea made of flowers.

But I have felt stupid enough times to not worry that much about feeling that way again, so I carefully covered the cup with a piece of paper, put a rubber band around it, and then just in case forensics could retrieve fingerprints from Styrofoam—and in case the prints were relevant to anything—I wrapped yet another piece of paper around it, and carried it to my car where it fit, with a little jiggling, in the cup holder.

I drove to headquarters filled with a sense of purpose that dissipated the moment I spoke with an actual human being who in no way shared my excitement over my find. I explained myself, the cup, my reason for bringing it in, then I reexplained, and then explained one more time. One of the principles of teaching is making your point three times. First, you mention the idea you're about to present, then you say your piece, and finally, you sum up what you've said.

That doesn't always hammer home the message in the classroom, either, so I'd seen his brain-dead-but-breathing expression before. "Honestly," I said, "I'm not a crank. If you get this to Owen Edwards—he was there this morning—and tell him I found it in my classroom, he'll understand."

The red-haired officer was passionately disinterested. "Let's see," he said. "You're reporting a cup you found." He had a checklist of categories of crime, and he read it through for a second time, his lips forming each item as he noted it. It named theft, aggravated assault, vehicle theft and the like, but obviously didn't have an entry for "cup, found." "You with Town Watch?" he asked. "Is that it? This is a littering offense?"

"I don't get it," I said. "Am I not supposed to do this?"

"Well, in fact, we have people—trained professionals, that is—who examine the crime scene and decide what's important and what isn't."

"It was an accident scene. They examined it. My classroom wasn't part of where the accident happened."

There was no indication that I was making sense to this man. The officer sighed and I had time to reconsider the situation:

Slightly disheveled citizen brings in old tea because maybe it's a clue in what has been declared an accidental fall down the stairs, which makes the concept of *clue* irrelevant.

I was lucky to have had all that practice at looking foolish.

"See," the cop said, "most people, they find something they think's important, a knife, a gun, mostly—they call the cops. Then we know how to handle it."

"It would have seemed a waste of money to have them come all the way to the school when I was on my way home and could drop this off."

He nodded wearily. "But the crime scene—you've messed with it now. You've moved evidence."

"It wasn't a crime scene—it was my classroom, and about fifty kids were in and out of it before I spotted the cup." I took a deep breath and tried one last time. "Owen Edwards was there. Philly Prep. You could check. Tomas Severin fell down the staircase. He's in a coma."

"Severin?" He scratched his ear.

"Right. Today. Two o'clock, thereabouts. There's got to be a report—there were investigators and detectives, and—"

"I didn't hear about any school crime today . . . Damn kids get their hands on guns and—"

"It wasn't that kind of thing—"

"Knives?"

"He fell down the stairs." I had said that, hadn't I? Several times?

"So a guy falls down the stairs and that makes this thing, this take-out cup—important how?"

"The way he fell was odd—"

"Police told you this? They asked you for this?"

"No. They didn't know—I didn't know—"

"But you—on your own—decided that cup might be important." He didn't actually laugh, but neither did he work hard to hide the vast, official derision that made his eyebrows rise till they formed an upside-down "V" over his nose.

"There might be something in it."

"You said that already, and you're right. There's some kind of fancy tea in it." He smiled and I knew what was coming next. I also knew why he probably hadn't been promoted to something more intellectually challenging than filling space in this spot.

"I don't mean sugar," I said. "The man's cheekbone was broken, but he fell on the back of his head, and—you have it there. I wrote everything down." I pointed at the lined paper sitting under the covered cup.

He looked at my notes without interest, but I suppose he'd had enough of me by now. "Okay," he said with the air of one dealing with the seriously learning impaired, "you've been a good citizen, and we appreciate it."

"You will contact Officer Edwards, won't you?"

"No problem," he said soothingly.

"And they'll send it to forensics?"

"You watch a lot of crime shows, do you?" He smiled.

I bit at my top lip. Do not react, I told myself. Had quite a battle with myself over that and then, because I knew I was losing the war, I did react. I switched tactics from earnest to bullying. "You've got the name, right?" I asked. "Severin. Tomas Severin. Unconscious, maybe in a coma from his head wounds. And yes, he's part of *that* Severin family, so odds are the family's going to be more than a little upset and quite able to express it if you, I mean of course, if we—miss something as important as the idea that he was drugged." It was difficult delivering my little speech with the passion due it, mostly because most likely there was nothing in that cup that didn't belong there.

The red-haired officer blinked and scowled, afraid to ask who *that* Severin family might be. "Edwards, right?"

"Right," I said, and he swiveled somewhat away from me and spoke into a phone, making hearing him as difficult as our limited space allowed. "Yeah," I heard. "Yeah. Pepper. Right. Really?"

"Wait a sec," he said when he was finished with his conversation. "You can hand it to him yourself."

I was surprised, but pleased that at least Owen Edwards seemed to think the cup might be significant.

Perhaps he did, but something else had propelled him down to where I was. He took the cup, thanked me, then said he'd walk me to my car.

"Thanks," I said, "but that's not necessary. I'm—"

"Right," he said, continuing to walk with me.

Once we were outside the building, he stopped walking. "A minute?" he asked. "About Tomas Severin?"

I waited. I had the uncomfortable sense I was being studied.

"He died." He paused, watching me again, waiting for something.

I didn't know what to say. It was terrible, in the way all sudden, needless death is terrible. But Edwards obviously expected a response, a reaction. "I—I'm so sorry," I said.

A hint of a frown creased the skin between his brows. I had failed a secret test. "And you still say you didn't know him, right?"

I'd answered that question at least three times this afternoon. "That was the first time I saw the man."

"Yes, but did you know him?"

If he hadn't had a relationship with Mackenzie, I would have let the full force of my annoyance out. I'd been an exemplary citizen, bringing in possible evidence and this man behaved as if I'd lied about something as irrelevant and simple as having known the man who fell down the stairs.

But he was Mackenzie's friend, so I took a breath and simply said, "I did not know him."

"Had you perhaps spoken with him?"

He wasn't that close a friend of Mackenzie's and I was losing my temper. "If I'd spoken with him, then I would have said I knew him. Or at least knew of him. The man at the bottom of the stairs was a total stranger."

He watched me with the intensity of someone trying to translate a new and mispronounced language. Then he looked away for a moment, stared at the traffic going by before turning back to me. "I know you're good with words—they're part of your profession, right? So I need to make this absolutely clear.

You never met him, never spoke with him, but—did you in some way have contact with him, or with, perhaps a secretary of his?"

"Officer Edwards . . ." I was pretty sure we'd been on an Amanda and Owen basis earlier in the day, but that was now ancient history. "I don't know how to make it any clearer. He was a total stranger. I never spoke to him. I never spoke to a secretary of his. Not to his mother or father or cousins. I don't have any idea why you're asking me these questions, either. I tried to do a good deed—dropping off the cup. What is this about?"

Once again, he did the overlong stare thing, then the look to the side; then he pulled a small piece of memo-pad-sized paper out of his pocket. "Because of this," he said. "Or, actually, because of the paper this is copied from." He passed the paper to me.

It read: *Calls—Amanda Pepper—Philly Prep.* There was also a small doodle that looked like a smile, and a *7* or it could have been a boat. I didn't think that was the part agitating the officer.

"This doesn't make sense," I finally said. "And where's it from?"

"It was in a notebook he had in his back pocket. We didn't find it till he was at the hospital."

I wanted him to stop looking at me that way, searching for a crack in my hardened-criminal armor. All I did was shrug and pass the paper back to him. "It doesn't even read properly," I said. "Shouldn't it be *call* me? Not *calls*?"

He wasn't interested in its grammar. "You wouldn't mind going over your exact whereabouts this afternoon, would you?" he asked. "From, say, the time you led your class to assembly to our arrival?"

"Oh, please! You can't for an instant believe I had anything—"

"Of course not," he answered politely. "Now, if you could begin with your class going into the assembly . . ."

Three

B y the time I got home, I'd simmered down. I was fairly certain I wasn't about to be taken away in leg irons. Nobody had even said Tomas Severin's death was anything but accidental. And, as I told myself several times, Edwards was only doing his duty.

Still, I admit I was shaken by the existence of that note. Perhaps it explained why Severin had been in my room, but not really because it made no sense. It was all I could think about.

I realized I could either drive myself crazy or busy myself with something else. Being an English teacher means never having to worry whether or not there's work to be done. There always is.

I thumbed through the seniors' essays. The novel had definitely touched them, and some papers were amazingly and painfully honest. It always shocks me when the generally guarded, self-protective teens allow a glimpse of their most personal selves, and it reminds me of how much so many of them need a confidante and friend, or simply a listener. Sometimes, an English class essay subs for a shrink.

From Cara: "My grandmother is like their father. She's always angry, and she told me I was born bad. I don't think that's fair, but if she's so sure I'm that way, then I don't care if I am that way . . ."

From John: "What does Steinbeck mean? Kathy seems doomed by something inside her. Her parents don't think she's bad, didn't tell her she was bad, and didn't favor somebody else the way Adam Trask is with his boys—so does this mean people really can be born evil?"

From Zachary: "When your parent doesn't like you, it hurts all the time and then it makes you mad because it shouldn't matter if your parents are divorced. They shouldn't be divorced from you, too."

From Amelia: "Parents can say the other child isn't the favorite, but maybe they don't even realize it, but the favorite child knows, and so does the one who isn't the favorite. When I'm a parent, no matter how I feel inside, I will never let my children think I love one more than the other."

Some of it might be adolescent hormones speaking, based on nothing, but I knew that most of it was honest evidence of a deep well of sorrow. And it was always there, ready to be tapped. I have a project I'd love to develop, a play called *Listen!* We'd use the actual words of these essays and others like them, though we wouldn't use any real names, and we wouldn't have any child reciting his own words. We'd invite the parents—maybe we could commandeer them. Order them to attend. Maybe it would make a difference if they really listened, and really heard. Or am I too much of an optimist?

I hoped the other set of papers would be less depressing. The ninth graders had been asked to write a page explaining an activity they knew well—anything they knew well—so that someone who didn't know the topic would now understand it.

I felt the cat eyeing me, and then he jumped onto the table and settled on the pages. "Share," I said, and with a green-eyed stare, Macavity allowed me to pull a few pages from under him while he shed on the rest.

I flipped through the ones I'd extracted. The first few eased my fear that they'd all have picked obscene or otherwise objectionable topics. There were some things my students knew well that I had no desire to know about. But they'd written about making cookies, playing soccer, babysitting, daydreaming, watching TV, bathing the family dog, and playing tennis. I silently apologized for doubting their integrity and sincerity, and thanked their desire to pass English.

I had not overestimated their ability to write, however. "To make a delicious cookie you need a lot of things, including flour and butter and sugar, many times lots of sugar. And an oven. Some of the cookies I like to eat I don't know how to make, like Fig Newtons, but I could probably learn, and at Christmas time, I like to make the ones with the sprinkles—red and green, the ones when I was a little kid my mother left out for Santa, which is when I asked the first time if I could make cookies, too, with her. So you start the oven, and—"

Happily, the young woman had never expressed a desire to become a cookbook writer.

Unhappily, composition is a reflection of the writer's thought processes. After years of attempting to unsnarl student sentences, I'm not sure it's possible to teach clear, communicative thinking without first doing a pedagogical brainwash. If we could get in their heads and clear the underbrush and put up road signs pointing straight ahead, teaching composition, i.e., teaching thinking, would be a cinch.

I spent too much time trying to restructure—and to explain why that was necessary—sentences such as: "It is important that you smell a lot, too, especially for burning." I was therefore relieved when the phone rang and I had a legitimate excuse to take a break.

Mackenzie said he needed to be at the library awhile longer, so he'd be a little late. That worked for me, too—those papers took hours to grade. He paused, then asked, rather delicately, "Was the tea still in your room?"

I explained its adventures, the redheaded jerk at the desk, the cryptic note, and Owen Edwards' suspicion of me. I don't know why I bothered. I knew what he'd say—the truth, the obvious, the thing I already knew. "He's only bein' a good cop and checkin' it out. You'd do the same. That's a weird thing to find in his back pocket."

I knew that. That didn't make me feel better.

I said we'd eat whenever he arrived, pledged my eternal devotion in the usual manner, as did he, and we hung up.

I put the phone back in its cradle and saw, to my dismay, the word *message* in the little box. I had no idea how long it had been silently trying to alert me, but I regarded the time of not knowing as the lost Eden. A day that had already included a full complement of adolescents, one dead man, and a cop who thought I was involved in the death had satisfied my daily anxiety requirements. I didn't need what I suspected was behind that word *message*.

We no longer have a machine that blinks and does everything but shout out the news that somebody phoned. Now, I have to lift the receiver and listen for an annoying sound or bend over and look at the tiny window on the message box. I therefore consider the process optional and I ignore the phone's environs for as long as possible, especially these days, when things have reached a point where I'm relieved when messages turn out to be from telemarketers.

But I'd looked at the little box. I knew I had four messages. Now I was culpable.

Every muscle in my body tightened to near spasm. I knew what was ahead. Four variations on a theme—arias from a very limited repertoire—the opera-in-progress called "Amanda's Wedding." We were ten weeks away from W-Day, with nothing resolved, and that seemed to unhinge my mother, my future mother-in-law, and my sister, Beth, now referred to as the Wedding Witches, the Marriage Mafiosa, the Bridal Bullies, the Nuptial Nags—you get the idea. Their questions and worries were endless, to the point where I often wondered how they'd filled their days before I'd rashly announced a date.

Macavity yawned mightily from atop the essays. "There's a definite advantage to being a neutered male and ineligible for any sort of wedding," I told him. "Also, in no longer knowing your mother."

He blinked and went back to sleep.

Yesterday, my mother had informed me about what she called the "blitz-diet"—guaranteed to get me into sylphlike perfection for my wedding day. She was on it, as was Beth, and therefore, so should I be. Until then, I was feeling fine about my size. I forget what it was she said I had to eat, but the call made me so anxious, I wound up devouring all the ice cream in the freezer, and I don't think that was the magic fat-dissolving food.

This go-round, my mother wanted to know precisely how many people would be on the guest list, what proportion of that number would be allocated to the parents of the couple, and was there some ratio between relatives and friends of the parents of the couple? This was a small dig at the size of the Mackenzie contingent—eight siblings and assorted step and foster siblings, all married, and who knew how many aunts and uncles.

She reminded me as well that my folks were now Florida residents. They therefore had many friends down South, including the entire condo association, of which she was secretary, an elected office. True, I didn't know them, and they didn't know me, but "a wedding is a bringing together of communities," my mother patiently reminded me.

Until recent days and the endless phone calls, I'd been blissfully unaware of the big picture, of the now-obvious fact that my private life was of enormous import to the greater world and that my nuptial decisions had major meaning and possible reverberations. "Not that the condo people would come—leaving Florida for Philadelphia in December is insane," my mother continued. "But all the same—"

We could create an invitation that said "If you promise not to attend, you're cordially invited," and drop them from a helicopter on all of Florida. I was afraid to even joke about that. My mother was too likely to think it was an efficient way to handle the problem she was creating.

She explained her many Floridian contacts and reminded me of cousins-of-cousins, and third cousins five times removed who were closer to home, and therefore more likely to attend. "Of course I'll see you next week, but if we can take care of this beforehand, it will be much better because—" I fast-forwarded to the next message, skipping her inevitable closing line, "After all, you only get married once."

My sister Beth was next. She, at least, hadn't suggested that I needed to lose weight before the wedding, only that she did. Her calls generally included progress reports or laments over no progress on her scale. "Listen," she now said, "I have a lead on a place with a spectacular room—all stone and a huge fireplace and it would look stunning in December with evergreens and lights, and the only reason it's available is that somebody had it reserved, but they haven't confirmed, and the deadline's approaching, so they apparently aren't taking it. It'd be gorgeous. A little pricey, but absolutely stunning, and after all, you only get married—"

I skipped ahead again. The trio's messages always gave me a headache and further confused me with urgent, urgent decisions to be made, none of which made particular sense. I envisioned them cackling over who'd bombard me with what question next as they stirred the cauldron in which they were boiling me.

The third message was from my future mother-in-law, a self-declared honest-to-goodness witch. The good news was that she wasn't interested in dieting. Other than that, there wasn't so much good news. Although she'd married off a small army of people already, and I'd have thought she'd be blasé about the event, she seemed at a fever pitch of excitement about marrying off her lone bachelor son. I think she also said that she'd see me next week at the shower, but I wasn't sure. When she's sufficiently animated, I can barely understand what she's saying.

She'd told me that the mothers of grooms were supposed to do only two things before the wedding: keep their mouths shut and wear beige. At the time, she'd laughed loudly at the very beigeness of the idea, as she was fond of the pulsating hot color combos last featured in the acid dreams of the sixties.

She hadn't even bothered to laugh at the other supposed obligation, that of keeping the mouth shut. She simply ignored it. And with her delicious, barely intelligible Louisiana accent, and her sweet Southern ways of being bossy in the most oblique manner possible, she was having a high old time planning my wedding. "Sweetie," she now said. That was a sign I was considered part of the family. She had mothered so many children that remembering their names all the time was too time consuming, so everybody's basic name was Sweetie Mackenzie. "Sweetie, I do hope you take this in just the best possible way, as an idea that maybe hasn't crossed your mind quite yet."

My extremities chilled in anticipation.

"I woke up with this vision, pure and simple, and I was overwhelmed by the beauty of it." It wasn't a good sign that she was rushing forward, her bayou words slushing one into the other. "So I thought—well, nobody's said otherwise so far, you know, so wouldn't it be absolutely the loveliest thing if Amanda and C.K.—" At this point, she was proving how much she cared about us by demonstrably knowing our specific, non-Sweetie names—"had a Wiccan wedding. And best of all, love—I could officiate! Wouldn't that be *fun*!"

It would not be fun. Or it might be fun. I didn't care. It was another suddenly-urgent-though-never-once-thought-of-before item in a basket already burdened with too many of them.

She rambled on. ". . . such an important day—after all, you only get married—"

Holy Wicca! What was I going to do?

The best that could be said was that the trio had now reported in. The fourth message couldn't be from them. They seemed to have a once-a-day pact, as if they were vitamins I dearly needed, but they were afraid of my overdosing.

The truth was, there were now four well-meaning pests. My friend Sasha claimed to have returned from England because of the wedding, and because she felt beholden to make me a shower. And even though the shower was not the main event, it had seemed to require almost as much planning, which translated into almost as many questions.

Even now that the shower was scheduled for next week, and notwithstanding our long friendship, the questions didn't seem over. As soon as I heard her voice, I tensed further, dreading the inevitable repeat of the already-asked and unanswered questions, about whether anybody attending had unusual eating habits, or allergies, or whether we should sing—sing!—or play games to break the ice. Also, as a tagline—of course—the concept that all this insanity was justified because I'd only get married once, a motto that became ridiculous when Sasha said it.

She'd been married and divorced twice in her twenties and for all I knew, she'd done it again while she was living in England and had simply forgotten to mention it. It was possibly genetic—her parents had, between them, half a dozen or more nuptials. But somehow, Sasha persisted in believing in romance, in the blazing, blinding appearance of Mr. Right, and in an ultimate permanency and bliss even if it had so far eluded her.

I grit my teeth, willing myself into patience, and concentrated so hard on not getting angry that it took me awhile to register that she was actually talking about something other than my nuptials.

"—thinking of you even when I've found a new, handsome prospect," she was saying when I tuned in. Sasha's optimism should be bottled. She is determined to have a good time in this life, and she always succeeds, at least for a while, and when her good time inevitably ends, her heart might need short-term EMT help—or chocolate—but she's a quick healer, and she's back in the ring for the next round. A good man might be hard to find, but Sasha wasn't looking for good—except as in good times, so she found what she called "love" everywhere.

I waited to hear about this new man, and how This Time It Was for Real.

"—he's in the process of separating—"

Not again. Perhaps I'm a pedant and overly concerned with the meaning of words, but I have tried to explain that a person is either separated, or not, and that a person who is still living with someone to whom they are married is most assuredly not separated. Siamese twins during surgery were in the process of separating. Sasha's "in process" guys were still married. But you can't interrupt a phone message.

"—and something was going on—weird phone calls. He said it like a joke, but he seemed bothered all the same. I mean, why tell me otherwise? So of course, I told him about you guys. That's okay, isn't it? I mean talking about you? I mean you're private eyes, but not so private I can't recommend you, right? It isn't a big job, but a job all the same. Help pay for the honeymoon, maybe. The man has bucks. What's my referral fee? Just joking. But if Tom Severin gets in touch, you'll know I sent him."

For once, one of her men had been as good as his word.

His last word.

Four

I sat down heavily on the kitchen chair near the phone and re-played Sasha's entire message to make sure I'd heard it correctly.

I had, and the net result was that now even less made sense. First, without a shred of false modesty, I'd have to ask—why me? Sasha had undoubtedly failed to mention my rank amateur PI status but still, she had to know that my work in the office was basically clerical. There were lots of fine, experienced investigators available versus me, an underpaid teacher with a second job, trying to make ends meet.

So once again, from the top—why me?

If Severin's note had read C. K. Mackenzie, then okay. Anybody with half a brain would want Mackenzie on the case. But the note hadn't said that, and it had specifically named Philly Prep, not Ozzie Bright's office.

Things that don't make sense give me hives. I enjoy the ridiculous, the far-fetched, and the positively insane, but when something is tilted and out of whack, pretending to be straight-forward, it drives me to the brink. Almost making sense doesn't count. It has to go all the way. I want to tidy it, label it, and shelve it, and I worry it over until I find where it belongs.

And then, somewhat belatedly, I thought about my friend and the fact that she'd been dating Tom Severin. I didn't know if she knew what had happened to him, and I didn't know how news of his death would affect her. Sasha was great with blowups, breakups, divorces, and amicable partings, but death was another matter altogether.

I considered the time and the stack of unmarked essays, checked the pasta supply and then the refrigerator for anything to put upon it, found enough, and lifted the phone to invite Sasha for dinner.

MACKENZIE RETURNED HOME before Sasha, and he opened the door when she rang. He bowed low, ushering her in. She carried an enormous bouquet of pastel ribbons and bows. "You look positively bridal," he told her. "Is there something we should know?"

She did look bridal, as long as we were talking about an alter-nate universe where wedding day attire included capes lined in fake leopard-skin and covered in brilliantly patterned patchwork worn over fire-engine red combat boots, a skirt that looked more like a long tutu with layers of chiffon in purple hues ranging from lavender to amethyst, and a black, loosely knit long-sleeved top that left one shoulder bare. She looked great. I wondered what my mother would say if I wore the outfit, including the bouquet, for my wedding. It would save us so many phone calls and questions and also take care of the "something borrowed" part.

My future mother-in-law's taste in clothes and color sense

was perilously similar to Sasha's, and I wondered if having both of them in the same room at the wedding would blind people.

At five-eight, I'm not at all short, and I'm happy with my auburn hair and green eyes, but all the same, when I'm around Sasha, I feel undersized and under-colored. Sasha is vivid: six feet tall, with big and curly black hair, extravagant gestures, and outrageous clothing. Her credo has always been, "Since I've got it, and lots of it, I will indeed flaunt it." It's a fine philosophy.

Mackenzie murmured something Southern and annoying about "girl talk," and excused himself to study while the sauce simmered.

"Um, pasta," Sasha said. "Except I shouldn't. Carbs. I want to be svelte at your wedding."

"Is there anyone in the world not on a diet?" I asked. "And since the answer is *no,* how come we all keep on having to be on a diet?"

"How come we're not all mentally serene and jolly and living happily ever after in romantic bliss?" she asked. "There sure are enough books about how to get that way. It's because we don't listen, and because I'll have the pasta, thank you." She thrust her ribbon bouquet at me. "What color do you want as your scheme?"

Before this wedding business, when I thought "scheme," I thought plot, preferably nefarious. I still did, though I didn't bother to say that. "Why does a shower need a color scheme?"

"I want to do this right."

"Are we going to have to dress in the color I choose?" I tried to keep the horror out of my voice, to remember what a nice thing she was doing, having the shower at her condo.

She shook her head. "Of course not, but I want to give favors—souvenirs. Little picture frames into which they'll put a group photo I create digitally even as we shower away. I'll print them out while you're still tearing wrapping paper and making the bouquet of bows and—"

"Sweet." She was too involved in my life and spending too much of her exceedingly small cash reserves on this event. "But . . .

would you think I'm awful if I asked that we avoid wedding talk this evening, including shower talk? I find it daunting."

"Typical." She settled on the sofa, chiffon petals floating into a purple haze around her. "It's the jitters. The cold feet."

"The boredom. The utter nonsense. The phone calls. The fact that they'll be here to make me insane in person next week. It's the overblown significance of the show of it—the public part, the—"

"Okay. I concede, but if we avoid wedding chatter, what's left to talk about except me?"

"That's kind of what I wanted to talk about."

"Me?"

"The man you gave my number to. Tomas Severin."

Her dark eyebrows pulled toward her nose. "I thought you guys were always looking for business."

I sat down next to her. "I didn't want to say this over the phone, and there isn't any easy way to put it, except to say I hope you didn't get too attached to him." It might sound a ridiculous concern, except that Sasha Berg was capable—repeatedly capable—of considering herself in a committed relationship before she was sure of the man's name.

"I know he's still married, if that's the red flag you're about to wave. But he's separating and getting a divorce, worrywart. You're going to be just like your mother someday."

I put my hand on her arm. "Sash, I really hate having to tell you this, but he came to the school today, presumably to see me, and fell down the staircase, and . . . he didn't survive the fall."

She opened her mouth, said nothing, closed it, tightened it as if to again say something, let it go slack. Her right hand picked at a lilac layer of chiffon. "Dead?" she said, intently checking my expression. "Really?"

I think that's a universal response, that irrational hope the news was a bad joke, or that you misheard. I nodded.

"Dead. That's . . . that's . . ."

I had seldom seen her at a loss for words and even less frequently seen her look frightened. I put my hand on hers. "I had no idea he was somehow connected to you, or to me," I said. "I'm sorry. So sorry."

The timer rang, and I jumped to turn down the burner. I gave Sasha a moment or two, and then I summoned the resident student. I not only wanted him to eat a meal that wasn't burned, but I also wanted him to hear and react to whatever Sasha could tell us.

The dead man had been, or had wanted to be, our client. There seemed a debt of some sort, of attention, if nothing else.

The putanesca sauce was not ruined. In fact, it wasn't half bad. Maybe the ladies of the night for whom it is named, hungry and tired after work, had built improvisation and inattention into the recipe. We sat around the table and made sociable, relatively meaningless chat, during which Sasha was silent. When she came out of her trance, even though we were talking about a new movie that had gotten good reviews, she said, "I thought it was a joke."

Mackenzie and I looked at each other, then at her.

"A bad one," she said. "A stupid one. I thought he'd hire you guys and you'd make money—he apparently had loads—finding out it was nothing."

We gave up on waiting and hoping for coherence. "What was nothing, what was a joke?" We almost said it in unison.

"The phone calls Tom was getting. I've been trying hard to remember exactly what he told me, but you know, he was cute, it was the third time we'd been together and we were reaching that point where maybe something for real was starting. The thing was—lots of what I was listening to had nothing to do with what he was saying out loud. You know what I mean."

Of course. What passes for conversation at the beginning stages is irrelevant. It's code. It's body language that matters, the speculation and the interest level that registers. "But still—what do you think he said?" I prompted.

"I think I was talking about why I came back from England, so I mentioned you and the wedding and the shower. And I probably mentioned how hard you both worked, how busy you were with school, and your day job, Manda, and I'm pretty sure that's how it came about that he knew you were private investigators. Forgive me, but I was talking mostly to fill airspace.

"And he said maybe he should hire you because he'd been getting prank phone calls. Only he didn't look as if he meant the word 'prank.' Not giddy kids at a slumber party picking out numbers at random. Actually, I'm not sure if he said *prank* or *crank.* I asked him what he meant and he shrugged and said he felt stupid getting upset about it. Didn't want to talk about it. But I used my Mata Hari ways and finally, he told me—I hope I'm getting this right—that the first call just said something like, 'I know about you, Tom,' and a hang up." She looked at the two of us, as if we could decipher the hidden meaning in a call like that.

I shrugged. Mackenzie said, "Not much to go on there. Not much to worry about, either. I get calls like that when somebody's cell phone hits a tunnel, or malfunctions. Maybe they meant to say 'Glad to know' something or other that was cut off." Then he shook his head, too. We were presenting a unified front, all right. A mystified unified front.

"That's what I thought, but there was a second call that said, 'Tom Severin, I'm going to tell everything I know about you. I hate you.' Then nothing, again. And a third that I think had just happened, and it went something like the same—his name and that he should be dead. Not those words, maybe, but like that." Once again, Sasha looked at each of us in turn.

Mackenzie said what I expected him to say, "It sounds like a prank—unless he knew who was doing it, and that someone was dangerous. But I don't think real threats make calls like that. That's kid stuff, timid person stuff."

"Maybe he did know, or thought he knew, because he must have been worried, given that he appeared at the school to hire you."

"Male or female?" I asked. "The voice."

"I asked, and he wasn't sure. He said it seemed almost familiar, but it was muffled, as if the caller was purposely trying to disguise it."

"Why the school?" I was still bothered by how that didn't fit. "Why would he come to school?"

"I don't know," Sasha said. "I told him you had an office."

"I wasn't there for long today," Mackenzie said. "I was back and forth to school."

She looked back at me. "That could be it, couldn't?"

"Our business phone is his cell phone. No message on it?" I asked, and Mackenzie shook his head. The choice of making contact with him via my room at Philly Prep still didn't make sense. "The note said my name. Very specifically. And the school. Call—or actually *calls*—Amanda Pepper. Philly Prep."

"We're never going to know, and probably none of this matters, anyway," Sasha said. "Except to make me feel bad for sending him to you. But if he died accidentally, then it doesn't matter who was phoning him." She sighed. "I finally meet an interesting guy. Just my luck."

"More his luck," C.K. said. "Of the really bad variety."

She smiled wryly. "He was good-looking. Fit, for a guy in his early fifties. Interesting to talk to. Charming. And his tailoring— I mean he never had to say he had money. His tailor said it for him. Eloquently." She poked her fork into pasta she'd barely tasted, but she forgot the part about lifting the fork's contents to her mouth.

I've known Sasha since junior high, and I half expected her to say, "easy come, easy go," and move on to lighter topics. That's her style, and if she grieves, she does it away from public scrutiny, so making light of losing a guy with great tailoring is very much her attitude. However, her relative listlessness and lack of appetite put the lie to her calm.

"Do you think he told his wife about these calls?" Mackenzie asked.

His wife didn't seem a topic Sasha was eager to approach. She frowned and finally said, "For all I know his soon-to-be ex-wife *made* the calls." Once again, she poked at her pasta.

I nobly held my tongue. There had been too many semi-married men in Sasha's life.

"She wasn't at the party where I met him," she said, slightly defensively. "Whatever they were, it wasn't together."

"At least not at the party." Mackenzie said it. I didn't. I thought it, and was glad my better half had expressed it and left me the good guy, the loyal pal.

"She sounded like a bitch, anyway. I mean I didn't break them up."

"What are you talking about?"

"Nina—that's her name—phoned me once, after the second time I'd seen him. Ranted at me, really. Like a fishwife, however a fishwife sounds. A drunk fishwife. I hung up on her." She was silent, seemingly remembering, and then she struck the side of her head. "Wait—I just remembered what else he said. He was acting like it was all a joke, but you could tell he wasn't taking it lightly. He said, 'You know that old expression, with friends like these who needs enemies?' I asked if he meant he knew who was making the calls. I mean until then, from what he'd said, I assumed he didn't have a clue as to who was calling. Wouldn't you?"

I nodded. "You think it was a friend of his, then?" I asked. "Or at least somebody he knew?"

"I think so, but I don't have any real idea because he clammed up, and I didn't ask anything more. It was weird, anyway. We were still working on flirting, and talk Lite. You know we met at a big party, did your basic chitchat: How was England, what do you do, what's your sign, how do you feel about feng shui—the usual fill-in-the-blanks—and then, we had dinner, and then lunch, way too soon for death-threat talk, so I got us back on track by invoking you guys, and then we talked about what kind of photos I take. I think that was the last mention of anything like that. Of course I feel bad about that now. Maybe he would have said more. Maybe none of this would have happened."

"You couldn't have known, and it probably was irrelevant, anyway. He fell down a flight of stairs. Nothing could have prevented that." I refused to think about the cheekbone. "When was that lunch?"

"Today," she said, as if I should have known that.

"Today? When?"

She looked worried about me, wrinkling her forehead and moving closer. "Lunch was . . . at lunchtime, why?"

"Because . . . was he injured in any way?"

She squinted. "His feelings, you mean?"

"No, I mean his face. Was he . . ." I was being ridiculous. Nobody had lunch with a new woman while his cheek looked raw and demolished the way Tom Severin's had.

"He was fine. And you—are you okay?"

"One thing," Mackenzie said. "You didn't mention anything more about us? About the PI offices, or anything?"

Sasha shook her head slowly, her forehead creased. "No," she finally said. "Like I said, Lite."

"He took our office number?" Mackenzie asked.

Recognition dawned in her eyes. "No," she said. "No!" And then she grinned. "That's why he came to the school! I never said where your office was, but he knew you taught there—I said so. When I told him you were an English teacher by day and sleuthette by night he asked me where you taught, and when I said Philly Prep, he raised his eyebrows. He looked impressed."

"More likely horrified, or incredulous." Our school's reputation ranged from mediocre to laughable.

"But you never mentioned Ozzie Bright," Mackenzie said.

"Correct. I couldn't remember his name. So that mystery's solved," Sasha said, and as soon as she had, she looked at her full plate with actual interest, although by now it was cold. Her emotional recovery speed remained amazing.

Now the note made sense. He was probably coming to ask me how to get in touch with Mackenzie. I felt as if some great psychic obligation had been removed. Now it was our turn to talk about her English adventures. She'd been back only a few weeks, and though we'd spent time together, it hadn't been enough. Sasha's life had always seemed a series of exciting but unrelated short stories. Having spent over a year in London and environs, and not being a particularly happy letter or even e-mail writer, Sasha was brimful of sagas needing new ears.

"You know," Mackenzie said when he'd finished his coffee, "those phone calls might well have been a prank, or from an angry employee who works things out that stupid way. People trip and fall all the time, and when a two-story marble staircase is involved in the misstep—people die. There wasn't anything you could have done differently, so don't go feeling guilty or as if you're somehow responsible." He kissed her on the forehead and excused himself to continue studying.

Sasha nodded. "I hope that's true. I hope it was all a terrible coincidence. Even that way, it's hideous news." She sighed, and finished her coffee, and we left it like that and did the dishes together.

You'd think after his gracious words to her she'd stop looking for his fatal flaws, especially given that she had almost no standards for the men in her life, but as soon as she was no longer thinking about Tom Severin, Sasha questioned my Mr. Right's absence from washing-up detail. I explained our every-other-night kitchen arrangement and defended him as a fair partner, and then, having done with death and love, I felt the inevitable next topic approach.

"About the color scheme," Sasha said, retrieving her ribbon bouquet.

My turn to sigh, too loudly. She looked hurt. I held up one hand to stop whatever she was going to say. "I know you all mean well, but I'm having a devil of a time with my mother's color scheme dilemmas, and my mother-in-law isn't helping given that she's wearing a lovely number she made herself. It's fuchsia and lime and guess how Mom feels about working that into the attendants' outfits and the tablecloths and flowers? And when I tell them—everyone—to wear whatever they like, that's not acceptable, either. So forgive me. My color-choosing nerves are frayed."

I poured us both wine, and sat back down at the kitchen table, under the best light, to choose a ribbon.

"Not that I'm making suggestions," Sasha said, "because I want this to be what you want—you and nobody else."

That, by the way, is how everyone prefaces heavy-handed "suggestions." Sasha included.

"However," she continued, "if you like this one"—she pulled out a mossy green that would not have been my first or second choice— "I have a coffee service from England that would go perfectly and I think it would look pretty as part of the picture frame . . ."

The telephone rang, saving me from noting that she'd become precisely like my mother and sister. My choice—as long as it was her choice.

A pleasant male voice asked for Mackenzie. "He's asked to not be disturbed," I said. "Could I take a message?"

There was a moment's silence, as the man on the other end of the phone seemed to decide whether he should trust me.

"This is his fiancée," I said, and then, hearing myself, I had to control a fit of the giggles. Fiancée! I will never get used to that silly-sounding word, but it seemed to give me cred as a potential taker-of-messages.

"Oh, sure. Right. Amanda Pepper. We talked."

Now I recognized the voice. "Correct, Detective Edwards."

"You're the one brought it in."

He was brimful of information I already had. This must be a social call. Getting back in touch with Mackenzie. But "You're the one brought it in" meant he had the cup of tea on his mind.

So perhaps not quite so purely social. Edwards was once again hesitating. I envisioned him staring at the receiver with that intense expression, then looking off to the side, deciding whether to tell me anything.

I hazarded a hunch. "Is this in response to Mackenzie's phone call to you?"

He grunted agreement. My surmise had been correct. My fiancé had been doing end-runs, helping me behind my back. I couldn't decide if I should be annoyed by this or not.

I opted for not. We were, after all, partners, in the kitchen and in crime detection. Now if he could also convince Edwards that I had not pushed Severin down the stairs . . .

Edwards obviously decided that no harm would be done if he trusted the messenger girl to transmit his words to the great sleuth himself. "Tell him he was right," he said. "There's a benzo-diazepine in it."

I had no idea what a benzodiazepine was. I needed a defini-tion, but didn't want to ask for one and allow Edwards to be still more patronizing. "Sorry to be dense," I said, "but how do you spell benzo—"

"Easier to just write one of its street names. Roofies," he said. "Got it."

He either didn't hear me, or didn't believe me, or didn't care, so he continued on. "Mackenzie will know. People call it a date-rape drug. Somebody takes it in a drink—can't taste it, can't see it in his tea, and he gets a kind of amnesia for whatever happens while he's sedated. Gets bleary, a little out of it and if he takes enough, he can pass out completely."

I truly had known all that, I just hadn't been sure of the sci-entific name. I'm the advisor to the school paper, the *Inkwire*, and we'd started this academic year with a bang—the first issue had a serious piece on drugs and their availability, a student-researched article that was exceptionally good because it was peer-to-peer straight talk. I was so proud of that article; I intended to enter it in a journalism contest.

"Not normally lethal, not that it was here, either," Edwards continued. "But if he had alcohol, say at lunch, and the autopsy's looking like he did, it'd make it much worse."

"I thought the tea might be significant," I said, blatantly of-fering my back for patting.

"Sure was, and since traces of it disappear quickly, thank him for the heads-up."

I resigned myself to the idea that this was a guy thing, and life was too short to start working on this problem at the moment.

"They're checking Severin for it now, and they wouldn't have otherwise. Or if they did tomorrow or the next day, it'd be too late. It becomes undetectable."

I knew that, too.

"What was that all about?" Sasha asked as soon as I'd put the receiver back on its cradle.

"Tomas Severin. Did you have wine with lunch?"

"I had a glass. Tom did, too. And a vodka martini beforehand. He'd had some kind of disturbing hour before lunch. Separate from the phone calls."

"Did you by any chance get tea-to-go when you left the place? Or did he?"

She shook her head. "It isn't that kind of place. Really—just a tiny bistro. No take-out."

"When did your lunch end?"

"An exact time? Amanda, I didn't check my watch, but it wasn't long. An hour, I'd say. We went our separate ways at one. He had another appointment. Very busy guy for somebody who basically didn't even work. Why?"

"It appears that somebody drugged him by dropping a date-rape drug in herbal tea he had in a Styrofoam cup." And if it wasn't at the café with Sasha, then where was it?

"Too weird," she said. "Why drug him? But why especially with that?"

"Beats me. It would make him dopey, slow to react. Rape was surely not the goal in this case, but you could do whatever else you had in mind more easily, I guess."

"What? What could anybody have wanted to do to him at your school?"

"In my classroom," I added.

"Tomas Severin, you don't deserve to live," Sasha said abruptly, startling me. "That was what the third phone call said." She paused, then nodded, and when she spoke again, it was so softly I could barely hear her. "Somebody meant it," she said. "Somebody meant it enough to kill him."

Five

PERHAPS the events at Philly Prep would have been news-worthy no matter who had died. After all, it's shocking—though sadly less so all the time—when violent death hits a school. But it's definitely worth a mouthful of sound bites when the victim's the scion of a local dynasty, and it becomes lead-story time when the wealthy and prominent middle-aged dead man has an infamous date-rape drug in his system.

Each time the media enjoyed another wallow in the story, they mentioned the "plucky"—absolutely not a word I'd want applied to me, ever—teacher who'd spotted the cup in her classroom.

I was given credit for my housekeeping—for finding the thing, but not for brains. The stories made it sound as if I'd simply noticed trash and mentioned it to the crime-fighters.

Needless to say, the excited newscasts and headlines did not make for a smooth workday. Now the students knew I'd discovered the body and the drugged cup—the latter in their very classroom, which became, therefore, a crime scene, and made them part of an investigative team. Each class in turn scanned for additional clues and evidence in corners and under desks. I could almost hear their excited thoughts: This time, they'd be the—plucky—ones to spot something and make the eleven o'clock news.

This is the result of too many reality shows. Or too much reality.

I felt as if I were hauling the curriculum behind me on a rope, trying to tug it into a room already overstuffed with yesterday's news. I didn't want to talk about the things the students chose as topics: how it felt to find a dying man; what the police asked me; whether I'd have to testify when they found out who had drugged Severin and probably killed him.

Now and then I tossed a little of the lesson plan into the *C.S.I.* talk and the day progressed. By the time my seniors entered the room, most of the crime-talk was over. Unfortunately, so was the day.

Even there, one adamant youngster came up with a new question. Faye Horrell, who was too cute and smart to be as afraid of speaking her mind as she appeared to be, protected herself by avoiding all direct statements. Every sentence out of her mouth was in the form of a question, even when she was suggesting that her teacher might be a criminal. Especially when she was suggesting that I might be in trouble with the law.

In her own interrogatory way, Faye delighted in all things deadly. I stood at the side of the room, where I could see the books stacked on her desk and, with her permission, I lifted the stack and looked at the titles. One was *Stiff*, by Mary Roach, one was *Corpse*, by Jessica Sachs, and one was *Declared Dead*, by Suzanne Proulx.

"For research?" she said. I didn't ask of what kind.

"So . . . have they said anything about your being under suspicion?" she asked in her tiny voice.

"Me? Why on earth? Because I found him?" I sounded just like her. Maybe my level of panic equaled hers then, too, because I flushed with the fear that she somehow knew about Severin's note, about Edwards's suspicions that I was involved in Severin's end.

"Because . . . the article?" she piped. "In the *Inkwire*? Remember?"

Of course I remembered it—with pride and pleasure in the students' accomplishments. It was the article I planned to submit in the journalism competition.

Faye wrinkled her forehead, looking pained and frightened. A "don't hit me!" face was one of her most-used expressions. I had worried about that, about her interest in all things morbid, about possible abuse, but Rachel Leary, the counselor, had quelled my fears. "She's pretty happy and normal. I had to ask her outright, and she basically told me that her cringing questioning style makes her distinctive. Kind of a trademark? As she would ask-say. She thinks it makes her cute."

Her writing was assertive and question-mark free. Someday I'd figure out a kind and polite way to let her know that the persona she'd adopted was annoying, not adorable.

"Nobody mentioned anything about the school paper," I said. "And even if they did, that doesn't make me a criminal."

"But wouldn't it have to be somebody who knew about the drug who did this? Somebody who knew where to buy it?" Faye's face scrunched still more intensely. I wouldn't have believed that such young skin could produce that many wrinkles. The child was going to need Botox shots before the semester was over. "You remember what Zach wrote?" she asked.

"Of course." Zachary Wallenberg, one of the outstanding seniors and one of our true success stories, had gone underground, with permission, and only to a preagreed-upon extent, and then had written an article that gave no specifics, but made it clear that close to a complete assortment of drugs—at least of the party and club variety—was available within five minutes' walking distance of the school.

"And wasn't that drug found in the dead man mentioned in the article?"

And yes it had been. I suppose Faye's mental scenario was that the police would assume I had a fit of temporary insanity and asked a student where to make a buy before I doped up this Severin stranger. Little did she dream that they had a far more logical reason to think I was involved, one that did not require a question mark at the end of the supposition.

"Thanks for your concern," I told her, "but there's no cause for it. Knowledge is power—not guilt. Only actions get people in trouble."

For the entire remainder of class, she'd look my way till I felt her glance and met it, and then she'd do the forehead thing and I'd smile, understandingly, and disengage eye contact. By the end of the period, I was no longer sure I was completely innocent.

As usual, before I left the building, I picked up the flyers, notices, ads, and general junk that mysteriously refills our mailboxes each day.

"Find everything okay?" Mrs. Wiggins asked that every day. I wondered if she'd worked in a supermarket before coming here.

"Just fine." I said that every day, too.

"And . . . about that . . . I saw on the news that—he was on drugs."

"Not exactly. The theory is that somebody put a drug into his tea and he didn't know it. It's tasteless and odorless."

She looked pale and overly anxious and she neared the office divider cautiously. "Do they know who?" she whispered.

I shook my head.

"Have any theory?"

"Me? Or the police?"

That choice stymied her, then finally she laughed, nervously, and said, "Either, I guess."

"I surely don't, and as far as I know, neither do they, but then, they wouldn't have any reason to tell me if they did. How about you?"

"Me?" She stepped back from the divider, as if it had become electrified. "What do you . . . ?"

I tilted my head toward Dr. Havermeyer's closed office door. "About . . . not seeing Mr. Severin come into the school. You know. Is it okay?"

She took three shuddery breaths, and nodded, then kept her gaze downward. "I think so. It was . . . embarrassing."

"You're only human. Don't worry."

She looked up at me and blinked. She was going to spend a long time analyzing what I meant, so I waved and walked outside, into the lobby—to the infamous bottom of the staircase, in fact. I thought about the remainder of the day, about putting in a few hours at Ozzie's office. Moonlighting under October sunshine. The office would be a welcome change. My tasks there were so routine my mind could go on sleep mode while I entered numbers and mailed out bills.

I'd stay two hours, I decided, then head home and mark those essays that, because of too much wine and talk with Sasha, had not gotten themselves read the night before. For about the millionth time, I wished math were my subject. I bet math teachers spent their evenings enjoying all the books English teachers, stuck marking papers, wish they had time to read.

But, I promised myself, today I'd zip through them and then I'd move forward with the wedding things, I'd pick an invitation, decide what it should say—except, of course, for where the event would take place, and I'd thereby bring a little sunshine into the bridal bullies' lives as well.

Making plans and lists and schedules fills me with energy and optimism. Carrying out the plans, actually doing the work, and being disciplined exhausts me. No fun at all, in fact, but I try to ignore that part of the equation when I'm high on planning, as I was at that moment.

I was nearly out the door when Liddy Moffat, carrying a mop and pail, shouted, "A minute of your time!" It was not a request but a demand. "What's up?" I asked when she was near.

I waited to see what precious item she'd extracted from the

trash this time, to hear the lecture on wasting not and wanting not, but her hands remained on the empty bucket's handle. "Somebody has to do something," she said gravely.

"That's pretty much always true. Want to be more specific?"

She cleared her throat. "Don't you get angry or anything."

Liddy did not generally concern herself with our potential reactions to her dictates. This, then, was troublesome. "I promise I won't get angry." I wondered what cleanliness infraction was this enormous.

"You think they're poisoning the kids?"

I did a classic double take, sure I'd misheard. "Who? What do you mean, poison?" I hoped against hope this was not more Tom Severin aftershock.

"The cafeteria." She put down the pail and folded her arms over her chest. "Have there been complaints about the food?"

"There are always complaints. Why?"

"Because maybe kids—my girls—are being poisoned, that's why."

"Miz Moffat, I appreciate your concern, but I don't understand it."

She drew herself up taller, holding the mop as if it were a ceremonial sword. "That's what I thought. Just wanted to be sure. So Miz Pepper, we have ourselves a mess of trouble. It gets fixed, or I leave."

And with that, she seemed to have said her piece. I waited, then finally confessed that I had no idea what she was talking about.

"The *vomit*," she said, as if of course I'd understand, as if vomit had been on my mind nonstop all day long.

I'd thought I knew my problems, but here, Liddy said, was another. One I really did not want on my list of concerns.

"In particular," Liddy said, "the ones who don't bother to get it into the toilet. You know they could. If they're not dying, or poisoned, then it's a sign of no respect, is all. I can't take it no more. There are other jobs. Next time, I'm working in a geriatric ward. Or a boys' school. Boys don't do things like that."

"Back up. What things? Who's sick?"

"Nobody's sick. If you say no poison, and I believe you—I only thought of that because of that dead man here. I heard on the news last night—"

"Yes. I understand." I could not bear one more retelling of yesterday's news.

"So I didn't really think it could be the food, but I didn't want it to be this stuff, that they're throwing up on purpose so they won't get fat. To be honest, I dread the period after lunch. Also makes me want to shake them silly—there's people starving in this world, and they're stuffing themselves and tossing it back. Dis-gusting!"

"Has this been going on for a long time?" I felt like those people at disaster scenes, the people interviewed on TV who say things like, "I knew this happened, but to other people, not to us." Of course I knew about bulimia and anorexia, about how frighteningly common eating disorders were among teens, how desperately they wanted to look "right," whatever that meant to them, to fit in. But everyone at school looked so healthy, so normal.

I felt a shudder of things missed, dangers unsuspected.

"It isn't that I'm lazy, or that I don't know sometimes in my profession, you gotta deal with unpleasantness. But when it comes to people being that inconsiderate, I have my limits." She planted her sturdy body even more securely, one fist now on her hips, the other still holding the mop like a staff and banner.

I nodded. "Of course. Well, I'll see what . . ." What? This was definitely out of my league and in fact, was in a league I didn't want to join.

Having vented, Liddy's instinctive kindness asserted itself. "I don't want them thrown out or anything. I understand how much they want to stay thin. Well, no. I don't understand it really, but I know that's how it is with girls today. Where I grew up, just getting food on the table and not being hungry was the thing. But I'm trying to understand. I just won't tolerate them missing the bowl, is all."

I looked at her, not sure whether to laugh or cry, and most definitely not sure of what to do about this situation. "May I ask why you came to me?"

She shrugged. "You seem like you care about things. Not everybody does."

I was flattered, but even so, it wasn't as if I could rationally expect help from the administration. I couldn't even imagine myself going into Havermeyer's inner sanctum and saying, "We need to talk about vomit." Did an uglier word than that exist?

This was emotional, psychological, not academic. That was the counselor's province, although the divisions were ultimately meaningless. A girl binging and purging, thinking always about what she weighs and what she can or cannot eat and how she'll get around the chemistry of hunger, can't devote her attention to learning grammar. A depressed child doesn't learn, a frightened child doesn't learn. There is, for better or for worse, a mind-body connection.

I hoped Rachel Leary, our counselor, would know what a school could and should do in this situation. She had three daughters now herself, and even though two were still in diapers, it was never too soon to think about the problem, because they might grow up to have teachers as oblivious as I'd been.

Or so I was going to tell her. And then I was going to leave her with the problem, turn my back, and bolt out of her office and away from this entire topic.

Six

"Yo, Plucky!" Ozzie Bright had clipped out a news story and he handed it to me within seconds of my entering the office. "For your scrapbook," he said.

I was touched. Ozzie was a man of a school so old he barely acknowledged that women had entered the workplace. In the several months I'd worked there—for Mackenzie, not Ozzie—he'd barely spoken to me, and then, only when I'd directly addressed him or asked a question. "Thanks," I said, flattening out my voice, demonstrating that I was not a flighty female ready to burst into tears at this show of consideration. "Gotta get to work now."

I'd scored points with Ozzie for that exchange. I always did when I made myself sound like the world-weary, emotionally void private eye in a thirties mystery.

"It's a bitch you don't get paid for the work," he said. "Free-lancing doesn't mean free, you know."

I hadn't thought of the cup-retrieval as freelancing.

"But good you mentioned the agency," he added.

I hadn't done that, either. My home phone gives the cell phone number in case of emergency and that, in turn, gives our names as part of the Investigative Office of Ozzie Bright. While Sasha was visiting, I had refused to answer the phone at all last night, couldn't stand the idea of more wedding agitation, but I had apparently supplied my caller with enough information anyway.

"Misspelled it though," Ozzie said before closing the door of his cubicle.

I looked at the news story. The reporter had written "Brite." First Plucky, then Brite. Strike two.

I hadn't done anything here except talk to Mackenzie and run out of the place the day before, and I had stacks of boring but necessary filing on my desk—reports, expense vouchers, printouts—plus bills and statements to prepare. I put the news clipping in my desk drawer and got to work, pausing only to kiss and greet Mackenzie when he showed up. I liked the days when we were both in the same place at the same time, even if we inevitably wound up doing our separate tasks.

I was preparing a bill for yet another hapless middle-aged man trying to find his first love when I heard the knock on the outer door of the office.

This does not often happen. Things have changed since the days of noir when the dame with the gams slithered into the office and hired the shamus. Most people phone their orders in because most wants are simple: find the girl I loved in high school; find out if my husband-who-I-know-is-cheating-on-me really is; find my child who has run away; find out who's stealing inventory or my daughter's heart or state secrets; find out if this guy's for real. Photos can be scanned and sent, documents faxed or attached, and much of our work is done without ever meeting the client.

Visitors these days are mostly delivery boys bringing Ozzie his nightly pizza, but it was too early for that.

Besides, the door wasn't locked. I shrugged and went to open it.

Instead of the acne-scarred pizza boy, I faced a tight-lipped woman in a leather blazer over a white shirt, tailored slacks, and chunky-heeled lizard shoes I immediately coveted. I gestured for her to enter, at which point I was able to see her handbag, which I also coveted. And while we were at it, I wouldn't have minded the jacket, either. It looked so soft, it was just this side of melting off her.

"I'm looking for"—she pulled a news clipping, that story again, out of her pocketbook and checked it—"Amanda Pepper."

I identified myself, and invited her to sit down. I decided, partly wishful thinking, that she wasn't from a newspaper. Her wardrobe suggested she had more money than most journalists, and her behavior lacked their self-possessed pizzazz.

She seated herself and found a paper-free corner of my desk, where she placed and smoothed the news story. "You found him," she said.

"If you mean Mr. Severin, yes. And you are?"

"Penelope Koepple." It was an awkward name, made more so by her speech, which had a discreetly European flavor, though I couldn't tell which country had spiced it.

"How can I help you?" I asked.

She smoothed the article again, unbuttoned her blazer, and leaned forward. "I believe I have information that might be valuable concerning Mr. Severin's murder."

Forget what I'd said—this was a thirties novel, after all. Unfortunately, I had no homburg and wasn't fond of mean streets, so I had to behave as if it was actually the present. "If that's so," I said, "you need to tell the police."

Her expression was stern and direct. I was sure I was supposed to quiver and quake under that fierce stare. "That isn't possible," she said. Her features and hair looked die-cut, and everything about her from the head down to those lizard shoes and the accent and modulation in between made it clear she was privileged, educated, and used to fine things. She seemed astounded to find herself here, in a poorly decorated, poorly maintained office. I was pretty surprised to find her here myself.

"May I get you a cup of coffee?" I asked politely. It didn't seem proper to mention how awful the house java was.

She shook her head. "Thank you, but no. If you have tea—perhaps with the smallest dash of cream?"

I offered up apologies, and thought of how Ozzie would view such a request. She was lucky he was still behind his office door.

I buzzed Mackenzie. "I'd like my partner to sit in," I said. "We handle our cases together." That wasn't true, but whatever she had to say concerned a murder investigation and those waters were too deep for the likes of me.

When C.K. appeared, I made the introductions, and he pulled up another chair. "Ms. Koepple was about to explain her problem," I said.

"It isn't my problem," she corrected me. "Except in that I'm the one who perceives it as a problem."

We must have both looked blank because she nodded, as if agreeing that she hadn't communicated anything clearly. "I am Ingrid Severin's social secretary," she said. "For the past fifteen years I have kept her calendar, though these days, in truth, Mrs. Severin requires more in the way of a companion. I still answer her mail, decline invitations on her behalf, and so forth, but Mrs. Severin is in decline, so she spends most of her time in seclusion."

I had been wrong about the thirties noir business. We were much further back in history than that. I purposely avoided glancing at Mackenzie to see if he was as entranced and surprised by the arrival at our humble office of a woman out of Jane Austen.

"I am here, therefore, of my own accord, but on behalf of Mrs. Severin, who doted on her son. However, if Mrs. Severin were to know of this mission of mine, I'm afraid I would be summarily dismissed. This is why I cannot involve the police. If they were to come question us, or in any way make it known that I'd gone to them, it would cost me my position."

Judging by her attire and accessories, her position was sufficiently lucrative. Things had improved for the help since Jane Austen's time.

"I believe you said you had information related to Tomas Severin's death," I prompted.

She tilted her head. "You didn't use the word 'murder.' Don't you think he was murdered?"

"I honestly don't know. I didn't know him, and we never had a chance to speak."

She held her head high and angled so that she was looking down the tidy slope of her nose at me. "He was drugged, was he not? That can't have been an accident. Tomas Severin was not a man to risk humiliation with a pitiable street drug. Midday! In the city! Something so low in a man so dignified and respectable. No. Absolutely not. Somebody wanted to humiliate him, to remove his ability to think clearly, make wise decisions." She shook her head. I coveted her haircut now, shaped so precisely that it swung, all strands synchronized, as she moved. "I believe that there was malicious mischief," she said, "as I believe anyone would surmise. And further, I believe I know who is responsible."

Before I repeated the fact that she was obliged to take this information to the police, I couldn't resist asking, "And that person is . . . ?"

"Cornelius Westerly. Or so he calls himself. He's the type to re-create himself at whim, and I'm sure his actual name is something rather less grand. Less traditional." She sniffed, regally, and looked from Mackenzie to me.

This had to be somebody's idea of a practical joke. Instead of the tough PI talk, give the English teacher an escapee from *Sense and Sensibility*. Cornelius Westerly indeed!

"And he is?" C.K. asked.

"Ingrid Severin's . . ." She paused and made sure she had our attention. ". . . betrothed. Her fiancé." She paused for dramatic purposes. "It is worth noting that he is thirty-two years old."

My age, and a decade or two younger than Ingrid's son.

"Ingrid Severin is seventy-eight," Penelope Koepple said crisply.

I could barely squelch an immediate response, a question as to how wealthy—or not—Cornelius Weatherly was. I was sure Ms. Koepple would inform us in time.

"Are we to take it that the age difference troubles you?" Mackenzie asked mildly.

Penelope Koepple appeared to be a well-maintained fifty-something, though it was hard to tell, and now she raised her fifty-something well-plucked eyebrows and considered that sufficient reply to Mackenzie's question.

"Age disparity is not a crime," he said in response. "And as they say, love makes for strange bedfellows."

She winced when he said "bed." I was sure he'd chosen his words carefully especially since the saying referred to politics, not lovers, and he knew that. I could feel his growing impatience, his eagerness to get back to actual paying work or to studying. In either case, to stop having his time wasted, and I had to salute his Southern politeness and savvy that hid his emotions from the prospective client.

"You perhaps don't comprehend the gravity of the situation," Penelope Koepple said. "Ingrid Severin fades in and out of lucidity, and she is often rather muddled. Further, as you may know, she is in possession of significant assets, so whatever papers she signs, new wills she makes, deeds she transfers—especially when emotionally diverted, one can't be certain she actually understands her actions."

Money. We were getting to the problem.

"That includes understanding the nature of love," Ms. Koepple continued. "The nature of the loved object. It is obvious to everyone except Ingrid that her young man is nothing more than a fortune hunter, but she apparently thinks she is half of the great love story of the century. She has said that it took nearly eighty years for her to find the right one. Although I never met Mr. Severin, senior—he died before I became his widow's social secretary—he was not, apparently, the most attentive of husbands."

"And Cornelius?" Mackenzie murmured.

"The most attentive of husbands-to-be. At least while he is embroiled in attending the financial aspects of the marriage."

"A prenup?"

"And worse. An altered will, or plans for same. Mr. Severin was quite involved in attempting to prevent the process, and need I say there was strife aplenty? Although Tomas controlled and ran the business once he was of an age to do so, and until, of course, he sold it, Mrs. Severin inherited significant assets when she was widowed, among which are apartment buildings here in center city. I am sure I need not say that we are talking about real estate worth many multiples of millions. I speak on behalf of her legal heirs—Tomas and his children. I should make it clear that I have nothing at stake here. I am simply a concerned friend of the family. And with Tomas gone, the poor addled woman needs someone to speak for her."

"And that's it for her heirs?" Mackenzie asked. "Tomas and his children. And his heirs?"

It was a logical question, but Ms. Koepple looked startled and nonplussed. It took her too long to say, "I of course am not a lawyer and am not privy to his will, but there are no other heirs I know of, except for the obvious charities and bequests. There might be issues with designated heirs. Mr. Severin has been married three times, and divorced, shall we say, two and a half times. The most recent severance was not yet complete. He was staying with his mother, briefly, while issues were ironed out." She paused, and sighed.

"The newpaper mentioned a widow," I said. "Is she the half?"

She sniffed. "Nina. Indeed. The current Mrs. Severin was not going to keep that title for very long."

"Discouraging to marry three times," I said. Ingrid Severin had obviously forgotten to tell her son the mantra, "Remember, you only get married once."

"All lovely women," Penelope said quickly. "Good women,

good families. It's simply that . . . well, possibly by coincidence, the first was quite young—in her twenties as was Tomas then, and the other two were also young, though Tomas had aged. People, including Tomas, seem to consistently undervalue mature women." Again, she looked at us each in turn. We were to understand that she was saying something negative about her employer's son, but she was saying it—she thought—obliquely.

I wondered for how long Sasha would have lasted. At thirty-two, she was probably just on the cusp of being overripe for Severin's taste.

Having editorialized, albeit mildly, Penelope returned to her point. "The children of the marriages would, of course, inherit from Ingrid, as I assume they will from Tomas himself, and possibly, his current wife." She waved away the idea of the looming legal mess. "Other than them, there's no one."

Perhaps Tom Severin's third wife felt the sting of his lack of interest in women as they matured, and perhaps it was worth doing anything to retain the title and the inheritance, including drugging the man and knocking him down a staircase. I'd have to think about that.

"Of course everything's in a muddle now with this tragic death. Naturally, it was expected that his mother would predecease him and that his children would inherit the remainder of Ingrid's estate at that time. However, Cornelius has replaced those children in her affections and attention. He's convinced her that he should inherit the real estate."

The millions of dollars' worth of apartment buildings in center city—gone to the fortune hunter? "She agreed?" I asked.

"She dotes on Cornelius the way she doted on Tomas. She used to think the sun rose and set simply to please her son, but of late, the discord between the two men was acute, which put a strain between mother and son as well. Ingrid was trying to sort out what she should do. Of course, this unscrupulous man—"

"Interestin', of course," Mackenzie said. "An' undoubtedly troublin', but I'm still unable to see what you want of us."

"Proof," she said firmly. "Proof that he murdered Tomas."

"He? Who?"

"Cornelius, of course."

"But he wasn't in the building," I said. "How—"

"How do you know who was there?" she snapped back, and I could sense how it must have been to deal with her when she was guardian of Ingrid Severin's calendar. "You weren't on the spot when this happened, and surely there's more than one exit."

"But why kill him there? Assuming anybody wanted to do such a thing, and assuming there was ongoing strife—why there?"

"I don't pretend to understand Mr. Westerly," she said. "Nor do I wish to. What I do understand is that he's an opportunist, and he has no scruples. If there was a sudden opportunity, he would seize it. Trust me on that."

"How would he even know where Tomas—Mr. Severin—was going to be?" I asked.

She looked at me, too quickly, and then at Mackenzie, and then down at her pale pink nail polish. "They had an appointment midmorning at the lawyer's office. I have no idea what was decided, but I do know there had been all-out war about the inheritance and time was running out. Ingrid's memory is fading rapidly, and it was apparent to all of us that if she didn't make the changes in her will soon, then it was probable no responsible lawyer would ever allow her to do so in the future. Tomas—of course he was concerned and trying to slow the process. Hence, the rush and the conflict. You see how reprehensible Cornelius is? And then—just when it appeared that sanity was going to reign and Cornelius would get nothing, which is precisely what he deserves—his opponent in the struggle dies in a most peculiar place and manner a mere hour or two after they'd had a meeting that was surely rife with discord."

Her theory was porous, to put it mildly. Without thinking about it, I came up with objections and questions about the motive and the drug, including how Cornelius would have administered it, where he'd have gotten it, whether she was suggesting that he always toted it in case he was going to a rave, or was in the mood for rape—or found himself with the opportunity to kill his fiancée's son. But I also remembered Sasha saying that Tom Severin had a vodka martini before lunch because he'd had an upsetting morning.

"The man is a disgrace," Ms. Koepple said. "A gigolo preying on a woman who could be his grandmother, and who is barely holding on to her sanity. Who will speak for her if not me? She's lost the son she loved above all things until her mind started going soft. And soon, the son's children will lose their rightful inheritance, thanks to this dreadful man."

I tried to generate compassion for the children who, after splitting up millions of dollars, were going to be denied the consolation of bonus apartment buildings when grandma died. "Has anyone in the family gone to the police?"

She shrugged. "This is not the sort of family you see on TV sitcoms. As I mentioned, Mr. Severin was in the process of divorcing his wife."

"How about his other wives?" Mackenzie asked.

She rolled her eyes. "Ex-wives," she corrected him. "As far as I can tell, they'd have killed him themselves if they could."

"Not friendly divorces?" Mackenzie said.

Once again she raised her eyebrows. "Tomas doesn't—did not—wear well with women, although there were always lots of them. Until a week ago or so, he had number four waiting in the wings. She considered herself engaged to him, although . . ." She shook her head slowly back and forth, not willing to actually mention, out loud, the simple fact that a man is not supposed to have become betrothed while he's still very much married to another woman.

"What happened to her?" If she was referring to Sasha, I'd know Penelope Koepple was prone to overstatement. Not even Sasha believed the relationship had gone that far.

But she was talking about somebody else. "He grew tired of her, of Georgeanne—or, more specifically, tired of the prenuptial agreement, of the squabbling over it, of the greed. That's what I understand. No great loss. From what I've observed, she's a better match for Cornelius than she would have been for Tomas, not to speak ill of the dead's choice in spouses, though he surely wasn't good at picking them. But the fact is, birds of a feather, and Georgeanne is Cornelius's friend. Childhood friend, she says, but I wouldn't be surprised if they're the actual couple and this combined attack is all part of their plan."

My head swam with wives present, intended, discarded, and prevented. Ms. Koepple's theory of Cornelius and Georgeanne working in cahoots—he'd take the mother and she'd take the son, and they'd have the billions together—was too convoluted for what I knew of reality.

And where did Sasha fit in here? Or had she had a niche of her own at all?

"I have to once again advise you to go to the police." Mackenzie's voice dragged at the edges.

"And I would once again remind you that if I were to do so, Ingrid would fire me the first lucid moment she had. And even if she didn't, I fear retribution from Cornelius. I consider him a dangerous man. Yet even so, if I had anything besides my convictions and the obvious two plus two of the situation, I would go to them, but what do I have? The fruits of long observation—a distrust of and disgust with this man and nothing else. They would laugh at me."

Mackenzie leaned closer to her, and in his most winningly soft-voweled Louisiana bayou voice, he said, "What is it you want of us in that case?" It was a sweet, almost lulling sound, and I could tell by it just how exceedingly, nearly critically impatient he'd become at this point.

"I want you to find whatever would give me a case to take to the police. Isn't that what you do? I have no idea how to find out who he really is, or what was or wasn't said in the meeting, but you do."

The money would be welcome, but not right now. Not with an already overflowing plate, with the wedding witches and their ridiculous all-consuming plans. I had already talked with Mackenzie about cutting back here until after the wedding, and he agreed.

In fact, he thought we both should because he, too, was feeling overburdened and pressured.

So no. Not possibly.

"I'm hiring you," she informed—not asked—Mackenzie. "That's what I'm doing."

He nodded.

What was this? I wasn't asking for us to have extrasensory perception or acute sensitivity, simply to remember what we'd talked about. Maybe Mackenzie no longer felt overworked. Maybe he'd reached a state of inner peace he hadn't told me about, and he felt ready to accept additional work on his own. I didn't see how, but what else could account for this?

"But you must understand, Ms. Koepple, that Ms. Pepper and I are a team, so when you hire one of us, you hire the other as well. We work together."

"I understood she was a schoolteacher."

I had obviously disappeared while I wasn't looking—to both of them. He didn't remember what I'd said about cutting back, and she didn't even remember that I was sitting beside her. I cleared my throat.

"She is also an investigator," Mackenzie said.

That wasn't 100 percent accurate, but a schoolteacher-clerk doesn't have the same punch.

"I understand." She looked at me this time, and nodded. "Actually, I surmised as much from the minute I read the newspaper story. I only meant your other duties might . . ." She let go of that. "Now I am sure there are practical details to be arranged, such as your fees and retainer, and how to bill me, as I would not like any bills arriving at the household."

Her efficiency and thoroughness were commendable. She must have been a hell of a social secretary. I wondered if Mackenzie would approve of a barter system. We'd handle Penelope's fears, and she'd handle mine. Let her deal with my mother. It would be just her cup of tea. With the smallest dash of cream.

Seven

THAT night, Mackenzie was occupied writing a case study. He had a head start on his classmates because in this instance, he could base his paper on an investigation he himself had done ten years ago. While he was busy with reminiscence and scholarship, I Googled the Severins.

The family had definitely made their mark on history, and they were all over the Web, with Tomases dotting time lines from the revolution to the present. Our Tomas was there in an article about his successful transformation of the family's venerable eighteenth-century company into what the writer called a "global model for the new millennium." And global it had become, possibly more than one would want. The new owner, the multinational firm, had relocated the main plants to five Asian countries and the corporate offices to a suburb of Berlin.

I wonder how many people that had displaced, and if any of them were apt to drug Tom Severin, bash his face, and shove him down the stairs.

I also found mention of the family matriarch, Ingrid Severin, though the articles were mostly from magazines a few decades old. Apparently, Mrs. Severin the elder had been the apotheosis of fashion in her day and circles, the "benign dictator" as one of her friends had put it, of what was and wasn't chic. "Always great fun and gracious," other friends were quoted as saying. "And always, always outrageously stunning." These observations were scattered through articles about banquets honoring her for her charitable work on boards, which I translated as gratitude for large donations. One brief piece mentioned a lavish birthday party Tomas had given his mother, though which birthday it celebrated remained a secret. "Who cares about numbers?" the businessman for the new millennium had asked the reporter. "She's ageless."

That explained a lot. You keep saying things about agelessness to your mama until she believes it and next thing you know you've got a thirty-two-year-old prospective step-daddy.

"Severin was worth billions," I said, just to hear how it sounded out loud. "*Billions.*"

Mackenzie looked up from his yellow legal pad. "Sure that isn't what his companies sold for? I mean there were shareholders and partners . . ."

"Okay. Make it a fraction of that. His portion—maybe only a single, lonely billion. I could run the household on that."

He stood up and poured himself a glass of water. "Is it time for me to spout all those clichés about how little he can enjoy the money now, and about how money can't buy happiness and look how happy we are without it?"

"I don't think so."

"Good, because I'm pretty sure it bought him a heap of happiness."

"A heap of wives, at least. Don't you wonder about that wife? The bad-tempered one who phoned Sasha?"

He ignored me. "Frankly, if I could think of a way to be a claimant to billions, I'd be sorely tempted."

"You could always shove Cornelius aside. Mrs. Severin the elder is still single. As are you."

He glanced my way, then went back to work, and I returned to speculation about what the feel of billions resting under you would be like. It definitely would provide the right degree of support. I imagined it would feel spongy—a perfect shock absorber, and definitely enough to cushion every fall. Except, of course, in the case of Tomas Severin, that final one.

I WOKE UP with three things on my mind.

First was relief that I'd actually marked both sets of essays the night before. That sense of accomplishment was short-lived, because right on its heels came the "but what didn't you do, Amanda?" daily reminder.

So, second was the depressing fact that I had not phoned my mother about the invitations. I had done absolutely nothing, in fact, about my pending nuptials.

And saving the worst for last—today was V-day. The day I dealt with the girls' room problem and those who'd created it. That realization hit me with sufficient force to push me back into my pillow.

I was an English teacher. I was supposed to work on language skills, to introduce young minds to the canon of literature. I was not trained or equipped to deal with psychological or emotional hangups. I was, in fact, not expected to, either.

That's how it went in theory, but I'm not sure who the theorists were or whether they'd ever seen a young person. A child, a teen, is a package, and one so intricately designed that all the pieces connect. The toe bone's connected to the foot bone, and the emotional system leaks right into the psychological and intellectual one.

None of that was news, and I couldn't lie abed regretting it. But I could resent the current conviction that the schools can cure every imaginable woe, make up for any cultural failings, any family pathology, plus unfortunate acts of God.

Nonetheless, there was nothing to do but get out of bed, reluctantly or not, and go to work.

There might be light at the end of the tunnel. Nobody could get me off the paper-marking treadmill, and nobody could take my place with the wedding belles. But there was a chance I could palm off the V-problem.

DESPITE MY DITHERINGS, I arrived with time to spare, so first thing after checking in at the office, I trudged upstairs and turned left, away from my room and toward Rachel Leary's office.

I hated doing this to her. She'd looked exhausted lately, and with good cause. She had three children under three and a husband who was becoming a long-term casualty of the burst dot-com bubble. But she was the school counselor.

"Sorry," I said by way of greeting.

She flinched. "Skip the apology, and hit me with it."

"Vomit."

"Boy, am I glad you didn't take my 'hit me with it' literally. But was that a command, a new way of saying you need help, or do you want to reminisce about my pregnancies?"

"None of the above. Regurgitation is the problem. Unless you count Liddy Moffat's threat to quit as the real problem."

"Ah . . . Liddy. Cleanup crew, so—are we talking bulimics?"

I nodded, and she waved me into the worn chair next to her desk. I started talking before my rear hit the dusty-looking upholstery.

"Everybody's worried about obesity," she murmured. "Me, too." She patted her abdomen. "I count calories, drink protein shakes . . . The mother's not the one supposed to be carrying the baby fat."

Nor the bride. I thought about the obnoxious ads I was suddenly receiving about getting in shape for The Big Day. Somebody—and I had my suspicions who—had put my name on a list so that I was blitzed with bridal lit. This included so many remodeling suggestions that I felt as if a groom-to-be became betrothed not to the woman as she was, but to his or her fantasized version of what else she could be. According to the ads, the engagement period was the time assigned to change the contours of hip, nose, chin, breasts, even feet if the desired slippers didn't fit properly. If exercise and portion control didn't do it, then implants, liposuction, and surgery could. There were special discounts for the soon-to-be wed, timetables of how far in advance of The Big Day each surgery would need to be performed.

It wasn't hard to understand how young girls acquired distorted visions of themselves, how they were trained to never be satisfied with who they were and how they appeared. After half a dozen of the ads arrived, I looked at myself differently and asked Mackenzie—only half in jest—whether I'd be a better me if I trimmed or augmented various parts.

He suggested that I should. In fact, he advocated that I add a Pinocchio-sized nose and remove my current boobs so that I'd stand out in the plasticized crowd.

He is definitely the guy for me.

I remembered why I was in this office. "So my question is, what are we supposed to do about the problem? Or maybe—are we supposed to do anything about something like that? Tell me we can't. Can we? And if so, what would it be?"

She exhaled loudly. "How about we DNA test the girls' room mess, and, of course, the entire student body so that we can track down the offender, tie her up, and force her to actually digest what she eats."

"Great plan. Do you have any suggestions that approach reality?"

"Nothing short of changing the entire culture. Eliminate all ads for fried and fattening and delicious and chocolate and beer and burgers—no wonder obesity's such a problem—but then, in order not to make them truly crazy, also eliminate all the TV shows with the incredibly thin stars, and all the airbrushed, Photoshopped, further thinned-out models in their magazines. How about if we stop saying you'll be happy and feel good if you eat this great-tasting fatty, salty, sweet stuff—and then, if you want to be adored, look like you're starving to death. What if women could simply look like themselves?"

She reached over to a teen magazine on her makeshift coffee table and flipped through it until she stopped and pointed at a page. "This!" she said. "Look at this model."

She was, of course, beautiful. Also, judging by her proportions, slightly over seven feet tall, and perhaps sixty pounds, and all of that in the chest. Her legs began at her neck. "This is who they want to be," Rachel said. "And she doesn't exist. I actually got a letter from the photographer who did a similar ad, lots of similar ads. He had repented and was trying to spread the word about how fake these images are. His mission has obviously failed and the images go on. I personally find it immoral, but there aren't any laws about it. He said that the photo of the already emaciated model had been further altered, at the orders of the art director, so that her legs were made longer and thinner, and her crotch lifted."

I raised my eyebrows at that last item. "A new kind of plastic surgery?"

"It's necessary to lift the region in the photo so as to convince you that her legs really are that long and thin," Rachel said. "Millions of dollars spent on ads for food nobody needs, and then billions spent forcing these images in front of every pair of dying-to-be 'normal' eyes, compelling them to believe this is normal, 'This is how you have to be!' when it's not only unhealthy, it's not only damaging what remains of their bodies, but it's also physically impossible. No wonder you wind up with Liddy Moffat ready to quit."

I let her rant. This was obviously not a new issue to her, or to this office. Whether or not it was one she, or we, or anyone could tackle with even a slim hope of success remained to be seen.

Meanwhile, I would stop wondering whether I really had to lose weight in order to become the right sort of bride.

At NOON, when I checked, there was a message from Penelope on the cell phone. "Please call, Miss Pepper. Ingrid is in a good phase, which is astounding given the shock of her son's death. I thought it might help you with your investigation if you actually met her and . . . Cornelius." She made his name have four distinct syllables and made it clear that each one of them left a bitter taste on her tongue. "I wondered whether you'd be at the funeral tomorrow. Please let me know." She gave me her private line's number and an e-mail address, and I phoned in my regrets, telling her that my partner would be there.

"Pity," she said. "But wait, is there a chance for this evening?"

Once again, I had to demur. "I've got an appointment," I said. "Concerning this issue."

She didn't ask me with whom, which I found strange.

"Pity." Her voice had lost its verve. And then her spirits rebounded. "Last try—have you a minute later today? She generally rests midday so that she'd be refreshed by teatime."

Teatime indeed. Why not? While I didn't think much of a practical nature would be gained by the visit, I was curious about the old woman. Definitely curious to meet the fabled Cornelius.

And a cup of tea never hurt.

If I say the day passed without much incident, you must take that to mean on this day, nobody died. There was, of course, incident aplenty. You can't be in a community of adolescents without hourly doses of high drama. Tragedy, comedy, and lots of farce are our daily fare, although most often, they hinge on less than Shakespearean themes, such as whether a given boy likes a given girl, or whether a given girl has erupted with an unfortunately located pimple, or whether someone's parents were allowing him to see the new movie the night it opened. The laws of physics are suspended in high school, because any action, no matter how insignificant, can produce a reaction that is operatic in intensity.

With the exception of schoolwork and adults, everything mattered to everyone, all the time, enormously.

The *Inkwire* staff met at the end of the day. Last year, we'd placed third in an all-city contest for design and layout. Not exactly the Pulitzer, but a start. This year, we were going for the gold, entering the actual journalism contest with the drug feature. When I told them the plan they looked as delighted as if they'd already won, and in a way they had, by being eligible for it. "We should specially send the part Zach wrote," a dark-haired girl said. For once, I was fairly sure this wasn't teen code for "I have a crush on Zachary Wallenberg." She was paying simple and honest tribute to his work, which was, in fact, the strongest part of the issue. "That's the one that could win," she added. "It's not like the usual 'just say no' junk. It's real."

We were not a school used to garnering awards, particularly in anything resembling intellectual endeavor. The possibility of a prize for a piece of research and reportage loomed large in all our minds.

Zachary, who'd found the dealers and established how frighteningly easy it was to acquire whatever illegal substance one had in mind, or to make some of them, looked both pleased and embarrassed. Then he succumbed to the excitement swirling around him and raised his arms in a mock victory salute. It was an intentionally funny gesture, since the show of strength was tempered by the cast on his arm. He'd broken it in a soccer accident the first week of school. Still, even an autographed and grimy cast can express triumph, and he'd earned it.

"The dude who died here," one of the other boys said. "The paper said he had stuff in him. You think he came here to make the buy? You think he found out where to go from your article, man?"

Zachary looked stunned.

"Just joking," the other boy said.

It was time to get to the business at hand, however, and we bounced ideas around for future articles: the vote on the senior class trip, the mural the art class was painting on a wall in South

Philly, the upcoming Halloween Party, whether we could have more elective classes . . .

"Definitely an editorial saying no more assemblies about Life!"

We all laughed guiltily, but did not put that on the list.

"How weird was that?" Carrie, an eleventh grader said. "We're all stuck listening to the talk about life while a guy's dying right outside the auditorium."

Lewis, a cute sophomore, broke the meditative gloom this produced. "What about a follow-up?"

"To that?" My mind was still on that ironic juxtaposition.

"To the drug thing. Why don't we talk to the police about how come we can find the dealers, but they're still there, like the cops can't."

"Excellent!" someone said.

Zachary, our new expert, smiled. "It's not like the TV dramas of the inner city. The dealers aren't hanging on the corner, waiting to make a sale. You know the dude, you say what you want, he gets it from somebody else. And he maybe only has a total of five pills at a time. Not that high on a cop's priority list. And who's going to tell, anyway? Aside from that, he's just a kid like us, making a few extra bucks. And he doesn't sell heroin or crack, only pharmaceuticals."

"But how about somebody like me?" I asked. I felt a twinge of guilt about using them as information sources, but I kept thinking about staid-looking, middle-aged Tomas Severin with that drug coursing in his veins. "Someone my age? Older? How would they find the person?"

"Like . . . for which one?"

"Like . . . the date-rape drugs." Like the drug in Tomas Severin.

"Ask any kid," someone said, and everybody laughed.

"Or make it yourself, if you're careful. Or so I heard," another boy said.

"You've got to know what you're doing, man," his friend said. He shrugged.

"I'm not planning to cook any up," I said quietly. "Not to worry."

At least the uneventful day had been well rounded. A start with girls destroying their bodies, and a conclusion about the ease of obtaining drugs. And somewhere to the side, a murdered man.

Who was it called school an ivory tower?

Eight

IN Hollywood they call them hyphenates. Writer-producer. Director-producer. Actor-whatever—you get it. There's a certain glamour to being a hyphenate there. It suggests a deliberate and chosen expansion of one's creative roles and life.

There is no glamour in needing a second job so as to pay the rent. Teacher-PI not only lacked the glamour of Hollywood's hyphenates, but sounded ridiculous. I felt competent and fine as long as the second job remained clerical. I know my alphabet, and I can file. I have also learned to work a computer relatively well. But Mackenzie was supposed to do the heavy lifting. He was the one with the license, and I was his trainee or apprentice. He supervised me, at least in theory. But while I thought of *super-*

vision as akin to teaching, something that involved pretty constant monitoring and guidance, Mackenzie thought of it as a casual dinnertime catch-up on how the day had gone. He said he trusted my instincts. He said I was smart.

It was a good plan if you wanted to save time and effort. I considered telling my students I trusted their instincts, and they could take the semester off to read great books.

I set out for my two interviews with my usual uncertainty, wishing I had a clear sense of purpose for either of them. Citizen Mackenzie had given Owen Edwards a heads-up about Cornelius, but I still didn't know any more about him than that he was engaged to a sporadically dotty woman forty-six years his senior. Included in what I didn't know was what I was supposed to find out or notice.

I drove out of the city into ever-increasing green and open spaces. Ingrid Severin lived in Villanova, in a sprawl of stone behind gates that bordered a city block's worth of lawn. My ancient, held together with duct tape Mustang so clearly understood that it didn't belong here that it stalled twice on the cobbled drive.

I was greeted by a silent, efficient woman I assumed to be the housekeeper, and led into a spacious room that overlooked another park's worth of careful landscaping. Autumn had been exceptionally warm, and only now, close to Halloween, were the trees turning. French windows lined the far wall, and through them blazed a velvety lawn studded with masses of chrysanthemums that seemed to reflect the trees' lemony, orange, and flame leaves.

Obviously, nature was one of the things that money could buy.

Penelope Koepple was standing when I entered the room, as was a woman dressed entirely in black, with hair to match. She was petite, voluptuous, and furious. "You are not in a position to make decisions," she told Penelope in a low and lethal voice. "Don't pretend *she's* in charge. I know this is your sort of meddling, your definition of propriety, but I will take my rightful place. I hope that's understood. Whether or not it is, I will take it at the funeral, so don't try to prevent me. I came here as a politeness, nothing else."

Penelope glanced at the housekeeper. "Mrs. Severin will be needing her coat," she said. "She was just leaving." She didn't push the petite widow out the door, not physically, but the effect was as rapid and efficient as if she had.

So that was Nina Severin, who, given her phone call rant to Sasha and this performance, might benefit from anger-management classes. And I thought I would benefit by putting her on my list of interviewees.

Meanwhile, Penelope retrieved me from the housekeeper and escorted me into the room as if I were a pet she'd just found. "And after that," Penelope called to the retreating housekeeper, "that" referring to young widow Severin, "you may bring tea."

She introduced me to the two people seated on one of the long chintz-covered sofas, though she needn't have. Who else could the emaciated woman in the dark blond wig and black knit dress have been? Who else could be the man who could have been her grandson had she not had her hand on his thigh?

Miz K. was less sure of herself here than she had been in the office. There was the hint of obsequiousness in her voice as she introduced me to her employer, the hint of the desire to not provoke anger or resentment, to have me be a good entertainment for today's teatime. "Miss Pepper is working with the police to investigate Tomas's death," she said by way of introduction.

"I'm so sorry for your loss," I said.

Ingrid Severin looked at me with the alert expectancy of a child at a puppet show. Maybe I'd be interesting, and maybe I wouldn't.

Penelope poured us all tea. "No sugar for me, no, no." Ingrid shook her head for emphasis.

"I know that," Penelope whispered.

"A girl has to watch her figure." Ingrid chuckled. I don't know how she watched hers, as it was close to nonexistent. She was acutely thin without a soft turn on her anywhere, and her black knit dress and jacket appeared to cover a loose arrangement of bones. Her face was smooth, her eyes wide, and the few lines between her chin and ears skewed, rising on an angle toward her temples in a way that said a facelift too many had trumped the laws of gravity. Her head looked borrowed from someone younger. It didn't match her hands, the crinkles in the flesh of her wrists, or any of the rest of her. It also didn't look quite human.

"And oh, my—none of those cakes that look so good! Not for me or I'll get fat!"

Her weight concerns, particularly given the circumstances, also didn't seem fully human.

"I know." Penelope let weariness into her voice. She didn't seem to care who heard it.

The cakes did look incredibly good, light and moist, with ganache filling and chocolate glazes decorated with candied violets. It was all I could do to keep from salivating, but I waited to be offered one. My mother would have been proud of me.

"Ladies do not want to be fat!" Ingrid said. "No, no, no!"

She seemed on automatic pilot. This is what one said when faced with edible objects. We could slip her into Philly Prep with the bulimics and they'd understand each other perfectly. She made me morose.

On the other hand, Liddy Moffat would probably make her a goddess. After all, Ingrid's face had been recycled enough times to win an ecology prize.

"I'll bet Ingrid would love one of these cucumber sandwiches. Wouldn't you, Li'l Thing?" Cornelius piped his voice up an octave.

Penelope K. sighed dramatically.

Cornelius ignored her, and didn't wait for Li'l Thing to answer, either, but used the silver tongs to pluck a waferlike sandwich onto a small plate he passed to her. She took the plate and beamed upon him.

I wondered if she was under sedation.

Cornelius was a surprise. I didn't have the sort of bank account or interests that exposed me to a lot of gigolos, so my imagery's out of date. I'd imagined Ramon Novarro or Valentino—a lounge lizard complete with pencil-thin mustache. Cornelius Westerly was nowhere near my fantasies. Given a room of men from which to choose my fortune-hunting fake, he'd have been close to my last choice.

He was strikingly average. He had sandy hair, a somewhat rosy complexion, and not a single feature you'd single out. Average height. Average weight. I could more imagine him coaching Little League than courting a woman who could be his grandmother and attempting to con her out of millions of dollars' worth of real estate.

Ingrid beamed at him.

Penelope fumed. I half expected steam to emerge from her ears.

Cornelius smiled back at Ingrid, patted her hand, and fed her bits of cucumber sandwich.

Ingrid's tiny right wrist held ivory bracelets that made muffled clunks when she returned the china plate to the coffee table. The bracelets were the only jewelry she wore except for a large emerald-cut diamond ring on her left hand. I glanced at Cornelius, wondering how he'd afforded it. Perhaps in arrangements such as this, it was customary for the bride to buy her own ring. To engage herself. Maybe all rules and customs were off when there was this much of a disparity between means and age.

"Cornelius always knows precisely what I want, doesn't he, Penelope? Isn't he amazing?"

Her mind might be going, but she remembered how to needle and torment. The wink she gave her social secretary emphasized the fact that she knew precisely what she'd said and meant.

"Have we met before?" Ingrid lifted her teacup, and holding it at chest level, paused to ask her question in a sociable melodic voice with a hint of the crackling of old age. I could imagine her a young hostess, and I could see how lovely she must have been. What was now starved and cadaverous must have once been willowy and svelte, and somewhere beneath the pulled tight, puffed-lipped face, there appeared the vestiges of real beauty. "Pepper, is it? I've known a Pepper or two. Are you one of them?"

I don't know what I had expected her to say or do. I don't know how families behave when one of them has been abruptly, cruelly, and murderously taken from them. I hope I never have to know it firsthand. But I would have thought the loss would be taken more seriously.

Life must go on, but must it go on quite this superficially, catered and politely low-key, as if purely social? Maybe it was a matter of propriety to keep up appearances, maybe women like Ingrid Severin were trained to keep a stiff—if artificially inflated— upper lip no matter the circumstances. I, however, didn't get it. The woman's only child would be buried tomorrow. Did she honestly feel in the mood for cucumber sandwiches, geriatric flirting, and social niceties?

Nobody offered the cakes to me. Perhaps they were saving me from becoming fat, or from Ingrid's reaction to my accepting one. She seemed numb to human emotions, except on that topic, but on that topic, she had enough emotions to produce a stroke.

"Now what is wrong with silly me? How are you expected to know if you're one of the Peppers I know?" She trilled a small, insincere laugh.

I thought she'd be consumed by grief. That she'd ask questions, demand I find whoever had harmed her beloved son.

"I never forget a face—or a pair of shoes, for that matter," she said. "But names . . ." She shook her head. Her dark blond hair— a wig, I had to assume—was cut in a straight bob. "Not that I was ever that good about names, was I, Penelope?" she added, to reassure us, or herself, that nothing was really wrong with her.

Penelope's murmur was unintelligible.

"I think this is the first time I've had the pleasure of meeting you," I said. "Meeting the both of you," I added.

Cornelius looked startled, as if he generally wasn't included in conversations.

I didn't know how to proceed and Penelope wasn't helping.

She'd asked me to come here to get a better sense of Cornelius, and I didn't know how to do that in this situation. "Tomas's death must be quite a shock," I said to the two of them. Connect! I mentally urged them—grab the thought and go with it. You know, the way people with emotional systems do?

Instead, they regarded me as if from a distance, as if whatever they might have felt was none of my business. Maybe if I mentioned calories she'd respond.

Penelope finally spoke. "Miss Pepper is the teacher who—"

"You're the one?" Cornelius asked in a tone that combined amazement and sympathy. I wondered how bright he was. He seemed surprised by everything.

"I wanted to convey my sympathy," I said.

"How sweet of you," Ingrid murmured. And without warning or transition, the cordial hostess mask she'd been wearing crumpled, as much as her lack of facial elasticity would allow, into a bereaved old woman's face. "My son," she said in a flat voice. She put her cup on the coffee table, but kept her hand on it, as if it steadied her. Then she looked at me. "My son died."

I nodded.

"He was such a pretty baby, such a pretty little boy."

"Now, now, L'il Thing," Cornelius said.

Penelope looked away from them.

"Don't upset yourself," Cornelius said.

"My lady friends oohed and aahed, he was that pretty. And at our soirees, his Nanny would bring him in, and sometimes he'd sing in that pretty little-boy voice he had. He looked like a Botticelli angel." She nodded and her smooth blond bob shimmered with the movement.

"Always a beautiful boy, wasn't he, Penelope? A shining jewel—prettier, even. Irresistible, wasn't he?"

Penelope wrinkled her forehead. She hadn't been with the family when Tom Severin was a boy. Ingrid was confused, but Penelope knew her role, and she acknowledged the memory all the same. "A very good boy," she said. "And irresistible."

"He was perfect. I was so proud to be seen with him. And then such a handsome young man and man. But the police came," she said. "He died. They think . . . do you think what they think?"

"I wouldn't have the expertise to say, one way or the other." Of course it was murder. She knew it; I knew it. A man doesn't drug himself, then bash himself in the cheek and then fall backward down the stairs. But I saw no reason to burden her with ideas that wouldn't change her painful reality and that, in truth, I was sure she already understood herself.

"There's no sense speculating and upsetting yourself. Think of good memories. Happy times." Cornelius sounded as if he was quoting a book of phrases for the newly bereaved. He sounded like someone thirty-two years old and happily ignorant of losses as devastating as this one.

Ingrid Severin ignored him, pulled her hand out from under his. "He was a graceful man, Miss . . . Miss . . ."

"Pepper," Penelope reminded her.

"Yes. I knew some Peppers. Are you . . . ?"

"I'm afraid not."

"Tom was an athlete. Outstanding ballroom dancer. Not the sort to ever, ever trip."

Everyone trips. How could even a mother believe that her son was the exception?

"And he did not take drugs," she said firmly. "He did not. He said, 'Mother, taking drugs is . . . taking drugs . . .' Well, he said something, and it wasn't good about taking drugs. *He* wasn't the one got addicted. *He* wasn't the disgrace. He knew—we all knew—drugs . . ." She shook her head again, the gesture substituting for a host of bad things that he'd said about drugs.

"Time to lie down," Cornelius crooned. "A little nap so you'll feel better."

I didn't know what impression Penelope had hoped I'd get of the young man, but I was watching an attentive, ineffectual, and unimaginative person try to ease an old woman's pain and confusion.

"*She* did it!" Ingrid hissed with such venom, it shocked me, as if actual snakes had sprung from her throat.

"Shhhh," Cornelius said.

"Who? Who do you mean?" Penelope looked alarmed, and I wondered who she was afraid her employer would name.

"*She's* the one who took drugs. Her." She lowered her lids, looked at each of us in turn. "Where is she?"

"Who is that, Mrs. Severin?" I asked.

Ingrid blinked, then ignored my question. She looked around the room wildly, craning to peer behind the sofa, as if "she" might be there. "Spite, that's all the fat pig ever was about. Ugly on the outside, ugly on the inside, I say."

"Nobody's there, Ingrid. You mustn't get yourself all upset this way." Penelope sounded worried now.

"Mrs. Severin must be tired," I said, but the tired woman glared at me and shouted, *"Her!"* so emphatically, I thought she meant I had killed her son.

The skin around Ingrid Severin's eyes had been tightened and, snipped so often I was surprised she could blink, but she could definitely still cry. Her startled-looking eyes welled. "She'd do it just to spite me—I know."

"Who?" Penelope asked yet again, but Cornelius stood up and, gently cradling her stick-figure limbs, lifted sobbing Ingrid Severin into his arms. "Time to rest," he said in a near-whisper. He walked, easily carrying his light burden, but when he was near Penelope, he spoke in a low, sure voice I could hear.

"You did this on purpose," he said. "She's fragile, and you provoked this. What was the point—" he looked toward me, including me in the circle of guilt, and then he turned to Penelope Koepple again. "What's wrong with you? Are you trying to murder her, too?" He took his ancient, sobbing fiancée out of the room.

Penelope turned to me, her mouth ajar. "Did you hear that? What he implied? That gold-digging schemer, that—"

I didn't want to hear any of them anymore. When a con artist courting a wealthy old woman is the most considerate and decent-seeming person around, it's time to leave. I felt contaminated. And the plain truth was, Penelope, whose eyes even now were round with outraged innocence, had "done it." She'd invited me to come, knowing what I couldn't have known—that it would throw her employer into the darkness that so often enveloped her.

Penelope demanded to know what I thought of Cornelius's "performance." I did not offer any opinions, but I promised a full report as soon as it was convenient. She threatened to fire Mackenzie and me, and I nodded and hurried out.

I had another stop to make, but then, I couldn't wait to be home with my trustworthy, ethical, surely-not-gold-digging Mackenzie. I wanted to be where I was sure the ground I walked on was stable. I wanted a shower, to wash off the residue of so many people hating and distrusting their closest ties.

I wondered who "she" was, the one who knew about drugs and hated Tomas. Was it Penelope, or the ex-fiancée Georgeanne, or one of the wives, or was it the wife, perhaps of one of Ingrid's lovers? Or was the whole idea of that person a figment of Ingrid's confused mind?

And then I realized I didn't care.

I wanted Penelope to fire us. I wanted out.

But I wished somebody had offered me one of the little glazed cakes first.

Nine

"THE Koepple bitch got to you, didn't she?" Georgeanne Errico blew her nose, which was so puffed and rosy she'd probably been sniffling for some time. She sat ramrod straight on her loveseat. A fluff of a dog so small my cat would dwarf him sat at equal attention on her lap.

Georgeanne had agreed to talk with me only after I said I was concerned with the legal aspects of Tomas Severin's death. I was fairly certain she'd interpreted that the way I'd wanted her to—as if I'd meant I was working on the financial aftershocks and her possible inheritance as an almost-wife with an almost pre-nup. She sniffled and blew her nose as necessary, she dabbed at her eyes, but she never explained her respiratory distress. I wanted to believe that despite their engagement having been so recently and unexpectedly dissolved, this was a display of grief at the loss of a love she'd hoped to recover, not the flu, an allergy to her dog, or despair at having come so close to billions, only to have them disappear forever because of her too-evident greed, if Penelope was right.

Unless, of course, she'd been so enraged—a woman scorned, a fortune unshared—that she was the hand that propelled Tom Severin down those stairs.

Her apartment was shabby-chic. Almost everything could have stood reupholstering and slipcovering except that then it would not convey the idea that these were long-standing family possessions, that each piece had a pedigree and distinguished heritage and, therefore, so did she. Even the art—uninspired landscapes darkened with time, and a fly-specked botanical drawing—appeared to be hand-me-downs because who would choose them now? The effect, real or carefully created, was that nothing had needed to be bought, that Georgeanne was the product of old and understated financial comfort.

Perfect for a man like Tom Severin who, according to Penelope K., liked his wives about Georgeanne's age and of his own social class.

Sasha had never stood a chance. She must have been an exotic amusement for him.

A suitcase, the rolling kind, stood by the door, and next to it, a pet carrier. She saw me notice it. "We were going to Boston for a shoot."

I must have looked confused about the "we." "Pickles and me, we go everywhere together," she said. "Doesn't always make little Mister Pickle-wickle happy to travel, but it makes me happy to have him nearby." Each time she said the tiny creature's name, or something that rhymed with it, his ears lifted and he cocked his head, which I had to admit, was fairly adorable. He was also much more tolerant of her icky baby-dog talk than I was, and that's one reason nobody lists me as man's best friend.

"I'm a photographer's assistant," she said by way of explanation. "Mostly in New York, but this shoot . . . Of course now,

now . . ." She shook her head. "I'm too devastated to do anything, to even unpack."

I would have found Georgeanne's plight more touching had she not been the victim of excessive prenup bickering with a man who was still married to someone. And had she not been dumped a week ago. "You saw Penelope, didn't you?" she asked. "What did the Dragon Woman tell you?" She blew her nose again.

I smiled and shook my head in a way I hoped expressed regret that professional ethics made me unable to divulge anything. That was a lot to lay on one rueful smile, but I wanted it to do even more—to also suggest that otherwise, we'd be new best girlfriends, swapping the secrets of our hearts. "Only that you were dating Tomas Severin, and that you'd been a childhood friend of Ingrid Severin's, um, fiancé," I said.

"I was Tom's fiancée, not just a date," she corrected me. "It hadn't been announced yet, because of his situation."

I liked that. A new one for the SAT's: a synonym for marriage is—situation.

"We were engaged. We were going to be married as soon as . . ." She waved off the obvious remainder of the idea. She was a pretty young woman, and not the flashy creature I'd anticipated. I should have known that Tom Severin wouldn't have had a visible bimbo as a serious consort. He could afford the very best.

Georgeanne's polished, aloof posture made her sleek black hair and chiseled features more impressive than they actually were. She was tall and thin and dressed completely in black, either for mourning or simply because that was the uniform of fashion photographers. One thing I could tell was that she was daring, holding a long-haired white dog on her black-swathed lap.

"You've known Cornelius for some time?" I prompted.

"We went to the same high school. He was two years ahead of me, but my folks and his knew each other, so he paid a little attention to me. He was on the basketball and tennis teams, big star, way popular. He wouldn't have noticed me without the family connection. We went out a few times, but there was nothing there, and then we went our separate ways. I never saw him again until after I started dating . . ." She swallowed hard, apparently unable to say the name. A tad histrionic, I thought, given the circumstances. "Tom," she finally managed. "And because I recognized him and said hello, and we joked about high school, the Dragon decided we were—well, I don't know what. *Intimates,* she called us." Georgeanne looked at me, her mouth pursed in obvious imitation of Penelope Koepple. "How she got to be such a priggish snob, I will never know. She's the lady's *secretary,* not her best friend."

"When you knew him in high school, was his name—"

Georgeanne waved away the rest of my words. "Yes. His name is Cornelius Westerly and always was. For some reason, the Dragon Lady is sure he changed it, and how stupid is that? She should talk to his parents. Their names are Arabella and Constantine. Cornelius's brother was Montgomery and he has a sister Isolde. You know, when you're operating on a budget, the one thing you can afford is the most ornate, gold-encrusted name in the universe. The Westerlys were plain people, aside from their names. His dad had a shoe-repair shop." She shrugged. "Probably still does."

I reconsidered her choice of furnishings. If her parents were friends of the cobbler, the furnishings here were probably not family heirlooms. Clever Georgeanne to create the perfect, canny backdrop from scratch, to make Tom Severin feel at home with Cinderella, even if he didn't quite know why. But how horrible to have an über-catch like Tom the billionaire slip away because of poor negotiating or diplomatic skills. We were silent a moment, and then she appeared to have thought something out.

"I'm not saying I approve of his . . . romance. And not only because of the age difference. I resent that she's using him more than he's using her. She's always had lovers. Dozens of them and as vague and confused as she gets, that part of her brain still seems to function. Forgets her own son's identity, but then she'll talk about her 'conquests.' That's her word, not mine. She sounds like a big-game hunter when she talks about them. How she spotted them, how beautiful each of them was, and she tells you in great detail. Ingrid is a great connoisseur of beauty. Self-appointed. Then she describes how she entrapped them—honestly, how she used them, God help us, and then, how she dumped them. She brags about it. And worse, she tells you how much each one cost. One cost a boat she bought him, one was dirt cheap, just enough liquor to keep him soused. And so on. That's how she thinks of people, lovers or no. Commodities. Things to be bought and paid for, used and discarded.

"Cornelius is one more toy, and she said he might be the most expensive. 'A few apartment buildings,' she said, and said it right in front of him, too, and then she laughed. So don't think of her as the poor old lady being snookered by a . . . a whatever Koepple called him. And don't think of him as a sleaze. Trust me, he'll have earned whatever she decides is his 'cost.' He can't be having much fun."

I didn't think "fun" was on Cornelius's current list of objectives.

"Not that Mama Ingrid was ever great fun from what I heard," Georgeanne said. "But now, it's like her social censor's turned off and the viper's out there for all to see. She only stops spewing poison when she sees—saw—that she's gone too far, that she'd upset Tom. She'd do anything for him."

"They were close?"

"The one problem I had with Tomas was how tight he was with his mother, but I figured I could ride it out. She's ancient and going, after all." She dabbed at the sides of her eyes, although I couldn't see any tears. "Who could have imagined that he'd be the one to go?"

"Did you think that Cornelius came between her and Tom?"

She shook her head. The little dog watched her every move, adoringly. "Nothing could have. Of course, she didn't always listen to Tom's advice once Cornelius was on the scene, and that made Tom furious even though just maybe Cornelius could have been right about a few things. It wasn't like Tom was going to be out on the street if she gave Cornelius a building here and there."

"You seem quite . . . I mean given that your engagement—"

She looked sulky, but only for a moment, and then she seemed to clear the darkness off her face and she hugged the little dog and lapsed into baby-talk again. I tried not to hear it, but "poor uggums whose mama . . ." snuck through my yuck barrier.

"Just to make sure I have it right—is it correct that the two of you ended the engagement recently?"

She waved her hand dismissively. "A speed bump. A lover's disagreement, not even a quarrel. We'd have worked things out." She looked at me defiantly. The little dog yapped, as if agreeing. "If you are suggesting for one minute that I am somehow responsible for Tom's death—"

"Not at all. Just trying to keep everything straight."

"We would have gotten past this. Every couple has differences, every relationship its ups and downs. I heard about the supposedly 'new' girl. Penelope made it a point to tell me. But I know Tomas. He's Ingrid's son that way and how could he be otherwise? He comes from people who don't have the same moral code as the rest of us. But she was nothing to him. He'd have been back." She opted to sniffle again. The little dog stood on his hind legs and licked her face.

Poor, poor Sasha. Or maybe lucky Sasha, to have not had the chance to become over-involved with this man and family. "Ms. Koepple suggested—"

"Don't talk to me about her. She's a vulture, picking at Ingrid's remains before the woman's gone. Those airs! So Merchant-Ivory—based on what? And the fake humanitarianism makes me sick. It's all about her, don't you see? She talks about how Cornelius is robbing Tomas's children of their birthright, as if she gives a damn. She hates them—and frankly, I'm with her on that. The twins are the whiniest, most spoiled . . . but then, if you look at their mother, you know how they got that way."

"Their mother is the current . . . ?"

"Nina, yes." Georgeanne nodded. "Penelope all but faints every time they come to visit their grandmother. She always finds things to do that take her away from home, and she was delighted to hear that Tomas was leaving Nina. Trust me, Penelope isn't worried about anybody's future except her own. She's picked on Cornelius and tried to poison Ingrid's mind about him every step of the way. Obviously, Ingrid bought none of it, and got angry with her. Penelope's rightfully afraid that she's pissed off Ingrid to the point where whatever was promised her is no longer in the will. I'd been led to believe Ingrid was leaving her enough of a bequest that Penelope never had to work again.

"That's why she wants Cornelius out of the picture. If nothing gets changed, and Ingrid keeps failing, Penelope's set for life. If they start mucking with Ingrid's will, who knows what happens to Penelope's bequest?"

I thought of the afternoon's contretemps. Was that why Penelope wanted me there? To upset and disorient Ingrid so that no new will could cut the secretary out? "You've gotten to know the family quite well," I said quietly.

She raised her eyebrows. "I knew Tomas quite well. These things worried him. You're thinking it's odd that I met his mother and his children, because Tomas is—was—still married, technically speaking, but it's an odd family. A sort of medieval fiefdom with dukes and empresses and intrigue and plots one against the other. Nina, his—the wife he was divorcing—she was history in that household. They don't have problems getting over people." She shook her head as if bemused. "Ingrid's the Czarina, all right, but all the Mrs. Severins, maybe except the first wife, are Grand Duchesses, or whatever high and mighty term exists. I get the feeling the first one was a youthful mistake, that's all. Quickly over and forgotten. But the other two, what a pair of harpies! I would not be surprised if one of them poisoned him with whatever that was. Whatever else you might think about me, I would have been his best-natured wife." She looked sniffly again.

She wasn't having an allergy attack. Her tears were, indeed, those of mourning, though I couldn't yet tell if they were about Tomas or his billions. She seemed so brittle and hard, she would have fit right into that family. No wonder she was upset.

"Had Tomas and Cornelius worked out their differences?"

She narrowed her eyes, as if to better see where I was headed.

"Now how would I know that, unless I was in close contact with Cornelius?" Her voice had lost any trace of warmth. "You've let the Dragon poison your mind about me."

She put the tissue to her dry eyes again. I took that as my cue to leave. I couldn't understand the script she was following, but her act was wearying.

Ten

MACKENZIE countered logically when I said I wanted to stop working with the wretched family. He agreed, but suggested that first we complete our report on Cornelius. That made sense, so even though I wasn't in the mood for making sense, I agreed to complete the project. We needed the money and the work was next to nothing.

Therefore, that evening the two of us returned to the land of Ozzie, and overjoyed his pizza boy by doubling the usual order, and while we munched pepperoni and mozzarella, we combed databases looking for Ingrid's fiancé and discovered that Cornelius Westerly appeared to be precisely who he said he was. He'd never been married, never been in prison. The only thing you could hold against him was a lackluster school record and a series of go-nowhere jobs, except for the most recent one as a paid "host" on cruise ships. That one had led directly to the Severin mansion.

His duties had been to escort single women on shore excursions, to be charming with them at all times, and to dance with them when the music played.

"How come I never heard about that job?" Mackenzie said. "What a life I could have had!"

"It must be tiring, like a boring party where your smile muscles ache, but one that lasts months."

Ingrid had apparently been wowed by her dance partner on a Caribbean cruise, and thus had begun their great romance.

Nothing criminal about that. Nothing criminal anywhere. Not that I believed Cornelius was profoundly in love with a barely-held-together woman pushing eighty, but strange are the ways of the heart and in any case, his actions were legal.

There were one or two more places to check, but Mackenzie was taking care of that, and we had no reason to expect any different results there.

Penelope was going to be disappointed, but I for one didn't care. We'd done what she asked, and our report would officially end our relationship.

I felt good knowing that as I entered school the next morning. It felt like starting over, ending the ugly chapter that had begun with my discovery of Tomas Severin Monday afternoon.

I had the sense that even the students had gotten sufficient distance on those events, and we were refreshed and reenergized. My first-period class actually had fun learning how to write a friendly letter. "Even if you break my heart and use e-mail all the time," I said, "make your goal being able to express emotion without spelling out things like *grin*. If you're being funny—be funny. No 'in my humble opinion,' no rolling on the floor laughing, and none of those little happy, sad, or whatever else faces. Use the language. That's what it's there for."

They humored me. It was an auspicious beginning to the day.

It was also an anomaly, a false indicator, and it was downhill from then on. The next class balked at taking a quiz, insisting I'd never assigned the section at hand, and what was frightening was that I wasn't sure they were wrong. We had a surprise fire-drill in the middle of a class that was going well, and that was it for that period. My tenth grade writing unit seemed to have detoured into incomprehensibility hell, and I could see no evidence that anyone had learned anything from the last exercise, and finally, in the afternoon, while the seniors were in the middle of an SAT-prep quiz, there was a knock on my door, and Mrs. Wiggins stood there, her arms bent up, palms facing me and fingers curled. Like a squirrel, only not as cute. I walked to the doorway.

"I wouldn't bother you," she whispered in her rabbit-speak voice.

"It's all right, but why not send up a messenger if—"

"Except that it's the police, you see."

I didn't see. I could only see this plump, gray woman who looked as if she were begging for nuts before winter arrived. "What do they want with me?"

"Nothing. Oh, no. I didn't mean to make you worry."

"Why are you here, Mrs. Wiggins?" I asked in the softest voice I could manage.

"Oh. Yes, of course. Well, dear, I'm here because they told me to come here."

"Because?"

"They're here for one of yours. If I read the schedule correctly, that is." Now she folded her hands over her chest, in a vaguely self-protective motion.

"The police want one of the students in this room."

She nodded.

"Who? Why?"

"They didn't say why to me, Miss Pepper," she said in her subdued voice. "They just said they wanted to talk with Zachary Wallenberg. That's all."

"They? How many?"

"Him, actually. One."

Zachary. My pride and joy and personal success story. Three years ago, his distraught mother had thought of this school as a last try. Ever since her divorce, which meant for most of Zachary's elementary and junior high years, her son had been what's so euphemistically referred to as "acting out." His grades were abysmal and he'd had petty encounters with the law.

But he was one of the reasons that teaching sometimes seems one of life's great gifts. The sullen tenth-grader slowly dissolved into a kid with a new vision of how he could live. He pulled out all the stops and determined to get into a top college. He wanted to study everything, and then to write about it. To travel the world and report back about it.

And he would. I was sure his grades and sports were going to carry him to whatever school he desired. After that, who knew, but the breadth of his ambition warmed my heart.

I couldn't bear the idea of his screwing up now. I had a momentary panic about his being in trouble because of the drug article he'd written. But finding out about something isn't a crime.

Then I realized that if he'd done anything really serious, the cop would have come for him himself. This was probably about an idiotic adolescent thing that needed a talking-to, and little more. In fact, it probably wasn't even about Zachary himself. He simply must know something about somebody who was in trouble. And so I convinced myself while the squirrel-woman waited.

She pursed her lips. "He—the officer—told me to tell you his name. Very formal and polite of him, I thought! But . . . the thing is, I can't quite remember it now. I should have written it down. I have trouble remembering. Old age, I suppose, creeping up on me." The rust-colored patches I'd seen there before once again formed on her cheeks.

She was too young for jokes about old age. She looked like someone in her forties who had, perhaps, lived a little too hard at some point. Maybe that accounted for the memory lapses. Or she'd never been overly powered in the first place.

"An unusual name . . ." She continued musing to herself, making me think she might have a hearing problem as well. "If only I could . . ."

I wondered why an officer would feel obliged to tell me his name, unless he was a friend of C.K.'s and simply wanted to say hello—but that seemed unprofessional, to say the least. Hi, I'm here to make an arrest and how's it going? Then I knew who it had to be. "Was his name Owen, by any chance? Owen Edwards?"

Her head bobbed assent before I finished the name. "Owen. Unusual. Not the Edwards part, of course. How did you know?"

"I heard the name somewhere." I didn't want to remind her of Monday's fracas, did not want her to associate Zachary with any of it, or to inadvertently or on purpose start rumors.

But what was going on? What could Zach possibly have to do with the man's fall down the stairs?

"Zach will be down in ten minutes, when the period ends."

"The officer wanted to see him right away."

"I understand, but everybody's time is of the essence, including mine. Including my students. Tell him the class is taking a timed test, and as soon as it's over, Zach will be down. I'll escort him myself."

"Are you sure?"

I nodded.

"Hasn't this been a week, though," she said. "Police and trouble and more police . . ." and she toddled off, holding very tight to the banister of the great and fatal staircase.

It wasn't a timed test, and it wasn't important, but I couldn't see the point of humiliating Zach by having him pulled out of class by the school secretary. He'd come too far from the days when that happened with regularity.

The ten minutes rolled by fairly quickly for me, and, I hoped, for Officer Edwards downstairs.

I stopped Zach as he was leaving. "I'm going to go with you now. There's a police officer here who wants to talk with you."

He pulled back, as if my touch burned him. "Why?" he

asked, but not with the level of incredulity and surprise I'd have liked.

"I don't know. I'm sure it's nothing. How could it be something?"

I wanted him to agree with me, to be indignant, or look really confused. Instead, he looked terrified. No other word for it.

As for Owen Edwards, his expression was sad and he seemed reluctant to make the next move. He verified that Zachary Wallenberg was the young man standing in front of him, and then he suggested that Zach go into Dr. Havermeyer's office. He made it clear that the headmaster was not in there, and they'd borrow the space for a minute or two. His voice was casual and light, making whatever business they had to transpire sound optional and non-threatening.

Zach walked into the office with the air of someone on death row.

"I came down to vouch for this young man. He's a good kid, a good student, and don't let his long-ago reputation influence you otherwise. I've watched him shape up and forge ahead these past three years and—"

"There's no lynch mob in the principal's office. I'm not even closing the door. I simply need to ask some questions."

"He's obviously terrified by—"

"Trust me to not be frivolous, or to jump to conclusions."

"Still, is this really necessary?"

"A man's dead."

"But what could Zachary have to do with—"

I'd thought Edwards handsome, but now he was simply a collection of chilled and steely features.

"Fine," I said. "Sorry." I waved farewell, and turned around, furious, but accepting the idea that I wasn't doing Zach any good by interfering.

Ben Summers was waving at me from the top of the stairs. When he caught my eye, he nodded and walked toward my classroom door, where he awaited me.

He was a small, rumpled man who taught and adored science

and had little time for those of us teaching what he'd called "frippery." "Name a poem that invented computers or cured cancer," he'd said during one particularly caustic meeting when the allocation of textbook funds was being battled out.

I wasn't sure if having him eager to talk to me was good or bad news.

"The police are here," he whispered without preamble. "They came to my room."

What was this, a general roundup? "Why?"

"Wanted to know about Zachary Wallenberg."

Maybe I'd been wrong. Cops worked on more than one case. Maybe Zach had committed a scientific prank that backfired or stolen chemicals.

Except that Owen Edwards was a homicide detective, not a prank investigator. "What about him?" I asked.

"About assembly. Monday. You know, the day that man . . ." He shook his head. "Zach was in my group that period. We should have been doing something worthwhile in the lab, not wasting everybody's time on that god-awful speech, and then maybe nothing bad would have happened."

"I'm not following."

"The cop asked me weird questions, like whether we take roll in assembly. Do you?"

"A head count, and as long as everybody actually made it from the room to assembly, why bother?"

"That's what I said, but that wasn't what he wanted to hear. Then he asked me when assembly began—why me? When precisely my class had arrived and when they left—I mean it was the same for my class as anybody else's. Did they ask you things like that?"

I shook my head. I felt slightly unethical not telling him that Mrs. Wiggins had come on the police's behalf, and for Zachary himself. Then I thought again of the textbook battles, and didn't feel all that bad. "About Zach," I reminded him. Ben was a methodical man who could take forever to get to the point of his story, the only part of it I cared about.

"Then he asked whether anybody had been excused from the assembly. Of course nobody had, though I'm positive everybody wanted to be."

"What was he getting at, and what about Zach?"

"Zach left assembly. The cop seemed to already know that. I mean he asked all those general questions, but he was just revving up to get to Zach. And I couldn't remember for how long Zachary was gone. What do they want of us? It couldn't have been that long, or I'd have noticed, but it takes awhile to get to the boys' bathroom, and then come back, and if he dawdled and was reluctant to hurry, who the hell could blame him?"

"Was—was he the only one?"

"The only one I remember. I'd barely have remembered about Zach if Edwards hadn't brought him up specifically. What do you think he wants? How could he think Zachary . . ."

We shook our heads in mutual dismay and confusion and went to our rooms. I waited, and just as I was about to go back to the office to find out what was going on, the object of my concern appeared. He looked ashen. "Is it okay if I come in?" he asked.

"Of course. Have a seat."

"I don't want to keep you or anything." He managed to slump even while he was getting into the chair. Having a broken arm didn't make him look less pitiful, either.

I sat down at a desk next to the one he was in.

I waited till he felt ready to say whatever had brought him to my door. We'd established what I thought was a good relationship. I trusted him to tell me what was going on, and to be honest about it.

He cleared his throat. "So I guess you're wondering what the cop wanted with me."

"Bingo."

"He wanted to know about the man who died here."

No surprise. "What about?"

"Where I was when . . . when it happened."

"Why you?"

I had never realized how large his eyes were, or how burning. "Because—look, I need to explain something. Wallenberg isn't my real last name. I mean it *is* my real last name now—it's my legal name, and all, but that's because when she divorced my father, my mother took back her maiden name, and changed mine to match hers. She—she said she didn't want any part of him. Except me." He paused, to make sure I was following.

"Got it," I said.

"So my name was once Severin." He watched me closely, obviously noting my confusion. "That man was my father," he said. "And I hate him."

"Oh, Zach!" I tried to keep my expression neutral, but the area around my heart suddenly felt frostbitten.

He shook his head. "But I didn't push him down the stairs, I swear. The thing is, we had a . . . kind of a quarrel a week ago by e-mail, and the cop, he knew about it. You think my—you think he—"

"He?"

"My—the dead man—went to the cops about it?"

I shook my head. "What was it about?"

Zachary swallowed hard. "College. I barely ever see him, or ever had. They made jokes, in fact. That the reason I wasn't a Tomas, like all the firstborn sons, was because I was a trial kid. An experiment, to see if he liked it. I guess he didn't. One of his new kids, one of the twins, he's Tomas. But two years ago, he said that if I didn't get into any more trouble, if I buckled down, he'd pay for whatever college I wanted to go to and got into."

"And you've worked your butt off, I know. He should be—should have been proud of you. Wasn't he?"

He shrugged. "Not exactly, because the reason we had that . . . disagreement was that he sent me this e-mail that said I was turning eighteen next August, and I would have therefore achieved my majority, legally, and he had changed his mind about all that. That he was under no further legal obligation to pay for my education and he wasn't going to."

"Why on earth not?" I shouldn't have let the words burst out, but I had.

"Because he didn't have to. The law says he doesn't have to. He pays for this school. Said that was enough. And that's all he said. Oh, yeah, and that he was having a cash-flow crunch, expenses coming up." He clenched his fists. "He's getting divorced again. That's the expenses. And anyway, he could get divorced ten more times and still afford whatever I would have cost him. I read in the newspapers how rich he is. But he said he didn't have to support me anymore, so he wasn't going to."

I could only judge how much his father's words had rankled, by the fact that Zach had repeated the "doesn't have to and wasn't going to" idea three times.

"Did you respond to the e-mail?" I asked quietly.

He inhaled deeply, and nodded. "I shouldn't have, I know, but I hit reply and said 'drop dead.' In big caps. In red. I meant it. I meant I didn't care if he didn't care about me. I wouldn't need his money. I'd find a way, or my mom would, and we'd show him. She's finishing school and she's working part-time because child support's going to end. We'll figure it out. But I didn't say all that. All I said was 'drop dead.' And then he did." He looked down at his hands, or more accurately, his one visible hand, and the other, in which only the fingertips showed from under the now gray and ragged cast.

I didn't want to think about that cast.

I stood up and walked to the window, giving him time to collect himself while I silently cursed Penelope Koepple, who had surely gone through Tomas's e-mail files. Tomas had been staying at his mother's, and probably using the house computer for minor mail, like brushing off his son. Penelope Koepple had combed through his personal mail. She must have been ecstatic to find Zachary's message.

She was expending a huge amount of energy keeping everyone's eyes on anyone but her.

In all fairness, however, I admitted to myself that given the circumstances of Tom Severin's death, I might have done the same thing, if the e-mail had involved anyone but Zachary.

And in ultra-fairness, the police would have gone through Severin's mail themselves, but that wasn't as satisfying as being angry with Penelope.

From behind my back, the voice was low and without animation. "The policeman—he thought I did it, but I swear I didn't. I wouldn't lie to you. People say 'drop dead' all the time. They don't make it happen."

I turned and walked back to the chair next to his, and sat down again. "I believe you," I said, and I meant it, but I could feel how difficult it might be to convince other people.

"I didn't do it. I swear I didn't. I left assembly and went out back and had a cigarette." He immediately put his good hand up. "I know it's wrong."

It was no time for an antitobacco lecture.

"Can you help me?"

I couldn't imagine what I could do, except get over my resolve to run away from this unfortunate event. But perhaps Mackenzie and I could hang on to Penelope Koepple's payroll a little longer. It was an excellent cover for a continued investigation, for finding out who had actually drugged, battered, and killed Tomas Severin—as long as it wasn't Zachary. "Tell me one thing. Did you also phone him?"

He shook his head. "We didn't talk much."

I suddenly remembered his composition, about how a divorced parent shouldn't also divorce his child.

Zachary asked again. "Can you help me?"

"I'll do my best."

He looked relieved, the poor, trusting child.

Eleven

I looked at the afterimage of his back for too long, willing my train of thought to halt halfway to its destination and wait there for me, for a time when I wouldn't feel as pushed, or frightened by where those thoughts might take me.

Besides, I was already late for the meeting at Rachel Leary's office.

Edie Friedman, the gym and health teacher, was there along with Geneva Kiel, who taught biology. We were trying to find the proper inroad to the starving girls' psyches. "It isn't about bulimia per se." Rachel looked exhausted and pale. "It's about their entire self-image. Their screwed up self-images."

"Screwed up by . . ." Geneva let the rest of the sentence dangle.

"The world. Life, Mom, ads, movies . . ." Edie herself worried incessantly about not being married and owned every spot-reducing device ever patented, and now she waggled her head. "Not enough exercise."

Thus spake the gym teacher. We each have our windows on the world, and perhaps mine looks like the tiniest of portholes to Edie.

"It would help, you know," she insisted. "Certainly more than upchucking!"

"What are we supposed to do?" Rachel's voice reflected the fatigue on her face. "Where do you start when the abuse is about food, a basic necessity of life being used the wrong way? Lots of wrong ways. It's obesity, and anorexia, and . . ." She rolled her head on her neck.

"Yoga!" Edie Friedman said. "Try it! Your neck wouldn't hurt that way."

Rachel regarded her blankly. I could almost hear her thoughts, and could only assume she was simply too tired to ask Edie precisely when she was supposed to find the time for yoga, as lovely as it sounded. With a full-time job, three children under three, and an unemployed and possibly depressed househusband, she must have thought yoga beyond her imagination, if only because of the silence of the sessions.

"So what are we really talking about here?" Geneva asked softly. "Can you name a woman who is happy with how she looks? I mean really happy? I don't think we're supposed to be. I think it helps business if we always feel incomplete, or over the hill, or out of shape—if we're always afraid, if we always know there's something else we should be doing to look better."

"That's so negative!" Edie said.

"All we have to deal with—all we can deal with, if anything—is the health issue." Rachel yawned.

"Sorry," Geneva said. "I only meant—"

Rachel nodded. "I agree with you. It's way bigger than the four of us or the school. It's way bigger than food. What's it about? Wanting love, approval? Wanting mastery over self, over all kinds of appetites?" She yawned again. "Sorry," she said. "But to tell you the truth, I've had some bad experiences trying to deal with this one-on-one. Parents who wouldn't admit their daughter was starving herself to death because Mama was just as concerned as the kid was that nobody put on weight. I swear, they wouldn't blink if their daughter became a terrorist, unless she was a fat terrorist."

"Okay—so I'll do a unit in girls' health," Edie said. "Not that we haven't tried that before. We can talk about fitness, different body shapes, fad diets, crazy ways of exercising . . ."

"I'll coordinate plans with you," Geneva said. "I mean we could really talk about what happens to the body chemically, physiologically, when it starves, or binges, or deliberately regurgitates. My classes are coed, however, and this is a ten-to-one girl's problem. So I'll have to do the general route. They're not going to talk as honestly is what I'm trying to say."

"My classes aren't coed, so I'll work on getting them to talk about body images, about being manipulated," Edie said.

"Help yourself to any materials I've got," Rachel said.

We were collegial, supportive of our own good intentions, but I'm sure not a one of us thought we could make a difference. Maybe the girls would stop leaving evidence of their problem in the school, but that wouldn't make them feel they were lovable and acceptable. That wouldn't cure a thing. I nonetheless would do my part. A week or so after the health and science units, I would structure writing or discussion—a debate, perhaps—about what a teen should do if she thought a friend was putting herself into jeopardy. Something like that. And I was going to find a way to interest the newspaper staff in writing articles about body image, about pop culture icons, and what the message being sent was. Maybe we could examine it as a form of propaganda, which I suppose it was, although I wasn't sure for whom.

"The bottom line remains that it's a profoundly deep problem," Rachel said. "Most of these children need counseling. Not once a week in my office—real, intensive psychotherapy. Maybe their families, too. Sometimes they need a residential program. We aren't going to cure slow suicide with classroom units and warnings. But you gotta try, right?"

And with those words we all knew to be true, we left to tilt against this week's windmills, and I was sure each one of us was saying, the way we do almost every day: Who knows? Maybe this time it'll work.

As soon as I approached the staircase, images of Zachary pressed back on me. Whoever administered the push was probably acting on a spur-of-the moment flash of rage and as much as I couldn't bear the idea that it had been Zachary, as far from his personality as that seemed, I knew that no one was immune from fury.

Of course, that still left the question of the drug unanswered.

On the other hand, one mystery had been solved. The ever-annoying question of why Tomas Severin had come to Philly Prep now seemed obvious. He'd either wanted to see his son, or come to see about his son. Maybe he'd meant to say *Call Amanda Pepper* rather than *Calls,* then decided to simply drop in. Easy enough to find my room. It was the first at the top of the stairs, and my name was on the board.

I wished I knew precisely what he'd wanted, whether he thought I could find something out that he couldn't get directly from his own child.

My cell phone vibrated against my hip. Since it was used only for business, I was sure it was Penelope Koepple, and I didn't want to speak with her. I took a deep breath. I thought about something I did want: to be able to pay the mortgage. To help clear Zachary's name. I took another deep breath and looked at the phone, at the number calling me. Then I needed to take yet another really deep breath, risking hyperventilation.

"Mom," I finally said, "this is a business phone. You're not supposed to use—"

"What choice do I have? You're not returning my calls, and

anyway, this is business. The business that prints invitations takes a long time to do it, and then there's the business of whether you will address the envelopes yourself or the business of hiring a calligrapher and in fact, the entire business that you haven't even chosen a design yet!"

It wasn't mean-spiritedness on either side, or stupidity, or anything malevolent. It was a simple failure to communicate, an illustration of what different meanings we give the same words.

Theoretically, Mackenzie and I were in charge. We made all the decisions. Everyone agreed.

In actuality, we made suggestions and choices and they were ignored or vetoed. We made plans and were told they really wouldn't work out. Meanwhile, the bridal banshees made countersuggestions—they called this "helping out"—and we were expected to rubber-stamp their ideas. If we didn't, then it was patiently explained to us why we were in error.

We'd long since reached an impasse and at this point, my preferred tactic was the Possum Strategy. Play dead. Do not agree or disagree. Pend.

I actually tried to listen to my mother, to get into the spirit of invitation urgency while I made my way down the staircase. It didn't work. The words became aural wallpaper to my own thoughts, and they were banging down these stairs, toward Tomas Severin's death and Zach Wallenberg's misery when I realized my mother had paused, either waiting for a response or, as I feared, stunned into silence because I'd just agreed to something. I had no idea what. "I'll call you later," I said, and hung up when she bemoaned the fact that I hadn't chosen bridesmaids yet.

I wasn't going to have bridesmaids. I'd told her—and Beth—that, but they had selective hearing problems. I wasn't going to force my friends to wear ugly matching dresses and dyed shoes. My sister would be my "attendant," and I found even that concept amusing, as if I were suddenly about to lose my ability to take care of myself in the most basic of ways, but so be it.

It had always been painfully obvious that my mother was

eager to see me married. What I hadn't understood was how literally she meant that. The act of getting married seemed more important than the meaning of it, than the lifetime following it. And what seemed most important of all was Doing It the Right Way.

My brain hurt. Too many voices clamored and babbled inside: Zach's pleas, Rachel's dark and true pronouncement about the limits of our ability to help, Steinbeck's wisdom, Penelope Koepple's haughty pronouncements, and, of course, my mother's nonstop plans and demands.

I stopped at the office on my way out as I was supposed to, to check for any late-breaking emergency directives from the headmaster. There were none, but there was a note written in Mrs. Wiggins's tiny, nervous script, saying that Liddy Moffat wanted to know if anything was happening about the "situation." I wondered if the euphemism was Liddy's or Mrs. Wiggins's.

"Find everything okay?" Mrs. Wiggins looked anxious, as if worried her note might have been substandard. It took a great deal of energy to make sure Mrs. Wiggins didn't become overly anxious.

She'd been chewing something. She usually was, and when she wasn't, she was sucking on something. She'd confessed to loving sweets, though she didn't have to tell me. Her body had a feather-pillow consistency without a single angle. She was obviously not the culprit in the great bulimia situation.

"You understand what she meant by that?" she asked me. "I told Liddy to be more . . . more clear, you know. I was afraid you wouldn't—"

"Thanks, but it's fine. Apparently, we have some girls who are mixed up about how to diet, or control their weight."

Her face mottled as I'd seen it do before, her version of blushing. "I hope I'm not speaking out of line," she finally said, "but I mean it's odd for a custodian . . . I mean what would a custodian . . ." And then she understood and her eyebrows raised. "Oh, my," she said. "They want to be thin, is that it?" Her arms went to her chest, as if to protect herself. "Everybody, of course . . .

everybody does but . . . ," she murmured. "Poor dears. Make themselves sick for life."

"It's going to be all right," I said. "We're going to help them as best as we can." At least we'll try, I silently added.

Most of the student body had long since taken to the hills, but ragged remnant groups—the student body parts—sat in the park across the street, or milled farther down the block.

A black sedan moved slowly down the street, then paused in the loading zone as I walked down the steps. Parents still car-pooled, even in the center of a city that had fine mass transporta-tion, so even though it was late to pick up a student, there were after-school activities, and parents were also known to keep their children waiting, I'd have ignored the black car had it not—abruptly and much too quickly for a school zone—pulled off again the moment I was on the sidewalk.

"Hey!" I shouted. "Stop!" I raised an arm as if that would make a difference. Teens were oblivious, so a reckless driver was a disaster in waiting. But luck favored the driver in the form of a clear path and the car moved across the intersection. I put my arm down with the retroactive sense that the car had been wait-ing for me, that somebody wanted to know where I was, and what time I left the school and had paused just long enough to find it out. Why?

Before I reached the corner, and despite having seen the black car cross the intersection and keep going, I checked and rechecked the street, glancing behind and to the sides of me, as if other, equally insane drivers were apt to strike from any angle. I'd lost my sense of safety and possibly was descending into para-noia.

On one of my swivels, I spotted Zachary talking with un-usual animation to a well-dressed, pretty woman—his mother. They stood near the school, out of the line of pedestrian traffic, and reading their body language, they were involved in a tense dispute.

Zach noticed me, then turned quickly back to his mother, who leaned close to him, her expression agitated. He tilted his head in my direction, then grabbed hold of the shoulder of her coat as she turned toward me. "Miss Pepper," she called out. "Please, a moment?"

"No, Mom," I heard Zach say. "Don't. You'll only—just don't."

"Miss Pepper," his mother said again, and before I could respond, she said, "I'm Carole Wallenberg, Zachary's mother." She put out her hand. "We've met before."

"Of course. I recognized you." I shook her outstretched hand. She was obviously upset, or she'd have remembered that for the past two years at least we hadn't needed to identify ourselves. "Glad to see you again," I murmured. Zachary looked as if he might bolt and run.

"I came as quickly as I could. I don't understand this at all. Why on earth would the police think that this boy—this gentle, good boy—could have murdered that man! God knows he's given us grounds for it, but still—this is insane!"

"Mom," Zachary moaned.

"You don't have to convince me," I said. At that instant, the black sedan reappeared, coming up the street this time, as if it had circled the block. This time, it moved slowly. I couldn't see the face through the tinted glass. I told myself that I was overreacting. The world was full of black cars. But I didn't listen to myself because I was sure this was the same car, and I couldn't convince myself that it posed no danger to me or to the students.

Carole Wallenberg grabbed my elbow. "How could Zachary have known, how could anybody have known, that Tom was coming here? He'd never come before. He only knows—knew— the name of the place because he paid the tuition." Her derisive laugh had a bitter, hard-edged sound. "When he severed ties with me, both of us became past tense. Zach and Tom had no relationship, and recently, he was turning it into less than nothing, deliberately humiliating my son." She turned her head away, her lips pressed tight, as if containing a further torrent of words.

"Mom," Zachary said, "she knows. You don't have to—"

"How? How could she?" Carole Wallenberg's head swiveled toward me at top speed, risking whiplash. "Who told you?" she asked me, her eyes wide.

"I did," Zach said.

Her head swiveled again, and then she shook it. "What did you tell her about me?"

"Nothing! Mom, we didn't talk about you, so stop it, you're embarrassing—you're—"

"What did you tell her?" She wasn't screaming, but the tendons of her neck looked as if she were.

"I told her about—about what . . . my father did."

She opened her mouth. Looked at me, as if she could read something through my skin. Closed her mouth. Took a deep breath. "When?"

"When did I tell her?"

"What thing that he did—he's been doing 'things' forever. I could list a million malicious, mean-spirited things. Which one?"

"About college." His eyebrows pulled together, and his mouth opened slightly even when he wasn't speaking. His mother had frightened, or at least worried him, and I couldn't blame him, though I wished I knew what she was afraid he'd said.

"Can you imagine that?" Carole spoke rapidly, with more animation than was necessary, running over her awkward gaffe, hiding it under a barrage of words. "A man with all the money in the world denying his firstborn child a college education, and for no reason except that the law allows him to do that. But that's what kind of man Tom is—was. So proper to the world. A pillar of society indeed, and privately, a . . . rat."

I had the distinct sense that she had censored words that came more naturally and, I suspected, often.

"And even so, Zach was going to go." She used her free hand to poke me, as if I weren't paying sufficient attention. "We weren't letting that man ruin his own son's life. We'd find the funds, and I told him that, didn't I? I've been in school, and I have a part-time job that has every chance of becoming full-time, plus, there are loans. We would have managed, so there would be no point, no motive. Even assuming he came here to see his son, which I can assure you with all my heart and soul he would not, did not, never would."

As she spoke, her tempo and tone returned to something closer to normal, but a mother-lion fire burned behind her eyes.

"Could you?" she demanded of her son who, for his part, looked as if he wanted to sink through the pavement forever. "Answer me. Could you possibly do such a thing? *Murder* someone?"

"Mom!"

"He's already told me that he didn't, Mrs.—"

"Carole, please. I'm sorry I'm so crazed, but my son did not do this. He simply isn't that kind. He didn't inherit Tom's meanness."

"Mom, *please!*" Zach could barely stand still, he'd become so agitated.

"I'm sorry Zach has to go through this mess," I said. "If I had the power to stop the investigation, turn it toward a better goal, I would. The police questioned Zach. They didn't arrest him."

"Hasn't he been through enough already? That man—his father—did everything in his power to destroy this boy. When Zach was . . . acting out, why do you think that was? It doesn't take a degree in psychology to understand what total rejection—meaningless, unjustified, unmotivated rejection—does to a child, does it? And now this, this—"

Her eyes glittered with unshed tears, but her words nonetheless had the feel of a prepared speech, or one that she'd been forced to deliver too many times, to school officials or the police during those earlier, rougher days. She was coming unhinged, preaching to the already-converted because she knew I'd listen, and she was afraid nobody else would. "If there's anything I can do, please, tell me," I said.

And then I must have shown some of the growing fear I felt when I again saw the black sedan cruise by. This time, I watched it more carefully. I couldn't see the license plate, but I saw that it was a Mercedes and it might as well have had a banner stretched around it saying, "I am watching you!"

Carole Wallenberg turned, following the direction of my eyes. "What?" she said. "What?"

"Nothing." By then, of course, the car had turned the corner. Once again, I told myself that I was imagining monsters, but it was getting really difficult to believe that.

"It's the drug part of it," Carole told her son, sounding half out of breath, as if she'd run to him with the message. "That must be why they're after—"

"They aren't really after—"

"—Zachary. He knew where you could get drugs like that and that they were easy to make, and he knew it because he wrote that article for you!" She glared.

I put my hands out, palms up. "And a great article it was," I said. "Fine investigative reporting, but exceptional as it was, I doubt that anyone on the police force reads the *Inkwire.* Even if they did, even if they thought that it was somehow incriminating, we'd make sure they understood that it wasn't. Anyone who reads it would know it wasn't." Zachary's article had condemned, in no uncertain language, the very idea of drugging a girl so that she'd be forced to have sex.

His mother wasn't listening. Perhaps she thought nothing I said mattered. "Zachary didn't drug that man. I know that. I can prove—"

"Mom! Jesus. Please. Miss Pepper doesn't—leave her alone."

I envisioned Zachary and his mother as poor rats in a maze, running frantically to nowhere, another dead end, and from what? Nobody had accused Zachary of anything specific, and his mother was windmilling, making claims she couldn't support, insisting she could prove things she couldn't and didn't have to in the first place. And she said nothing about all the silent indictments, the circumstantial evidence against him, though I couldn't keep them out of my mind.

Zachary's unfortunate past history of problems with the law.

His unexplained absence from assembly at just the right—or wrong—time.

His recent blowup with his father, whether or not it was justified.

The cast on his arm. Tomas Severin's dented cheekbone.

I wondered whether Zach was in Tomas Severin's will and whether he'd be better off with a dead father than a living one. I thought again of the Steinbeck quote: ". . . live so that our death brings no pleasure to the world." So far, with the exception of Tomas's muddled mother, and even she, only sporadically, nobody seemed to be grieving about his death.

The drug had been peculiar and juvenile. A date-rape drug. Not a typical poison, not fatal. A stupid choice if the intent was to kill, but stupid, alas, brought us back to teens. Zachary's own article had said it would take no more than five minutes to find a source. All anybody had to do was ask.

On the other hand, logic also weighed against Zach's involvement. For starters, according to what Sasha said, Severin's visit to Philly Prep must have been a spontaneous lunchtime decision, so Zach couldn't have planned anything.

That left a big question of how and when he could have administered the drug, and why he would have had access to it in the first place. He was out of assembly, according to his story, long enough to smoke a cigarette in the alley behind the school. I played the necessary steps through in my head: He'd have to have known about and then found the café his father had chosen to drop into en route to the school, and this was a man whose locations and habits he didn't know. And then, he'd have to have secretly—how?—drugged the tea, then have lured the man who wanted next to nothing to do with him back into the school, avoiding Mrs. Wiggins's notice. And then he had to convince him to go up the stairs and into my room, and then back out so he could be pushed down the stairs.

And then he would have had to return to assembly, as if nothing had happened. As if he were an experienced assassin.

Completely ridiculous.

"Just because somebody knows where a drug can be found doesn't mean he—my God, anybody can find or make that stuff. I studied chemistry. Why didn't the police come to me? Or you? You know, too." Carole faced me directly. "You assigned those stories. You set him up."

This time when Zachary put his large hand on her narrow shoulder it had an instantaneous impact. She spun toward him, and then she shook her head in small, palsied movements and burst into tears. "Who will believe him? They're so powerful, so cruel—and it's just us, our word. But he didn't do it!"

I tried the hand-on-shoulder technique, very softly. "I believe you," I said. "I believe Zach. And I believe the truth will out and we'll learn what really happened. You should try to believe it, too."

Once again she was like a wobble doll as she mimed a silent "no." But there was nothing funny about Carole Wallenberg's motions. She could barely catch her breath. Silently, except for the hard breathing, she was saying no to everything in a world that she saw poised against her son.

I stayed with them a little longer, hoping to hear what hadn't been said, the feared revelations Carole or Zachary Wallenberg had pushed aside, the just below the surface words, but I didn't learn anything more, and after a polite interval, I left them.

One block away, I saw the black sedan.

Twelve

I walked on automatic pilot, giving free rein now to a major paranoia attack about the car and its driver, about who it might be and what it might want with me.

I saw it, or I thought I did, one more time, from a distance, as I approached the office. It—if it was it—kept moving until it blended into traffic and I couldn't find it anymore. I still wasn't sure it was the same Mercedes, but that didn't lessen my anxiety.

To my delight, Mackenzie was once more at the office. I tried for professional calm and detachment. I tried to remember what I'd wanted to say before I was distracted by Carole Wallenberg and an anonymous black Mercedes. "There's a hole at the center of this Tom Severin mess," I said by way of greeting. "It's driving

me crazy. We're circling something missing, only I can't see what
it is."

"Circling something that isn't there can be a real problem,"
Mackenzie said. "So hard to know how large to make the circles.
An' I believe that seeing something that's not there is generally
considered mental illness."

"Logic is what isn't there. The pieces don't fit."

Mackenzie bent forward to stretch out his back. The chairs in
Ozzie's office were anti-ergonomic, sadistically designed.

"What are we forgetting?" I asked.

"First we're circling something not there and now you want
me to remember what I've forgotten? This is taking on the feel of
a Zen koan."

"The illogic bothers me. How could Zachary know where
and when his father would buy a cup of tea?"

"Maybe the question is—who did know? How fast does that
drug act? If it's instantaneous, and the man brought tea into the
school, and the stuff was dropped in it there, how long would it
take to affect him?"

He was not too subtly implying, correctly, alas, that I hadn't
done my homework. I should have researched these questions,
but I hadn't even thought through the implication of the question till I heard it coming out of my mouth. That didn't stop me
from reacting defensively, from picking up a virtual chip and
plunking it on my shoulder. "Why would anybody put a drug—
that particular drug—into a man's tea? It would disorient you,
make your reaction time be off, but it isn't lethal, so if you had
murder in mind, why that?"

"They said a big enough dose could be fatal."

"But it's iffy. And he didn't drink all the tea. There were too
many variables. He was able to walk to the school, go upstairs—
that isn't the way to kill somebody. That isn't the drug to use. And
if you were going to push the man down a staircase—"

"And do a mite of bashing beforehand, too." He tapped his
cheek. "But maybe that was an improvisation. Maybe there were

other plans in mind, but that huge staircase was there, an open invitation."

We were back to zero. And to me, zero looked like the hole at the center, the one we were circling. Or the spot where the cheese was sent to stand alone, and Zachary was the cheese. Mackenzie had been kind enough not to use words like "sudden impulse" or "rage," but I knew who he thought had improvised.

He'd been studying the computer screen before I started talking, and he was sneaking glimpses again, tracking, or trying to, a man who'd disappeared six months ago. The classic story of going out for cigarettes, though in this case, it was ice cream. He never came back, nor was there any sign of foul play.

He'd never used his charge cards again, and he'd never applied for a job that required his Social Security number. The logical assumption was that he'd been killed while on his domestic errand except for the discovery, days after his disappearance, that he'd removed his entire collection of antique watches, kept in the safety deposit box.

That's when his wife knew he'd never intended to bring home dessert.

Mackenzie was sure that when the man ran out of ready cash, he'd sell some of his valuable collection. And after that, he'd bob to the surface as a collector. He'd be selling or buying at a show or a dealers' convention, or online, or he'd participate in a real or virtual antique watch collectors' discussion group. A man will change just about everything, the theory went, except the thing he can't—his true passion, his obsession, so Mackenzie was deep into the world of antique watches. At the moment, they seemed to entertain him more than the Severin saga.

"Look at this." He pointed at the screen. "Eighteen thousand for that one, eleven thousand for this one. The guy had two hundred at least, his wife said. We're talking millions. And you should see the wife, the house, so ordinary middle-class. Wife works as a library aide."

Which reminded me, of course, of Carole Wallenberg with her part-time job and college studies vs. Tomas the billionaire, but that connection didn't seem to occur to Mackenzie, who exclaimed at each new watch—the man had collected only pocket watches—and its price. "Even if some of them were only worth ten grand—"

"Only!"

"—that was incredible wealth. Wonder for how long he had this planned."

I saw the appeal of the missing watch collector. It was a story that made sense in all its parts, and it was probably going to be solved by my trusty, brilliant guy. On the other hand, whatever had happened at Philly Prep was murky and amorphous and therefore less fun. What's the joy in a puzzle with no underlying logic?

I respected his choice, but I didn't have the same options. I was stuck with the one that didn't make sense. I figured that if I couldn't see any other logical suspect aside from Zachary, then the police were surely not going to look further. But somebody had to. "Has she fired us yet?" I asked Mackenzie.

"What? The guy's wife? Why would she? She's not so sure she wants him back, but she wants those watches."

"Not her—Penelope, the Social Secretary. Has she fired us yet?"

"She never was going to. You were the one wanted to quit. And by the way, I tried reaching Nina Severin three times today, as per your request."

"Thank you."

"Only got her answering machine. Now why do you want to know about being fired?" He turned the chair back toward me. "Do I sense a change of heart? Why?"

Did he really have to ask? The police had questioned Zachary, that was why.

He really did have to ask, and he did. "Do you have more about Cornelius?"

Cornelius. The one we were being paid to investigate.

He had to ask more. "New ideas?"

He was so single-minded, so annoyingly linear. Now, he

waited, smiling expectantly. "Cornelius? New ideas? Yes," I said. It was partly true. Maybe only one percent had to do with Cornelius, but that was a part. "I think we should find out about that meeting with the lawyer Monday morning. How did it go? Maybe Cornelius hung around and saw him go buy the tea and drugged him."

"Why would he? What did he have to gain by something that inept? That wasn't what killed the man."

"Unless it made him trip and fall, which it most definitely could have done."

"Was he prescient? Drugged the tea because he knew the man would then climb a marble staircase he could fall down?"

I admit it sounded foolish when said out loud. I tried a new tack. "It wouldn't hurt to know whether the meeting left Cornelius expecting to get zilch—no prenup, no changed will because his fiancée is cuckoo—or expecting to become a multimillionaire real-estate tycoon someday. Talk about a motive!"

This time, Mackenzie gave a half-nod, half-shake that meant grudging, incomplete agreement.

"Penelope will know the name of the lawyer," I said. "And they'd talk to you. Nothing confidential, simply whether or not the meeting happened."

He sighed.

I was failing to impress him with my deductive—or was it inductive—powers. I tried harder. "You have to take into account that so far, we're relying on what Penelope chooses to feed us about the two men's relationship."

I heard a nice grunt of assent from my partner, but his attention had wandered back to the antique pocket watches on his computer screen.

"And so, in order to do what our client wants, that is, to ascertain Cornelius's guilt, I'd have to eliminate other potential suspects."

C.K.'s eyes were doing the visual equivalent of holding their breath, refusing to budge, but he finally forced his gaze from the screen to my direction. "Who are these other suspects?" he asked.

"There's only one, far as I can see. Penelope's got a bug up her about Cornelius. Nobody else thinks he's involved. They might think he's contemptible, but that doesn't make him a killer."

"He had millions at stake. But there's also Nina Severin. She's way better off as his widow than she'd have been as his ex."

"That may be true, but the idea of her following him into the school and beaning him there—does that make sense? There's a wide world of possible places to get rid of your husband, particularly when you've got money, so why there? Why that way?"

Of course it didn't make sense, but neither did the Zachary scenario, not in the way things make sense in your emotional core. "Maybe that's the brilliance of the plan," I finally said. "To make it so illogical that no theories make sense, and yet the man is dead."

Mackenzie rolled his blue eyes.

I rushed on. "And speaking of rich, speaking of opportunities, here's something that bugs me. Why us? Of all the investigators in all the world . . . why choose us? Just because Sasha knew me? That doesn't make sense. A man that rich would research his options, find the most famous detective, whoever was considered the best. Once I found out Severin was Zachary's father, I thought he might have come because of his son. That it wasn't about the phone calls at all. But after hearing Zach's mother, it's obvious that parenting didn't matter much to Tom Severin. Sounded more as if he was finished with Zach."

That got no response.

"Anyway, if we're still employed, I owe it to Penelope to ask a few questions," I said.

"Questions about how it doesn't make sense to arrest Zachary?"

"I never said that. But our client thinks Cornelius is behind this, so that's what I'm trying to find out. If in the meantime, I happen to clear Zachary's name—where's the harm in that?"

He grinned. "It veers toward the unethical side of the fence to pursue alternate goals on a client's dime."

I raised my eyebrows and tried for Penelope-like authority.

"Indeed! If that were what I was doing. But I'm simply trying to get to the truth, to be as comprehensive as possible. Can't blame me for trying extra-hard, can you?"

He had an oddly bemused expression.

"What?" I asked.

"You ever realize how much you've picked up from your students? Like that explanation, right now. That excuse was sufficiently self-serving and twisted and phrased so as to avoid the charge I made altogether to have been written by one of your little darlings." He returned to his screen.

Teaching is a give and take. They learn from me and I learn from them. I made a list of questions including who had been with Tom Severin when he bought the tea, and where he had bought it, and what he had done after his morning meeting at the lawyer's office, and what, if possible, the meeting was about, and what Carole Wallenberg had thought her son might have told me about her, and what Nina the widow Severin was like. And then I thought of another question, the biggie of who Tomas Severin had truly been. Aside from his business acumen and his astounding monetary assets—who? What if there was no underlying logic, and the school setting had simply been a lucky break for someone who saw the man walk into the building? What if that someone had nothing to do with the family circle, but was an enraged acquaintance, or someone who felt personally harmed by Severin's sale of his companies?

The possibilities were endless. I could only hope that Penelope's purse was equally vast.

Thirteen

I told Mackenzie about the black sedan, hoping he'd treat it as the imaginings of a ninny, discount it, say something like, "You're being silly." All the things I hate for him to think, let alone say, I wanted him to think and say.

Instead, he said to be careful. Be alert. And most important, get the license number. He didn't mention the obvious, that I should have thought of that myself and have done that already. He is a kind man.

So when I went outside, and started walking home down Market Street, I was both careful and alert.

And I saw it again.

I was nowhere near school now, and in fact, was headed in a completely different direction from it.

He was after me.

I kept my hand on my bag, on a notepad and pen, and I managed to see and write down the first three numbers before the car was too far away.

But on the next block, it was back. I grabbed the notebook again, but I needn't have hurried, because the car slowed down, then pulled into a parking space at the curb.

I considered turning around and running toward the office, but instead, doubled my pace, dropped the notebook back into my bag, and grabbed my cell phone while I looked for a safe harbor. The pickings were slim: a restaurant not yet open for the evening meal, a locked up realtor's office, a dusty sporting goods shop that looked so deserted I was sure it was a front for something and not a place to find protection.

A luncheonette across the street was no more prepossessing than the sporting goods shop, but it was open and might at least have more people and better lighting. I crossed the street against the light, horns honking as I dodged and ran. I pushed open the door—and he barreled in behind me.

I didn't even have time to use my phone. "Call the po—"

"Wait! Don't!"

I squelched myself mid-shout and turned around.

He looked puzzled. And familiar.

Cornelius.

I clutched the phone and waved it in front of him. "What are you doing, following me around? You want to scare me, but you aren't!"

"You sure? You look scared right now. And why did you run across traffic to come here? That's not safe! Do you love this place that much?"

The restaurant looked as if it had been sprayed with grease, and every inhalation was the equivalent of an oil and lube job. A lone customer sat at the counter, and two or three more were in the leatherette booths lining the other wall. They seemed permanent, shell-shocked fixtures vacantly pleased that entertainment had popped through the door.

"Lady, are you all right? He bothering you?" The burly man behind the counter looked willing to go for Cornelius's throat. I felt vindicated in my choice of safe harbors, but I assured him that I was fine.

"What do you want?" I asked Cornelius in my most authoritarian teacher voice, one I kept in my arsenal but almost never use.

"I want to talk to you." His voice wasn't surly or intimidating. It was, in fact, mild and matter-of-fact.

"Then why *stalk* me? My God—outside the school, circling the block, tracking me on the street, what on earth did you have in mind?"

"Finding a parking spot. This city gets worse every year. I thought in front of your school, but then I saw it was a loading zone, and then I couldn't find anything till right now."

"Did you ever hear of honking? Letting me know you were trying to reach me?"

"Didn't want to scare you."

"You wanna booth or what?" the man behind the counter asked. His apron looked like the "before" part of a detergent ad.

I reminded myself that Cornelius was a con man, currently charming an old and addled woman out of her property. I was to ignore the open innocence carefully arranged on his face, the suggestion that he wouldn't even park illegally, let alone do anything more malicious. "What do you want to talk to me about?" I asked.

His forehead wrinkled in puzzlement, real or feigned, and he waved his arms. "Everything. What's going on. Why you're checking up on me."

"Lady?" the man behind the counter said. "This ain't a museum or something. The booths and stools are for sitting on."

"A booth," Cornelius said softly. "More privacy, okay?"

I shrugged, and picked the cleanest looking one and tried not to look at the ripped part of the vinyl, or think of what microorganisms dwelled inside it.

"Two coffees," Cornelius told the man. Then he looked at me. "Okay?" He was polite, or pretended to be. But of course, that would be part of a paid escort's bag of tricks.

I waited, my hand still on the telephone, even though I had no idea what I would have said to the dispatcher. "A man wants to talk to me and he ordered coffee for me without asking first!" lacked a certain urgency.

"I know you're checking around about me," Cornelius said. "And I resent it."

"It's what I do."

"I thought you taught."

"That, too."

He bit at his bottom lip. That first impression I'd had of him, that he wasn't particularly bright, was reinforced as he deliberated, rubbing his hand over his chin, wrinkling his brow. His expressions suggested that thinking hard wasn't something he attempted too often.

"You spoke with Georgeanne," I suggested.

He nodded. "She called me right after you visited her."

Interesting. I'd gotten the distinct impression—she made sure I got it—that they were casual friends of long ago, not currently close at all. Penelope's theory that the two of them were in cahoots might have more weight and truth than I'd allowed it.

"Why me?" he asked.

"Not you," I said. "Not you exclusively or for any specific reason. We're talking to everybody."

"No. You aren't. Or at least you aren't listening to them. And that includes Ingrid. You didn't really talk with her or you'd stop thinking I'm some kind of criminal. She trusts me. She knows she can." For the second time, he added sugar to his coffee. I wasn't sure if it was intentional or not.

"I know that Ingrid doesn't think you've done anything wrong," I said. "She thinks a woman did it. Do you know who she meant?"

He stirred the coffee and looked unhappy with the question. "No," he finally said. "And I wouldn't want to get anybody in trouble by guessing."

"People are already in trouble. One of them is dead."

"Nina, then."

"Who?"

"Nina Severin. Tom's wife."

"Why?"

"Because Ingrid said stuff about drugs. About knowing about them."

"Tom's wife is addicted, or what?"

"Not her—her brother. I don't know if he was addicted or not, but he was in prison for being involved with the stuff. He's out now, and . . ." He shrugged. "He's not an okay guy, and Nina . . . she's crazy lately. She won't stop talking about Tom or screaming at him. I mean I guess now, he's dead, sure, she stopped, but she would call the house and scream at anybody who answered the phone. It didn't even have to be Tomas. Even her brother called. I picked it up one day—I didn't have a clue who was talking. He must have thought I was Tomas, and he says, 'You're going to pay.' Something like that. Freaked me out till I realized he wasn't talking about me. It was Tomas and the divorce. Tomas was—he had a reputation for not giving his ex-wives much."

There was too much meat in that one sentence. I didn't know where to start. Why a phone call from the brother? What did "You're going to pay" mean? A literal divorce settlement—or death? And the entire idea of a phone call again. Nina's brother as avenger? Also as insurer of a large inheritance? "What's his name?" I asked. "Nina's brother?"

Cornelius looked worried, and I suddenly was afraid he'd made the entire incident up. "I said I didn't want to get anybody in trouble. I mean the guy's just out of prison not all that long ago, and—"

"You aren't, and I can certainly find it out myself. I just thought I'd save time." I tried to sound casual, as if I didn't really care one way or the other.

"Jay," he said. "Jay Kress."

I wrote it down in my notebook and thanked him.

"You're patronizing me," he said.

His vocabulary was better than I'd expected. "Why would you say that?"

"Pretending like you think I'm telling you the truth."

"But I—"

"I resent your whole attitude." The shy-boy aura that had surrounded him until now was gone.

"What attitude? We're trying to reconstruct who was where when. Trying to find out as much as possible as to what happened. There's nothing unusual about that, is there?"

"You're trying to figure out if I killed Tomas Severin so that he wouldn't stop me from inheriting from Ingrid, right? You think I stopped him from having her declared incompetent before she could change her will."

I tried not to let the "aha" show on my face, but lots of pieces fell more neatly in place with that.

"And that's because you're sure I'm around only so I'll inherit from Ingrid, aren't you?"

"Of course not." Of course yes. How could that not be what I thought? But he looked so upset by the idea, I was suddenly unsure about even that. "You had a meeting that day, at the lawyer's. I'm sure it was full of tension."

"And a few hours later he was dead."

"Right."

He put both hands up, as if he'd made his point and he was angrily giving up, surrendering. "I wasn't ever inside that school."

"He was trying to prevent Ingrid from leaving you buildings worth a fortune."

"And you think I'd kill him so he'd stop interfering, because he was trying to split us up?"

Interesting how he'd made Tom's intention out to be breaking up the great romance instead of keeping the family fortune intact. "Look, Cornelius, I'm simply trying to do my job, investigating what happened."

"I think you—all of you—are the ones with the problem. You look at her and decide that nobody could love her."

"That's not fair." Did I think that?

"Because she's old. You have this image in your head of how a woman has to look to be loved."

"No!" Hadn't I been thinking just the opposite in fact?

"And," he continued, "she'd better be young, fresh, new."

Again I demurred, but of course hadn't I—hadn't one of us—said precisely that at the meeting with Rachel? And wasn't it at least partially true? Even all my bridal junk mail advocating pre-ceremony plastic surgery said it. And most of all, pathetic Ingrid herself, with her pulled-tight face, plumped-up lips, and emaciation said it with every iota of body language.

"You think that just because a woman's not young anymore nobody can love her."

I wasn't sure what I thought anymore. Wasn't I operating under an unarticulated rule that said an old woman could not be attractive to a young man? Even if it was generally true—where was the logic in that? Who was I to impose a statement of what was possible and what was not for all humankind?

"You think it's all, one hundred percent, about looks, and nothing to do with experience, or personality, or interests. Do you realize how prejudiced you are? All of you are? How unfair?"

I sipped my coffee. It was bitter but it bought me time. Then I cut to the chase. "Do you love Ingrid Severin?"

He nodded, and with the nods, his righteous anger seemed to evaporate. He looked at me defensively, as if expecting me to laugh at him, or explain why it was impossible or even criminal for him to feel that way. "You don't understand love," he said softly. "You and that cracked secretary of hers, and her son—"

"Tomas?"

Cornelius nodded. "She acted like he was a—a—I don't even know what. He could do no wrong. He was the best. Maybe that spoiled him, ruined something in him, because he barely had time for anybody, including her. She'd die before she'd say something bad about Tomas, but if she waited for attention from him, she'd die waiting." He considered his words. "I mean, of course, when he was alive."

I was hearing a lot of feeling and not a whole lot of brains. Did that make him truthful, stupid, or crafty?

"She doesn't have anybody," he said. "Don't any of you get it? She's all alone."

"Except for you."

"Yes." He looked at me directly, quietly defiant.

I nodded. "I'm not challenging your feelings toward Mrs. Severin."

"Yes you are. And so is that bitch, Koepple. You think she likes Ingrid? That she cares what happens to her? She just likes the people Ingrid knows, or knew, and the money she gets paid for doing next to nothing. Do you really think Ingrid has a social calendar that needs keeping anymore? Only things on her calendar are doctors' appointments these days, and I'm the one who goes with her. Koepple isn't even kind to her. She gets short-tempered with Ingrid. I've heard her chew her out, but she knows that Ingrid won't remember it by the next time, and if she does, Penelope will say she's making it up. Poor Ingrid knows she gets confused. She'd believe that bitch."

"Is this what you wanted to talk to me about?"

"What else did you think? I had this grandma. She was the best. She was the world to me." He shrugged. "I like old people. They know things, know about things. So as soon as I met Mrs. S. on the ship where I worked—"

As a dancer, I reminded myself. A hired companion for vulnerable and financially solvent elderly women on cruises.

"—we clicked. She made me laugh. She can be funny, you know. And she stood out from all the other women on that cruise. She was special in every way."

He looked at me as if daring me to contradict him. I wasn't about to. "She knows about the world," he said.

I was surprised, both by the sophistication this implied, and by the idea that Ingrid Severin paid attention to the human condition, or foreign affairs, or cultural patterns.

But that hadn't been what he meant. "She has style," he said.

"She knows what's good style and what's . . . cheap, or flashy, or bad design. She knows when something's quality or not."

Things. Stuff. She knew her objects which, to him, made her the final authority on aesthetics. I thought of the saying about the person who knew the price of everything and the value of nothing.

"We aren't . . . it's not like . . . you can love somebody without—there can be a higher plane, or at least a different one."

"You're talking about sex."

He nodded. "But that doesn't mean you don't love the person."

"She's not always coherent," I said. "Not always able to remember what's going on. She's got—"

"Problems. And you know what? Lots of times, I take care of those problems. It's what you do if you love somebody, not turn your back the way they do when the going gets hard. And that included Tomas. I'm the only one who's kind to her. The only one, you get that?"

I nodded again.

"So I'm sick of being made fun of or worse. Why shouldn't she be allowed to leave me something? She likes me, too. Who else deserves it more? The others, they're like . . . like . . . they're the ones circling around whatever they think they can get their hands on. Why come after me? Why listen to Koepple? Long ago, Ingrid promised her a bequest. I don't know the details, but I heard them squabbling about it, and later, I asked Ingrid what was going on. It would be enough money so that Koepple wouldn't have to worry about working anymore. Now, Koepple's crazy afraid that Ingrid is going to take away the bequest when she changes her will."

"And might that happen?"

"When a new will's made, who knows? Certainly Ingrid's hinted that. If you ask me, Koepple's been living off Ingrid for years. But she didn't need to lose the bequest. If she'd stop attacking me it wouldn't be in danger."

"You mean it really is?"

He looked surprised. "She didn't say?"

"Say what?"

"That she'd been fired? Told to leave at the end of this month? I thought it was nice of Ingrid to give her time to look for something new. I wouldn't have, because Koepple's nothing but trouble. But she told her to take her time, get her things in order, and look around, and she said she'd write her a good recommendation, which sounds a whole lot like maybe Ingrid isn't so hot about setting her up for the rest of her life anymore. Doesn't it? Me, I'd have booted her out on the spot. She's been coasting for too long already with nothing to do except spread rumors and badmouth people."

Fired. I knew this shouldn't be my first consideration, but I admit I felt as if an elevator had just crashed in my insides, and what I thought about was our bill for services, stuck under the debris. Who was actually paying us, or was anybody going to do so? "Cornelius—"

"Most people call me Neil."

"Neil, then. When was Ms. Koepple given her notice?"

"What?"

"Fired. How much time did Ingrid give her to look around?"

"Last week. She pushed too hard. Told Ingrid I was cheating on her. That I was romantically involved with Georgeanne, the woman Tomas—"

"I know who she is. She says she was engaged to Tomas."

He nodded. "That did it for Ingrid. She told Penelope that she was so unhappy about everything that she was making Ingrid unhappy, too, so for everybody's benefit, Penelope had to leave. That was Friday."

Three days before Tomas Severin tumbled to his death. But of what possible gain could that have been to Penelope? It seemed, in fact, that she was the one person who'd have done anything to keep him alive and fighting any change in the will. Her real motives in hiring us, however, were now murky and suspect.

"Ugly scene, all right," Cornelius said. "And it proved she never even liked Ingrid. She's a user, just like all of them."

"What do you mean?"

"She got all hissy. I could understand. She's losing her job, after all. But she said something that gave me the chills. She said that her job was her life and how could Ingrid turn her back on years and years of devoted service. I don't know. I wasn't there for those years, but since I've been there, I've barely seen her lift a finger for that woman." He shook his head, upset again at what he'd perceived.

"And that gave you the chills?" I prompted.

"No. Not that. It's what she said after that. She said, 'and I know what's *your* life. I know what *you* value more than anything. What if you lost that, Ingrid? Maybe you'd understand suffering a little more.' " He sat back in the booth and waited for a response.

"What . . . what did she value more than anything?" I asked, although I'd already been told the answer by more than one person. "Was it you? Was she threatening you?"

"Me? I was a good thing, but not the thing. There was always only one thing for Ingrid and everybody knew it. And that one thing was her son. Three days later, he was dead, and Ingrid knew what suffering was."

ALL THROUGH DINNER we talked about my encounter with Cornelius, about the ever-escalating pile of potential suspects. Nina Severin, who was still refusing to answer any calls, with the help of her brother Jay, had become the frontrunner, although Penelope Koepple was neck-and-neck. For me, that is. For Mackenzie, Zachary Wallenberg was the odds-on favorite.

"If it was an act of rage, we shouldn't forget Georgeanne— the woman scorned," I said. "Especially if she really is in cahoots with Cornelius, and for the life of me, I can't decide whether he's for real or not."

We went over the timetable, and C.K. said he'd try to find

out where things were with the investigation and would check Nina's brother's whereabouts. "Everything fits for him—the drug, the propensity for phone calls," I said.

"The school?"

"He must have followed him, seized the opportunity."

By the time we were on our nightly pre-bed prowl, the entire subject went stale. "Too much," I said. "No more Severin talk till tomorrow." Mackenzie nodded.

The prowl might sound more exotic and interesting than it was. It was not to be confused with a promenade, or the nightly sociable strolls of Italy and the Latin countries. The prowl was our repeated though futile attempt to remember and organize everything for the next morning's rapid exit. Kind of like Mom laying out your clean clothes for school next day, but we had to think of clothes plus teaching materials, papers marked or un-, textbooks for Mackenzie, notebooks, work-related notes—the whole shebang with a lunch or two tossed in.

We never completely succeeded. Morning dawned and something we'd forgotten—clothes for the dry cleaner, a shopping list, a gift that was pathetically overdue—caused a last-minute flurry.

But on we went, talking to each other, gathering, sorting, and doing our best. We had exhausted the back and forth of whether we should believe either Cornelius or Penelope, and had settled in some indeterminate "none of the above." Time to switch topics. "You're going to the funeral, aren't you?" I asked while making my rounds. I was sorry they'd scheduled it for noon, when I couldn't possibly be there.

He put a hand up and shook his head. "Severin talk alert," he said. "Forbidden topic."

"It's preparation for tomorrow."

He shrugged. "I'm going," he said. "Not that I know why. I'm sure it's going to be enormous and formal, and I don't expect that kind of family to be overly demonstrative. Certainly, nobody's going to stand up and proclaim guilt or whatever happens in old dramas."

"Still, I wish I could go," I said. "The situation itself interests me. Is it protocol for all the ex-wives to come? How about the estranged son? The soon-to-be-deposed wife?" I thought that was what Nina had been insisting on—her funeral rank and position—when I crossed paths with her at Ingrid Severin's.

"I can't find my highlighter," C.K. said. I am bemused and annoyed by the fact that like so many women, I waste lots of valuable brain space with a complete household inventory. I am almost always the finder of lost things, mundane objects such as highlighters, socks, tickets, and pens. I'm sure there's an anthropological explanation for this—Mackenzie's ancestors were trained to look for large things with big teeth. Mine were trained to hoard whatever they found, or to know where our stock was so as to grab it and run if the thing with big teeth entered the cave. It was as good a theory as any.

I walked over to the little drawer near the phone which was, alas, where lived the blinking message light.

It was so easy to ignore the little box on the wall that blinked in one pattern if there were no messages and in another when there were. I admit that if Sigmund were here, he'd be jumping and pointing and giving a Viennese lecture on avoidance, but on this issue, I dwell in a pre-Freudian world where sometimes forgetting is just plain forgetting.

I tossed him the highlighter, and reluctantly lifted the receiver, pushed in our code, and listened. I tried not to be pessimistic. It was possible to receive messages that had nothing to do with impending nuptials. Other people did. Maybe this was my lucky day and somebody was trying to sell me aluminum siding.

Instead, there was a message from Beth, with further details of the marvelous, but pricey, place she'd found. "But given that cancellation, or I guess it's more like a no-show, they haven't even been able to reach the woman, let alone gotten a confirmation from her, and who is going to rent it now if not you?" Then she once again made her point about my being the only person in the known universe to believe it was possible to set a wedding date three months in the future. "Do you have time tomorrow to go look at it with me because I need your go-ahead."

Now that Beth worked, she tended to forget that I did, too.

The second message was from Sasha, who used to be a lot of fun, and unpredictable. Not anymore. "I'm going with the moss green," she said, "so is that really okay with you? And your cousin Betsy called, she's going to miss it because her sister in Cleveland is due any day now and she—"

I hung up. I cared, but not that much. Not right now.

"The Mafiosettes?" Mackenzie asked.

"I'm sorry to have brought them upon you."

"My side's contributing confusion, too, so it's more or less mutual. What were the topics today?"

"The usual. Color schemes, rental halls, and while I was still at school, my mother called—on the cell, which I told her was only for major life emergencies—anyway, hers was about invitations and calligraphers, and I promised her something, but I can't remember what. I think I agreed to something, too."

"Why not simply pick an invite? Any one, or do you really care?"

"Of course I don't." I shook my head for emphasis, then realized I was lying. "Yes, I do. I care. I don't like any of them. They're formulaic. Predictable. They're not us, not special. And in so saying, I become like every other whiny, picky, stupid bride-to-be agonizing over the least significant part of what's going on in her life. Remember how enthusiastic they were about our planning our own wedding?"

"Imagine how awful it would be if they were planning it," he said, and it broke the tension enough for us both to laugh. He is such a good man, he almost makes this wedding lunacy worthwhile.

And in gratitude and for expediency's sake, I decided to gift him with a decision that would please his third of the trio. "Your mother's been lobbying about the joys of a handfasting ceremony."

He looked up at the ceiling, perhaps through it, for Divine Guidance. "Wiccan," he finally said. "She wants us to have a Wiccan wedding. A witch's wedding?"

"It sounds more peculiar than it actually is. It's really the original wedding, according to your mother."

"Far as I know, the original ceremony involved a club and dragging the pretty one by her mane into his cave. Is that what she has in mind? A reenactment?"

"Not quite. She thinks it would be nice if we all—guests included—dressed as medieval country folk, but she's willing to negotiate on that."

"There's a break." He packed a heavy text into his backpack.

"You'd look smashing in tights."

He put down the backpack. "You're serious?"

"I'd think you'd like the part about our setting the term of the contract. Traditionally, you commit only for a year and a day, she told me. None of that 'till death do us part' business." I thought of Tomas Severin's many wives, particularly the enraged Nina. If they'd had a Wiccan handfasting, they could have parted amicably and easily. "Will you take this woman for three hundred and sixty-six days? How's that sound to you?"

"It sounds like she never gives up. She's done a hard sell every time there's a marriage on the horizon."

With eight kids and many foster-children, all grown and much married, I was sure Gabby Mackenzie was a pro at Wiccan weddings by now, and at least I'd be pleasing my future mother-in-law with a wedding that'd be anything but rubber-stamp generic. Maybe I could even get into the medieval thing. We could rent costumes and save choosing the gown, and dithering over color schemes. Pretty at Christmastime, with evergreens and tiny lights.

"And medieval!" he said. "The Middle Ages—everybody's favorite time period, right?"

I immediately envisioned my wedding complete with hay bales, donkeys, and dirty children in raggedy clothing. Fleas, beggars, bare feet. No tiny lights, no electricity . . .

"How much of it did your brothers and sisters do? Did they truly handfast? Tie the knot with the ties that bind the hands together? Did they have the Maypole? Costumes? How did it look?"

He laughed and led me to the sofa and guided me onto it. Then he sat down next to me and took both my hands. "Miz Pepper," he said, "nobody has ever had a Wiccan wedding. Only a Yankee like you would be wacky enough to agree to her suggestion. It's sweet and lovable of you to try and please my family this way but for God's sake, any God of your choosing, but definitely for my sake, and our sake—Just Say No. Okay?"

I felt a rush of guilty relief, and a little disappointment, too, because there went the one plan I could use to make my mother and sister back off.

"The truth is," Mackenzie said, "my mother feels a quasireligious-feminist obligation to lobby for her special ceremony, but nobody wants it. Not even her. She likes the party part of weddings. She adores the toasts—and the dancin'. She loves the ceremony, the part where she gets to snuffle and blow her nose and murmur about what a cute baby the bride or groom had been and how time flies. She adores it when they play that old Wiccan favorite, 'Sunrise, Sunset,' and she gets to wallow in memories. She loves telling embarrassing stories about the child who's marrying. She loves the flow of champagne. Lots of it. She has never shown the slightest regret or other negative reaction at having her Wiccan suggestions declined."

He came over and kissed me. "As for your mother, and your sister, and your girlfriend—and my mother—consider them an initiation test. I'm sure that's why it's so forbidding and complicated. If we survive this with good grace, then we're a match."

"You are one in a million," I said. "Better than I deserve."

"I like your attitude. That's why I'm signing on for longer than a year and a day."

Fourteen

'M not the kind of person to be duplicitous—except when absolutely necessary, of course.

Never with a friend.

Unless there is absolutely no other way.

Which is why, when I was barely awake, still half-dressed but already mentally cluttered by the ever-expanding to-do list, I picked up the phone and called Sasha.

We've been friends since ninth grade, when we bonded for eternity because teachers said she wasn't the sort of girl I should befriend. There was nothing wrong with her except that she was not particularly interested in studying, but was precociously interested in boys and they in her, while I was still on the sidelines envying her bad girl reputation and wondering what all the ruckus was about. My approach to puberty was not a lovely thing to behold, and the real question was what on earth Sasha wanted with me. The chemistry of opposites attracting must hold for female friendships as well.

And though I owe this long friendship to that meddling teacher, I have tried to never replicate that kind of interference with my own students. But the point is, Sasha and I go way back, through the traumas of her nutsy parents' multi-marriages, and then her own. Her family is genetically incapable of learning from others' or their own mistakes when it comes to the opposite sex. And this morning, I realized I could capitalize upon that trait. Duplicitously.

I reached for the phone, too early, but she would simply have to understand.

She didn't, not for a long, yawny while.

"I adore the idea of moss green," I said. "It's different, and the fact that you have china that matches it—well, it's perfect."

Mackenzie had the bathroom door open, defogging the mirror after his shower, and he poked his wet-haired head out and said, "Am I hearing correctly? You've had a conversion experience?"

Even Macavity, snoozing on the duvet, opened one yellow-green eye in amazement.

I waved off both my skeptical males while Sasha mumbled that she was glad I'd made up my mind, but in truth, the announcement could have waited a few hours.

If she'd been wide-awake, she would have been as sharp as the feline, and would have been suspicious of my chipper bridal zest. But she was seriously sleep-fogged, which is why I was calling at this hour. "I wanted to catch you before I went to work, because I thought we could hang out today during my lunch hour," I said. "Settle everything and maybe I could help with something. I mean it's happening in a matter of days and you must be swamped."

"Can't," she said. "That's Tom Severin's funeral. I'm going. I'm not sure why—respect, I guess—but I am."

Good. "Really? Then after school? We could take a walk. It's pretty out, I think." It was never easy judging the weather from the loft. We could tell whether it was wet or dry through the sky-light, and we could get a sense of how bright a day it was, but temperature was gauged by the attire of passersby three stories down. "Combine that with last-minute shower talk, and TGIF and new sights you missed while you were away."

"That'd work."

"It'll be fun."

"Can't wait," she said. "Girlfriend talk, a glass of wine, a sight or two. Who could ask for anything more?"

She could have, that's who. She could have asked for honesty and forthrightness.

MACKENZIE LEFT A MESSAGE on the cell. "Severin and Cornelius met at the lawyer's office for about forty-five minutes, till just before noon when Severin ended it to keep another date, the one with Sasha, I have to figure. Beyond that, of course, I couldn't get any information about what they said, what the tone was, whether it ended acrimoniously or with the two men embracing. My guess? From the way I was told 'Mr. Severin had to leave for another appointment at noon,' I had the feeling the meeting could have, or should have lasted longer, but when he left, nothing was resolved between them."

Sasha had said it was a quick, short lunch. He had an appointment afterward, which, given how soon after that he'd come to the school, and given that he hadn't had the school in mind until that lunch with Sasha, had to mean the appointment was at the coffee shop, and brief. So brief that he got his tea to go.

Or did he leave with the other person? Could that person have come to Philly Prep with him?

Finding a take-out for tea between the restaurant where Sasha had met him and Philly Prep wasn't that difficult, but how to find out who else was there? That seemed close to impossible.

Penelope drank tea. Was she the date?

I heard myself thank the message for the information and felt like a fool. The nice thing about the omnipresent cell phones—and there are a few nice things about them—is that nobody knows if you're actually speaking to someone, or having a psychotic break and talking to your hand.

I turned off and closed the phone and tried to forget about everything except my day job. Friendly letter writing—as if people still did that. Oral book reports. The slithy toves.

My ninth-graders were wending their way through a poetry unit, and I was hoping to actually help them feel the human urge to make music with words, and the joy of it. We'd reminisced and reread childhood favorites from Mother Goose et al, then read and listened to ballads, and it felt time to toss in "Jabberwocky," that nonsensical mock-ballad that's so much fun.

And, continuing my day's theme of deception and duplicity, I sneaked into their minds and planted a secret grammar lesson.

"Jabberwocky" substitutes delicious nonsense words, but slots them precisely and in the manner of our actual language, so it can also quietly teach a lesson or two about how differently functioning words build into meaning.

Imagine the groans and sighs if I told them we were going to talk about syntax. Thanks to Lewis Carroll, I didn't have to. "Twas brillig and the slithy toves did gyre and gimble in the wabe," I read. "What do you picture when I read that peculiar sentence?"

I knew their first instinct was to picture me in a straitjacket. Gibberish, nonsense, silliness. Sometimes the most difficult lesson was getting them to loosen up, enjoy the games of language. "There is no wrong answer possible," I said.

"Slithy sounds slimey," someone said, and "Brillig—sounds like a weather report," another person said, "because 'twas'—it was something. Rainy? Hot?" "I think a tove looks like an elephant seal—you know the ones with the huge trunk? They're so ugly they're cool. I think they'd gyre and gimble, and shake their noses."

We talked amiably about the role different sorts of words play in sentences. We had syntax without tears.

O frabjous day!

SASHA HAD BEEN BACK for three months, but this was the first time I was in her apartment. "It's so different," I said, feeling vaguely cheated. I wanted to go home again—to her home—and once more, had found out it wasn't possible.

"Like it?"

I nodded, though I still wanted it to be a place of tossed scarves and the green tufted chair with the carved mahogany arms that had been painful to sit in, and slightly ridiculous, but very Sasha. Now, as spacious as the place was—Sasha's condo was the guilty spoils of one of her parents' many marriages and divorces—it seemed overstuffed, and its contours covered with chintz and wildly rampaging flowers. About as un-Sasha as it gets. "A man is involved in this, right?"

"A lesser member of the nobility," she said. "He not only offered me a container's worth of furniture, but he shipped it here for me. He had too many houses, and he was consolidating a few, and there I was. We were briefly engaged." She put a hand up. "It wasn't a long enough betrothal for me to get around to mentioning it."

"I assume the new china is from him, too?"

She nodded. "He was shipping stuff over to his daughter, and she didn't want everything he wanted to get rid of. My pieces filled out the container. Kind of a pan-Atlantic Goodwill donation." The room looked as if it were waiting for antimacassars.

"But I don't know," she said, "I keep having the oddest sensation that I should be gardening, or visiting the vicar."

This furniture was doomed. I asked no more about the minor royalty and the engagement. Since she'd been home, Sasha had casually mentioned at least seven men with whom she'd been involved during the year she was away. As she herself has said, if you lower your standards sufficiently, you can really have a good time.

She filled two glasses with white wine. "Why go in search of a bar?" she asked. "We can take a walk later. TGIF indeed. This has been a hell of a week."

"How was the funeral?"

She shrugged and settled herself on red-flower-splashed chintz. "How can funerals be? Sad, but oddly unemotional at the same time. Very large, but you didn't have the feeling it was because he was beloved. More because he was important. Or more precisely—rich kind of important. Not because he invented anything or was leading something. He was just plugged in."

"Did they give talks—eulogies?"

She shook her head. "Strictly formal. The minister gave the eulogy and it was . . . I thought I'd find out more about him there, but I didn't, not really. That was kind of sad. Nobody personalized the loss by saying what role he'd played in their life, or anything like that."

I'd hoped to find things out secondhand because both Sasha and Mackenzie had been there, but I could see that I wasn't going to.

"The most interesting part was beforehand," Sasha said. "The couple sitting next to me. The woman, I assume the wife, kept half-rising, looking around until her husband would yank her back down and say stuff like 'Nonsense,' and 'You're being too obvious!' I thought for sure somebody famous was arriving, but eventually I heard them whispering—but the way old, slightly deaf people think is whispering—about 'her' and whether she'd show up, and that it was only right that she should, but she probably wouldn't and was she locked up somewhere or maybe not even alive, and why wasn't she mentioned in the obituary." She looked at me and raised her eyebrows.

I was hooked. "Did they ever say who they meant?"

"What do you think it was? A stupid TV crime show? Of course they didn't say! They knew perfectly well who they were talking about."

"You think he had a fourth wife who wasn't mentioned in the obituary?"

"I thought maybe they meant his fiancée—the ex-fiancée," Sasha said, "except that I think somebody said she was there. Georgeanne, right?"

I nodded.

"And of course then they got into the maybe she's dead business."

"A mystery."

"Indeed." She sipped more of her wine, then leaned back farther on her busy country-house sofa.

"And now . . ." Sasha said with something close to the sound of a drumroll, "Amanda Pepper will, if she wants to live, reveal the true purpose of her mission here today."

"Me? What are you talking about? I'm here about the shower."

She slowly shook her head back and forth. "Nooooo," she said. "Not in this lifetime, bunky."

"How long have you suspected?"

"Not suspected. Known. And only since you phoned this morning. Here's a hot tip for your career as a sleuthette. If you're pretending to be here for a reason, mention that reason. You haven't remembered to say a word about the shower since you got here."

"What can I say except whoops?"

"Plus," she said, "I saw Mister No-First-Name at the funeral. Why is that? Am I to believe you stumbled over Tom Severin's body and that bonded both of you to him forever, so that C.K. felt compelled to witness his interment?"

"We were hired."

She nodded acknowledgment. "I appreciate your candor, albeit belated, but who hired you? The wife he was about to dump? Oh, no—wait—the fiancée he had already dumped. She had it in for me, all right. Not that he ended it with her because of me. He would have, of course, but not quite that instantaneously. But the wife—you following this?—she phoned me. Me! She called me 'a bitch from England.' Moi." She grinned. "Being a bitch from England is so much more fun than being a bitch from Philly."

"It's not about you."

"I am so a bitch from England."

"Being hired, I mean. It wasn't about your relationship with Tom Severin."

Her shoulders slumped and she looked altogether disappointed by the news. "Then who could it be about? The police haven't arrested anyone, so you can't be working for the defense."

"Mrs. Severin Senior's social secretary—"

"Is this a limerick?"

"—wanted us to look into something."

"What?"

I shook my head.

She tsked and sighed. "Okay. But what did you really want with me? Not the description of the funeral because your man was there."

"Right, although he wouldn't have heard that couple next to you, so thanks."

She waited.

"I don't know, Sasha. Honestly. My hope was that he said something to you—pillow talk, perhaps—that didn't seem significant at the time, but that might be a line of investigation nobody's thought about yet."

"He didn't just fall down those stairs? He was murdered?"

"Looks that way because he was drugged. Not a fun-time drug that he might have given himself. And not a fatal poison, at least not normally. A stupid date-rape drug."

"Makes no sense."

"Nothing makes sense in this. But I thought you might remember something he said. After all, he told you he was being bothered."

"By the phone calls. Yeah. But he didn't know who was calling him."

"Anything else?"

"Anything useful? Not that I can think of right off the bat. We only had three times together. We talked about my London

year, we talked about his trips there, we talked about foods we
liked—you know the drill. It wasn't till that day when I mentioned your wedding—I was hoping he'd be my date, Manda . . ."
She grew quiet.

"The phone calls," I prompted.

She shrugged and poured more wine. "I told you what I remembered. He didn't want to talk about it anymore after he told
me about it, so I didn't push."

"I don't know what to do," I admitted. "I don't know where
to go with this, and I don't think the police do, either."

"Don't worry about it. It'll work out."

"I'm afraid it will work out that one of my students is arrested for this."

"Why would he?"

"Because it turns out he's Severin's son. From the first marriage, and Severin treated him with contempt."

"Maybe the kid really did do it. It makes sense."

"No." I refused to accept that. "He had motive, the drug's
one that every kid in my school says they can get hold of easily,
but he couldn't have been where the drug was administered and
in the school building at the same time." I kept the cast and the
broken cheekbone to myself. "The police have questioned him,
though. I'm sure he's a suspect."

"Well, they make mistakes." Her expression suddenly bright-
ened. "Hey—here's what to do. Tell them—"

"Who?"

"The police. Tell them they're ignoring the obvious and in
this case, the so very obvious!"

I had no idea what she was talking about.

"Detecting one-oh-one, girl. Come on—what's the bottom
line of sleuthing? Surely you take a break from great lit every so
often and read a mystery."

"You want me to tell the cops that the butler did it?"

"Did he? That wasn't what I had in mind."

"You've had too much wine."

She poured herself still more, then leaned close. "It's a *literary* convention, and I'm shocked and dismayed by your ignorance. What do we do when faced with crime? We *cherchez la femme*! And hasn't this particular dear departed provided you with a bevy of femmes for which to cherchez? My God, there are three wives, a fiancée, the limerick lady—"

"Who?"

"The Severin Senior's social secretary—and me. And don't forget his mother, who is known to be something of a nightmare. And those are the ones we know about, so cherchez, cherchez, and remind those cops to do the same thing."

Imagine, the teachers in junior high hadn't thought Sasha was bright.

Fifteen

Penelope Koepple did not respect the sanctity of the weekend. She phoned at twenty-six minutes past seven A.M. That would be annoying on a workday, but on Saturday, it was first alarming, and then . . . alarming, because the only rationale would be an emergency, Penelope telling us either that the building was on fire or that we ourselves were fired.

I yawned audibly into the receiver. It was possibly unintentional.

"Did I wake you?" she asked, not sounding at all concerned.

I was by now so perturbed by her imperial manner that I used the snarky response that forced apologies out of people. "Oh, it's all right," I said. "I was going to have to wake up at some point, anyway."

"Good, then," she snapped. I was sure there were Prussian generals on every branch of the Koepple family tree. "In that case, let us have our status conference within the hour."

"Our . . . ?" No matter how groggy I was, I knew I'd never have agreed to anything called a "status conference." What did it even mean? An update? Did I have to teach her to communicate more clearly? Why didn't she say she wanted to know what we were doing with her money and what we had found out about or fabricated against Cornelius Westerly?

I would have told her on the phone. Later in the morning.

I had planned, I had fantasized, I had anticipated with great pleasure, a dawdling morning, the kind where I didn't have to do anything immediately. Anything I didn't want to do, that was.

And Penelope was most assuredly not on my "want-to" list. She was, however, pressed for time, she said. She didn't say why, but I remembered the news that she was being let go, and I'm sure she felt that pressure day in and day out. At least we'd get some more of our fee up front today, and that in itself was reason enough to meet.

My partner in crime-solving was not overjoyed by this re-scheduling. He'd planned to spend every free minute of the day studying for a looming midterm and finishing a paper. Such were our wild weekend plans.

I must admit walking to the so-called status conference was almost as enjoyable as dawdling around the loft would have been. The glorious autumnal weather was hanging in there, with air so crisp I could almost hear it crackle, and even in Center City, it carried the scent of cider. We walked south on Second Street, then turned up Chestnut to Independence Mall, which always feels like time travel of the best sort: Carpenter's Hall, the First— and Second—Bank of the U.S., Independence Hall, the Phila-delphia Exchange, the new democracy's political shrines in all their unprepossessing red brick glory, the shrines to money ve-neered with marble and built in classical style, as if afraid to try anything too new.

While we crossed through Washington Square and the preserved brick facades of Society Hill, Mackenzie mentioned that he'd talked with Owen Edwards after the funeral, and would probably get information later today about Nina's brother, Jay Kress. "At a civilized hour," he said. "Even when life and death's concerned some people—professional people—understand about days off."

We were there on time, washed and semi-starched. Penelope checked her watch as we entered, and the gesture made me want to slap her. Instead, I sat down and waited for the unhappy-looking waitress to notice her two new customers.

It was eight-fifteen Saturday morning, and she'd driven in from the Main Line at seven A.M. And yet her coal-dust hair looked sculpted into a stiff pouf that made her resemble an Edward Gorey drawing. She wore a tailored dove-gray suit with a burgundy silk blouse and looked ready to run a corporation, not talk with two sleepy part-time detectives.

"What have you found?" she asked before a single sip of caffeine could reach our lips and brains. She already had a small teapot in front of her, and she made no mention of actual breakfasts. Fine. Mackenzie and I would stop at Reading Market on the way home and stuff ourselves. Hot, freshly baked soft pretzels sounded a reasonable way to start the day, and if we topped them off with homemade ice cream, we'd have our dairy allowance as well.

"Surely you've found something by now," she said. "Poor Tomas is dead and buried and it can't be that his murderers are going to profit from it."

"We've found out a lot." Mackenzie slathered Southern on his vowels. That usually calms savage organisms, but I wasn't sure Ms. Koepple was soothable. "Unfortunately or fortunately, none of it incriminates Cornelius."

"And by the way," I added, "that is his given name."

She leaned back in her chair, as if to remove herself from me. "You've spoken with his cohort, then."

"If you mean Georgeanne Errico, yes. But that wasn't how we verified his name."

"But as a character reference . . . well—what would she say? They'll cover for each other. They have this all planned out."

"We checked Social Security records and birth records, ma'am," Mackenzie said. "School records. Work records. That's his given name, an' he has no criminal record."

"It will all be in the report," I said, "but the bottom line is— nothing criminal, nothing even unethical."

"As far as you can tell," she said with a slight sniff.

"It's understandable if you don't like him," Mackenzie said. "Or if you don't think this engagement's the best idea. But he's legit, and we've done about all we can—"

I kicked him gently under the tabletop and interrupted. "—in the preliminary investigative phase. Who knows what we'll turn up next?"

"You should have already . . ." She didn't bother finishing the thought. We had failed her.

Mackenzie waited a moment, then spoke in a low voice that was close to a whisper. "You strike me as an upright, law-abidin' woman with a strong desire to see justice—true justice—done. You don' want us to falsify anythin', do you?"

She didn't answer instantly, which was answer enough. "Of course not," she ultimately said with no conviction. And then her facial muscles realigned into an expression that looked hungry, though not for food. Hungry to tell.

Mackenzie, no slouch he, saw it too, and he waited, like a predator outside a cave. And when the silence stretched tendrils into the discomfort zone, he said in that voice that's so low you're surprised you're hearing every word, "What is it you want to tell me?"

She shook her head, then looked down at her hand on the table.

"Can't help as much as possible if you don't say what's on your mind," Mackenzie said.

"It's simply that . . . I know he was involved in Tomas's death." She twisted her paper napkin until it looked like a cheese straw, then she untwisted it and began the process again. "I find it, I find it unbearable if you can't . . ."

"What makes you positive?" I asked.

I was sure she'd say something about character, or woman's intuition, or something along those lines, but instead, she dragged her eyes up until she looked levelly at us. "I saw him at the crime scene."

"Saw him?" we said in unison.

"Saw him push Tomas down the stairs?" Mackenzie asked.

She shook her head. "Saw him following him."

Mackenzie put down his coffee mug and held up his hand like a crossing guard. "Let's take this step by step. Where and when did you see him? An' I take it the two 'hims' means you saw Cornelius following Tomas."

She nodded.

"So where? When?"

She took a deep breath. She no longer looked us in the eye. "Tomas came out of the café near the Square, about two blocks north, on Eighteenth."

I thought I knew the place she meant. Cute, with small green awnings and crisscrossed curtains at its many-paned windows, and a constant flow of people in need of nonalcoholic beverages and a sweet. I always suspected that they piped the scent of freshly baked cinnamon rolls out onto the street.

"Did he come out alone?" Mackenzie asked.

She was silent. "I'm not sure. I actually saw him across the street from the coffee shop, but he was carrying a cup—the take-out kind, so it was obvious where he'd been. I was surprised. I thought he'd had a lunch date, and the coffee shop doesn't serve real food."

"But he was alone," I said. "Not with a companion."

She hesitated. "Nobody was talking to him. There were people on the sidewalk, men and women, but I didn't see any inter-action."

"And Cornelius?"

"Half a block later, I realized that there he was, on the other side of the street, pacing himself so that he was like a mirror image, moving just as fast as Tomas and no faster." She looked first at Mackenzie, then at me. I had no idea how to respond, or to know whether I was upset or delighted by this news.

"What happened next?" Mackenzie prompted.

"I followed him or rather them—"

"On foot?"

She nodded. "That brought us near the school, and I saw Cornelius cross the street, and then I was afraid he'd see me, so I left."

Of course it could have been coincidence. The Cornelius and Tomas part, at least. They'd both been nearby at the lawyer's. They had both presumably done something nearby—eaten, gone somewhere—for an hour, and if they then happened to be walking in the same direction later on in the day, so what? She hadn't seen them leave the café together, nor had she seen them enter the school together. So of what was this evidence?

Aside from that, there was an obvious question, but it seemed impolitic to ask it outright. I was still working on how to phrase it when Mackenzie, in his half purr, half growl, saved me further deliberation. "How'd it happen that you were following Tomas?" he asked.

Once again, she looked down at her hands, now folded on the table. She waited awhile then spoke with none of her customary arrogance. "I wasn't. Not really."

"You happened to be downtown walking around? In the same area as the lawyer the men were seeing?"

"Yes," she snapped, looking directly at Mackenzie, her eyes unblinking. I was sure that boring-through-you look had been effective many times. But not this time. "I spotted him—Tomas, I mean, and I wanted to ask him what had happened at the lawyer's. I meant about his mother's decisions, her mental health hearing. He wouldn't tell me. Sometimes he seemed to care about pursuing a hearing, and sometimes not. Entirely too much hinged on his whims." She pursed her lips, silencing herself.

"What hinged on his decision or his ability to deal with his mother?"

"Isn't it obvious? Her estate, the apartment houses, control, if he had power of attorney, if she was declared incompetent—" She was spluttering, very un-Jane Austen now, trying hard not to mention the part that touched her directly, the bequest that would allow her to safely stop working, that would free her of all this. That couldn't be changed if the will remained as is. If Ingrid couldn't change it.

It was hard believing she'd accidentally stumbled across the men that day and it was painfully apparent that she had never once mentioned the fact that she'd been fired, that her days with the Severin household were numbered.

If Cornelius had been telling the truth. There was not one single person involved in Tom Severin's life and death whom I believed or fully trusted.

Except Zachary.

"Did the two men speak? Did they go into the building together?" I asked.

"I couldn't say. I didn't want Tomas to see me, nor Cornelius, for that matter. As soon as Cornelius crossed the street, I felt obliged to leave the scene."

"You didn't ask Cornelius why he was there?" Mackenzie had perfected the art of asking hard questions in the softest, least threatening manner.

"Of course not! I didn't speak to him—I hid when I saw him! And when I reemerged, neither man was anywhere to be seen. Had I spoken to Cornelius, he'd have run directly to Ingrid, and she's besotted with him. He's charmed her into idiocy, so of course not! What would I say? What would be my explanation?"

"That you'd seen him accidentally, the way you said you did." I widened my eyes and made my voice innocent, outraged on her behalf. "I assume you had appointments in the city . . ."

She said nothing for much too long, and when she finally spoke, she mumbled. Her Prussian ancestors would have been ashamed of her. "She wouldn't have believed me," she said. "She—

she's short with me lately. He's poisoned her against me. My whole life . . . my . . . everything I hoped for . . ." She shook her head, looked back down at her hands, but I saw the glint on her lash.

An actual tear. A most un-Koepple-like response.

She was a wretched, insincere, sycophantic, pretentious, and completely annoying woman. She had dragged us from bed in order to plant further suspicion on somebody else, and that effort had backfired, at least for me, so that I wondered precisely where she'd been at the moment Tomas Severin plummeted. Maybe Tomas had decided to let his mama do as she liked, to change her will every day if she wanted. Maybe Penelope found out and was enraged.

That would take care of everything. Penelope wouldn't have to worry about providing for her future because she'd be a guest of the state, and I could sleep late again on Saturday mornings.

But still, watching her plaster-of-paris face work—and fail— to keep its facade, seeing generations of stiff upper lips and straight arrow posture crumple, I felt sorry for the woman. I didn't want to, but then, you don't always get what you want.

Sixteen

THAT evening, we met friends, as planned, for a meal out and a movie.

The meal was more expensive and less tasty than hoped for, and the movie was the sort that leaves you squinting and headachy, older, and sorry to have once again learned that just because nothing whatsoever happens over the course of a film doesn't mean it's art. I thought I might never again attend any movie that had the word "exquisite" in its review.

Still and all, at no point in either real life or the movie did anybody tumble down a staircase, prove to have been drugged, accuse anyone else of murderous impulses, or talk about wedding preparations.

We considered it a fine and jolly outing.

Next morning, nobody phoned before we awoke, and I thought my fortunes had changed and that I was truly in control of a wide-open day. While C.K. studied, I'd get school- and housework done, the cat brushed, e-mail answered, a letter written, and then, and then . . . who knew what else? The possibilities were endless, and the day felt that way, too.

Of course that wasn't meant to be, but before I knew that, I had settled in to mark papers, contented for once to be doing so as I sat at the oak table, a pot of coffee in front of me, the golden autumn sun flooding the loft, Macavity catching the edge of a sunbeam on the carpet next to me.

That's when the buzzing began. It's a sound that digs into and claws the small canals of the ear. It means somebody at ground level wants to visit, so it should be welcoming and pleasant, but it sounds instead like a warning to immediately evacuate the premises.

The only buzzees out and about at this hour would be people I didn't want to admit or even know, so I ignored the noise until I could no longer stand it, then I left the sunny table and stomped to the door. "Who is it?" I snapped into the intercom.

"Me! Who'd you think?"

"Who'd I think? I thought a serial killer, a Sunday morning drunk or druggie, a thief, a—"

"Are you going to let me in, or are you going to leave me out here until one of those guys really does come along?"

So I let my sister in and listened as the elevator cranked its way up to the top floor of the building.

She opened the door and looked surprised. "Arms across the chest, teach? What did I do?"

"Why did you ask me who else it could have been downstairs?"

"Because it's me! Because you said you were free and that we'd go look at The Manse."

"I said that?"

"She said that?" The near-echo was from C.K.

"Of course!" Beth said.

"I said come over on Sunday, Beth, and we'll go see a mansion?"

"The Manse."

No way could I imagine wedding invitations that said anything resembling "see you at The Manse" unless it was meant as a joke.

"You didn't say those words precisely, no," Beth said. "But on Monday, I asked you when we were going to check the place out, and you said as soon as you had a free day."

Monday. All I remembered of it was Tomas Severin's body. It was possible Beth was bamboozling me, but there was no way I could remember what had or hadn't been said, wedding-wise. And I couldn't say what I was thinking—that I hadn't spoken to her Monday because I'd ignored her phone message. That would be opening a separate can of worms.

"And Wednesday," she continued, "when we were talking, I asked you what your weekend plans were, and you didn't mention a single thing for today. Therefore—your first free day!"

"The dog that didn't bark in the night," I said.

C.K. chuckled. "Ever considered investigation as a sideline, Beth? You're pretty good puttin' clues together and noting what wasn't said."

"You promised Mom you'd come." Beth sounded too much the teacher's pet good-daughter for my liking, but I realized with a sinking sensation that she was probably telling the truth. That must have been what I'd agreed to on the stairs, when my mother had phoned me at school.

Beth's smile had too much of an edge of self-satisfaction.

"I never realized how wily you are, Beth. How cleverly you set your trap. And if this is a potential wedding site, well, I don't think I could get married in a place that called itself The Manse."

"It just means lodging, a house."

"Oh, please. It means—" But her expression stopped me. Her smile had disappeared, and a crease appeared between her eyebrows. She glanced at C.K., who seemed once again mesmerized by his book and his highlighter, and then she looked around, and back at me. "There's no place here to be private!" she said in an irritated whisper.

"About what? What's going on?"

"The bathroom," she said. "Come with me."

She reached for me, but I pulled away. "That's beyond ridiculous. What's the big secret, and from whom? The only other person here is the one I'm marrying."

She sighed and sat down at the oak table, back toward Mackenzie, and patted the chair next to her, so that I, too, would be facing away from my intended. When I was seated, she took a deep breath, exhaled, then put her hand atop mine. "We're sisters. I'll understand. Be honest with me." She was almost inaudible.

"About what?"

"Shhhh," she whispered. "About *him.* About your feelings. It's well and good to joke about the bride having cold feet, but your feet are frostbitten. You seem upset about so many things, lethargic about so much else, that I realized I haven't been sufficiently sensitive to what you're trying to say. So I want you to know that you do not have to—"

Oh joy! She'd gotten it, and it would not be necessary to go through this sea of froufrou to reach the golden shores of matrimony. She was giving me a get out of jail card.

"—marry him." Her level of earnestness could flatten mountains.

"What?"

"You don't have to marry him."

I had to stop and try to rerun the tape, figure out what we'd been saying to each other. "But I want to," I said. "I like the getting married part."

"You don't have to say that. There's no shame admitting you've made a mistake. Even after two people have been together awhile, it can take something like setting the date to realize they're about to make a mistake. He's a lovely man, but other people's opinions shouldn't color yours in any way. This is about you, and your future, so—"

"Beth, I don't feel that way." She sounded as if she'd memorized something from a talk show. "I'm only—"

"Only anything but subtle about your reluctance," she whispered. "Good Lord—I have to trick you into looking at your own wedding site. And Mom says the same thing about the gown, the invitations, about everything. You said you wanted to plan your own wedding, and yet, you plan nothing. You haven't registered at a single store. You haven't even thought about it, have you? What else could it mean? I phoned Sasha this week—"

"Did she mention a dead man?"

"That's precisely it." She pursed her mouth.

"Dead men? Wait—I'm lost now."

"Your own life, your *wedding day*—just about the most important day of your life!—is secondary to—"

I could not believe she meant what she was saying. I mean I knew she meant it, but I couldn't—wouldn't—believe she meant the subtext, that a murder was not as important as the choice of lace or satin trim on a wedding gown. Or as a visit to a place so infatuated with itself that it named itself The Manse.

She. Meant. Well. That was becoming my mantra for all of them. And I knew it was true. Beth was a professional events planner, so she couldn't contain herself when faced with a celebration. Gabby Mackenzie created chaos while also meaning well. So did Bea Pepper, who had drawn up blueprints for my nuptials while I was still in the womb. So did Sasha, who believed in love and marriage and proved it repeatedly. They. All. Meant. Well.

That didn't make the barrage easier to endure. "So many decisions," I said. "I'm overwhelmed with work—two jobs, and, yes, the dead man who has become part of both my jobs, and then, to think about guest lists, and—"

"It isn't him?" Her whisper was barely audible.

"That's the one thing I'm sure of."

"I'm so glad!" She smiled. "And I'm glad we cleared the air."

Did I dare hope I'd therefore have a day or two without wedding imperatives?

"You're stressed," she said, "but I'm here for you. I'm here to make it easy for you. To relieve you of the burden."

No. Nothing had changed. "I don't see the point of all this."

She put her hand back on mine. "It's a cultural tradition. It's bigger than we are."

"As if that were the only day of my life that counted. Need I say how I feel about that concept of my existence?"

"It brings the two families together, and you get to be even more gorgeous than you usually are and there's this huge party for you."

I tilted my head in the general direction of the in-house student. "What about him?"

"Well, of course, him. But it's really Your Big Day. You are the center of attention."

I have no problem being the center of attention when it's appropriate, but I did have a problem with the idea that finding a man willing to join you in marriage was IT. A woman's big day, and then, if you really bought that idea, that left all the rest of her days doomed to be little. I wanted the marriage, not the ceremony, to be the big and long IT. But I knew when I was beaten. "And I only get married once, right?" My turn to speak softly.

"Absolutely," Beth said. "Okay, then. Get a sweater—it's brisk—and let's go. If nothing else, it will be a beautiful ride on a positively glorious autumn day."

When the phone rang, I was rooting around for something to make my jeans and T-shirt look more acceptable at the sort of place that would make Beth flip.

"I've got it," Beth called out. Either she assumed it was our mother, or she herself had become as meddlesome as our mother.

"Then you come, too!" I heard her say in her professionally animated voice.

Not our mother, then, I hoped. She was supposed to stay in Florida until the shower. I'd found my rust-suede shirt jacket and thought I looked sufficiently countrified to enter The Manse. "Who?" I shouted.

"Sasha. She wanted to talk to you about the shower, so I said I'd pick her up en route, and that way you won't feel over-whelmed or harried. We'll have lunch and go into the country and look and see and discuss—and we'll get everything taken care of today."

Even she knew that couldn't happen, and Beth is, if anything, honest. She amended her promise. "We'll get a lot done today."

There was another pause. "We'll get something done." She left it at that.

THE MAIN LINE RECEIVED its name by virtue of being the area along what was once the main line of the Pennsylvania Rail-road, and it runs from Overbrook to Paoli. We drove its woodsy streets—Beth avoided all expressways whenever possible—ogling the sprawls of homes, with admiration for the many elegant and understated beauties, mostly older homes, and a silent thumbs-down for the new and raw-looking pretentious temples to wealth.

The Manse was located just beyond the end of the Paoli local, in Malvern, on a vast expanse of land. Even as we entered its long drive, I knew its pedigree and credentials were as deep-rooted as the ancient trees that lined the road. I wondered what had become of its original inhabitants, and that made me think about the Severins's homes and what would become of them. Tomas's properties must have been in some dispute because he'd moved out of his marriage into his mother's house. What would become of the place after Ingrid moved on? Given Tomas's pat-tern of wife-shedding and child-ignoring, I wondered who, if anyone, would make a claim.

Could Carole Wallenberg stake out a right in the name of her son, Tom's firstborn? Unless, of course, said heir did in his father, which would crimp any legal claims.

It was situations like the Severins's that turned homes like this into rent-a-ballrooms.

"Isn't it gorgeous? Imagine it with tiny lights all over it, and greens and holly."

"Um." I ummed so much I sounded like a quietly operating appliance all the way up the drive as Beth and Sasha blathered about the loveliness surrounding us. I continued umming as we walked through wide double doors, and into a perfectly splendid entryway.

Perfect, that is, if I were royalty, or marrying into it.

Glorious it was, but—I didn't belong here. I wasn't going to have a good time here. The scale was enormous, the ceilings too high and serious, the thick walls and stained glass panels suggesting a citadel, a cathedral to acquired wealth, not a celebration of love.

The booking agent, though surely there's a more elegant upscale job description when booking mansions, hustled up to Beth, who'd obviously made our appointment in advance.

We were not her only guests. A rather awkward and grim couple, a sort of urban American Gothic, stood in the middle of the enormous ballroom looking as if they'd been abandoned there. They were tall and solid looking, serious, both with short gunmetal gray hair, and both slightly squinty-eyed, as if we three women might be an invading army. They were alert and wary. Then I became aware of a third person, a woman in her late thirties or early forties, pacing the perimeters of the room, as if inspecting every square inch.

". . . waited till the last minute," the agent whispered to Beth. Her smile, which she flashed after almost each sentence, was tight, nervous. She turned to toss another smile at the waiting couple, but when she turned back, her voice, even pitched low and confidentially, was filled with disapproval. "Literally. As you know, today was the deadline."

She had to be talking about me. Sounded as if I'd forfeited the place. I controlled the urge to cheer.

The agent shepherded us toward the gray-haired couple. They frowned as we got near, but in puzzlement, I thought, not displeasure. The agent introduced us to the Arbussons, Philip and Meredith, and them to Beth, and she to me and finally, to Sasha.

It all took a great deal of time and I had no idea why we were being introduced to the squinting Arbussons in the first place. Furthermore, the agent said, with a weak smile, "I'll be just a minute," and hustled off to the woman who was still resolutely examining the room and making notes on a clipboard.

"Haven't we met before?" Meredith Arbusson asked. She was speaking to Sasha, though they did not look as if their social orbits occupied the same universe. Meredith A., in a royal blue knit suit, pale cream silk blouse, and proper black pumps, awaited Sasha's answer. "Perhaps at the . . ."

Sasha peered back. She was at least six inches taller than Mrs. Arbusson, and she'd chosen to wear an ankle-length brown velvet skirt with a burnt orange vest embroidered in gold thread, a green long-sleeved blouse, a chiffon scarf in blazing oranges and hot greens, and her favorite suede boots. I thought she looked great, and fittingly autumnal, but I was fairly certain Meredith Arbusson wouldn't agree. Nor, of course, would she approve of my jeans and suede jacket. We didn't belong here.

"I don't think . . ." Sasha began.

"Perhaps at Sylvia and Donald's?" Mrs. Arbusson said. "I know I remember you. I never forget a face."

"Unfortunately, I don't know a Sylvia and Donald."

"I know, then—I volunteer most afternoons at the library, the main library. You know, after school, when the children are there. I was a librarian, once, and I suppose it's in the blood, though I'm past working full-time, of course. Past working, in fact, but one does get bored, and I don't play golf. Or bridge, so—"

"Meredith . . ." her husband said.

"Oh, Philip thinks I go on about everything too much, and he's right. I absolutely do, but still—I must have seen you at the library, right? So many people there every day, I remember their faces, but—"

"Actually, I've been in England . . ." Sasha tilted her head, and moved slightly to the side of the woman. "Aha," she said. "Were you—I don't mean to cause you any pain, but were you at Tomas Severin's funeral this week?"

Both Arbussons looked as if his name had indeed caused them grief, but they nodded.

"I sat next to you," Sasha said. "Recognized you as soon as I saw your profile. We didn't talk." And she introduced herself.

This, then, must be the couple who'd been looking to see if somebody was there, somebody who should have been there but apparently wasn't. I wished I remembered more precisely what Sasha had said.

"You were his friend?" Philip Arbusson asked.

Sasha nodded.

"My condolences."

"And mine to you, too. You were there. Are you relatives, or were you his friends?"

"We knew him, of course," Meredith said. "We knew all of them, from the time they were newlyweds and the children were born. Philip worked with Tomas Senior, years ago. He left the firm when this Tomas took over." She looked as if she were still pissed about whatever had caused her husband to sever his ties with the family. "It's been awhile. We came out of respect for his father's memory."

I wondered why they'd felt the need to make it clear to strangers that they had not come on behalf of the deceased or the deceased's mother or wives. Confusing, but interesting, as was mention of "the children." Whose? Hers? Or plural Severin children and if so, who and where were the others?

And then Sasha flicked me a glance—no more than a shift in her eyelashes, it seemed, but with it, she'd hit the invisible ball to me, and I knew that she'd hooked on to her memory of that day, too. It was a definite "dare you."

"Absolutely lovely ceremony, didn't you think?" I murmured.

"Ah, so you were there, too," Meredith said.

I nodded. Who was to know?

"The crowd was impressive," Philip said. "But of course, Tomas Senior and Ingrid were very social."

"Beyond *being* social," Meredith said with a brief laugh that didn't seem all that happy. "Ingrid was the arbiter of what *was* social. If she bought it or wore it or ate it—then it was fashionable." She sighed. "Oh, but that was long ago."

"She's still quite . . . stunning," I said. On this, I was on firm ground. Her looks had stunned me. Even the memory of them left me light-headed.

Meredith didn't seem to care. Ingrid was no longer arbitrating anything for her. But she looked like a woman who needed to vent about something, and I wanted to release that steam valve. I remembered Sasha telling me that she and her husband had talked about a missing someone, but I couldn't remember if they'd said who it was, or even what sex the person had been. I thought female, but we'd also talked about Nina, and I was afraid I was mixing the memories.

"I hope this isn't out of line," I said, "and the truth is, I couldn't see everyone who was there, of course. It was too large, except that I could see the family, and I paid my respects, and I wondered . . . well, you know . . . I had thought, given the seriousness of the occasion, that . . ." I shrugged. "You know."

A teacher learns so much from her students. This was how they often answered test questions, saying nothing, hoping that by dancing around the idea, they'd find the outline of it.

It worked about the same way for me as it generally did for them, which is to say, not very well.

Meredith Arbusson stared at me as if I were an alien species.

Now my panic was authentic, so that my starts and stops were no longer faked. "Somewhat upsetting—if I'm right, that is. Of course, as I said, I couldn't see, so many people there, but—" I was going to have to use a pronoun soon, a "him" or "her," but which? Who was it that had been missing?

Meredith nodded, her lips tight. "I thought so, too, but I

didn't see her. I think she must be dead. I heard she was living a . . . hard life. In and out of trouble of one kind or another."

A her! "Let us hope not," I said. "Let us hope she found peace somewhere." Let us please be told who this is and what she's about and also why I was speaking in this horribly stiff manner.

"Of course," Meredith said, her mouth curled and angry, "Ingrid behaves as if she never existed—and he was just as bad."

It's quite amazing what people think they hear, the way Meredith Arbusson thought she'd heard me say something tangible, something that proved I was intimate with the family and its history.

Sasha watched the exchange with undisguised admiration. At one point, her brows lifted, and she looked surprised. She'd remembered something more. "But of course," she said with great emotion, "it's also possible she's still—or perhaps again—locked up."

Locked up? Had Sasha told me that before? Where, in prison? Name erased from the family rolls because of a crime? Was she, perhaps, one of those rich young revolutionaries?

"No wonder she had to be committed," Meredith said. "No wonder. The authorities should have been brought in a long time ago."

Committed. I tossed the image of the Severin revolutionary. A mental institution.

"Meredith," Philip Arbusson said.

She ignored him. This had obviously been bottled and left to ferment in her for a long time, and Tom Severin's death had pulled the plug. "I found it disgraceful that she wasn't even mentioned, even if she is away somewhere—even if she's dead! Not during the ceremony, not even in the obituaries. If Tomas Senior had lived this would never have been allowed to—"

"Meredith, these people came here to look at this building. To rent it. Isn't that so?" he asked me directly.

"I'm enjoying talking to—"

"But they must agree," Meredith said. "And where's the secret, anyway? It's been a long time since I worried about making Ingrid Severin angry. Why shouldn't I say that I find it monstrous that any mother could turn her back on her flesh and blood that way, could treat her so—"

"Meredith," her husband repeated softly, urgently.

She applied the brakes with a long, deep breath. I knew that we'd hear no more, but Philip would, later on.

At that point, the agent bustled back to us. "Sorry to have had to leave you both in the lurch, but I had to be certain. Dorothy—" she waved toward the woman who was still at her measurements, "has decided to be married here."

"Nice," Sasha said. "So has Amanda."

"Dorothy decided months ago," Meredith said.

"Unfortunately," the agent said, "her wedding's the same date you'd proposed."

"Wait a minute," Sasha said. "We—"

"It is the only time Dorothy can be married, given her schedule," Meredith Arbusson said.

I wasn't in a mood to be pushed around by any more arrogant members of the social register. I was ready to stomp and carry on and inform them all that the same applied to me—the teaching calendar was not going to bend on my behalf. And all that though I didn't want this place at all. But I was saved from making a fool of myself this one time, and saved from The Manse, when Meredith completed her sentence.

"She's a reconstructive surgeon, you know, and she's about to begin a stint with Doctors Without Borders in the Congo. So sorry we weren't able to confirm the date till now, but it's taken forever to be certain when precisely she was leaving, and—"

"I understand." I kept my eyes on the polished inlaid floor, trying to look as if relinquishing this setting required a great deal of backbone and moral strength.

We shook hands, said how lovely it had been to meet, wished the bride well, and walked to the door with the agent. "I'm sure we can find another time for you," she said. "Maybe a weeknight?

Or next spring? I am so sorry. I truly thought she'd . . . I was positive . . . I told your sister—this morning was her deadline with us, and we'd heard *nothing*. Not a peep."

"It's all right," I said. "Honestly. My sister is amazing, and we will find a place. Or we'll change the date and be back to you again." I was elated. I'd made my escape without needing to be the guilty party. Not My Fault. I didn't want it to show, so I managed a slight tremble in my voice, and felt I did a pretty convincing act of being brave despite adversity.

And for the rest of the afternoon, through lunch and bridal shower discussion and even through all Beth's reassurances, based on nothing whatsoever, that we'd find another place, I controlled the bubbles of joy popping inside me as I replayed Meredith's words. I didn't know what precise relevance they had to anything, but I was sure they were important—why else such a secret?

Ingrid Severin had two children: a boy, Tomas, and a girl.

I hadn't lost a Manse. I'd gained a daughter.

Seventeen

I wasn't sure how Mackenzie would feel about my Sunday excursion. I had been supposed to make decisions and come home with a little checklist completed. Instead, I spread the joyous word that I hadn't gotten what everybody else thought I wanted.

"You're an odd bride-to-be," he said. "For which I'm grateful."

"You aren't upset that we're still in wedding venue limbo?" I didn't wait for an answer because I knew he wasn't. I decided on a quick meal of omelets—brides-to-be are busy people. I chopped onions and mushrooms and sautéed them while we spoke. "Beth, on the other hand, is practically in mourning."

"You had a phone call," he said. "A woman who refused to leave her name. She sounded upset."

"A woman, not a girl." My first thought was of strange miracles—that the mysterious daughter had contacted me. My second thought, closer to rational possibility, was that a student had called. "Nothing said about grades? Absence? Papers due? Did she say 'so she goes' or 'whatever'?" I scooped the mix out of the pan and put it aside and poured the egg mixture in. I loved that first buttery sizzle.

"Woman," he said. "Upset. Sounded tentative, unsure of herself. Talked in half sentences and let things dangle, like 'I only wanted to . . . I guess it won't . . .' and she never hit the subject part of the sentence. I asked about your calling her back, but she said she wouldn't, she couldn't, and anyway, she would be gone the rest of the day. Ask me, she wasn't being evasive so much as falling apart."

I put the filling into the first omelet. It was nice that C.K. had paid attention, answered the phone, attempted to take a message, and even tried to analyze the lack of any hard data. I couldn't fault him for that. But I really didn't see the point of messages like that one. Why tell me about it, except to drive me a little crazier, make me a little more apprehensive?

"Sasha said we should cherchez la femme," I said.

"A breakthrough at last."

"Maybe that was *la femme* herself. Maybe Nina finally returned our calls." I slid that omelet onto a plate and worked on the second one.

"I'd think that cherchez la femme theory would raise your feminist hackles. What does it mean? That every crime since Eve has a female at its core? If she didn't actually do it, then she made him do it? And isn't it usually because she's been spurned?" He grinned. "Do people get spurned anymore? Or just dumped?"

"The late and oddly unlamented Tomas Severin was an expert spurner. Sasha would have experienced spurning, had he lived long enough to do so. He was not a model of constancy."

The omelets were done, and quite beautiful to behold, and I

went from mildly crazed to vastly contented. This was how it was supposed to be. Omelets, salad, a glass of wine, music in the background, and the guy.

He must have felt the same way, and he even suggested a lunch date—a pack your own food sort of lunch date—for the next day. His schedule was open, and I had no clubs or meetings at noon. Life was good.

I relaxed to the point where I forgot to obsess about the Arbussons and their amazing daughter, and about the Severins and their mysteriously missing daughter, and didn't return to them until we were washing up.

"It's odd, isn't it?" I said. "The unmentioned daughter?"

Mackenzie doesn't find as many things astounding as I do. Perhaps he's seen too much, knows too much about human nature. He washed the omelet pan and passed it to me for drying. "Lots of families have squabbles and estrangements," he said.

"I get the feeling it was a particularly nasty variety of that. Meredith—"

"My, but you develop relationships with great speed."

"—was on a rant about how the authorities should have been called in long ago because of the way Ingrid treated this daughter. That's extremely harsh, and Meredith's a most staid-looking woman. She also said that had Tomas Senior lived, none of this—but she didn't say what 'this' meant—would have happened. Unfortunately, her husband shushed her up, so there was no way to find out why she felt that way, or what was done, or whether anybody knew what had become of this daughter."

"Is it important?"

"Couldn't it be?"

He was silent for too long. A polite way of letting me know he didn't feel a particular urgency about this information.

"Well," I admitted, "most people think she's dead."

He nodded. "I keep thinking about Cornelius following Tom Severin."

"I don't think it's such a big deal. They were together at the lawyer's, so it doesn't strike me as particularly weird if they were continuing on, each to his own destination, in the same direction. It's not that big a city."

"Simply seems he had the most motive and, if she's telling the truth, opportunity. Edwards more or less agrees."

"You spoke to the cop?"

"*The cop?*"

"I didn't mean to insult the individuality of every member of your former profession. Saved time, is all."

"I told you. At the funeral. We're friends, after all."

"You didn't tell him what Penelope said."

"Not yet." Of course he hadn't. We were private, not public, investigators.

"You didn't tell him what Cornelius said, either, right? About Nina's brother?"

He shook his head again. "Didn't want to get the fellow in trouble if there's no need. In the big scheme of things, his crime wasn't that much—a little marijuana farm, for which he served his time. Let's wait and see."

"Wait—if Edwards said something about Cornelius, then he can't think Zachary killed Severin." My private black cloud dissipated. "Tell me I'm right."

"Apparently you are. I only hope Owen's right, too."

THE NEXT DAY went smoothly enough for a Monday, when teachers and students all have trouble being back in harness. Expectations are so high on Fridays, and we never are willing to remember how insufficient any weekend is to hold all our dreams for it.

But my students' Monday morning grumpiness seemed minimal, and I had not a trace of Monday morning blues. I'd deflected The Manse, learned a little, and with one week between us and Tomas Severin's death, and despite the confusion surrounding it, things were approaching proportion again. Even Rachel Leary looked as if she'd gotten some rest over the weekend. "I have more ideas for the eating disorders campaign," she said. "We'll talk later."

I liked her optimism, which was catching, and the idea of calling it and thinking of it as a campaign. Who knew? We might actually make a difference.

And now, with the enormous relief of having Zachary off the list of suspects, I thought we should stop pretending that we had more investigating to do for Penelope and call it quits. The income was nice, but it was time to move on. Besides, the police were now directing their attention to Cornelius, so she had achieved her desired goal and, I suppose, so had we. We could eat our sandwiches and talk about it.

My lunch date arrived promptly at noon. I was waiting downstairs for him, so as to avoid the student messenger and the peculiar giddiness engendered by any suggestion of a private life on my part. Mackenzie said that he had a lead on Nina's brother's whereabouts, and if I wasn't too busy after school, we could visit him then and have our second date of the day. And the good news was that we could bill for the after-school date.

His car was in the loading zone outside—the very spot where Cornelius, our prime suspect, had been afraid to break the law and park because all he'd had to unload were his grievances. I didn't want to think about that.

"I had an idea," Mackenzie said as we pulled away from the curb.

"Can't be too exciting of a one. I have just under an hour."

He grinned. "We have what—three days before your mother arrives for the shower?"

"I was in such a good mood, do we have to talk about that?"

"Yes," he said with too much solemnity.

"Okay, yes, three days. She's arriving and so is your mother. Don't forget."

"As if I could . . . but I thought of something that might let them ease up on us, at least not feel that you don't want to get married."

"You were eavesdropping!"

He glanced over at me and looked vastly amused. "Shocked? Listen, here's a hot tip: When somebody is totally aware that there's no privacy—so that she comments on it—"

"Somebody like my sister?"

"—then she's right, and there's no privacy. Got that? Not a great place to share secrets you don't want the other person in the same space to hear."

"She was whispering. Her back was to you."

"I am a trained eavesdropper. Besides, I knew everything you said."

I couldn't remember what I'd said, and I told him so.

"Basically, you made it clear that you're crazy about me and frankly, even though you were swapping confidences with your sister, isn't it a little late for you to be embarrassed about my knowin' that? I had, in fact, suspected it already."

"Okay. Then what about our mothers, and when do I get to eat this sandwich? I am starving."

"You can eat any time."

"Lunch in the car is our intimate tête-à-tête?"

"No, City Hall is. We get our work taken care of there, then we can go up to the viewing platform and survey our city—and finish the sandwiches. Would that be sufficiently intimate?"

"Are we searching records? Going to court?"

"We are preparing our defense."

I opened one of the sandwiches, turkey with mustard and Swiss cheese, and passed him a half while he circled, looking for a parking lot. Walking would probably have been faster. I knew that there was no way to defuse my mother once the rocket fuel was in place and the starter button pushed, but I thought it was delightfully innocent of Mackenzie to think he could do so, and learning the error of his ways was something he'd have to do on his own. "May I ask how?"

He found a lot, took the ticket, and pulled in. Only when the car was in a slot did he turn to me with the look Columbus must have had when first he spotted land. "We're getting our marriage license."

"Now? Today?"

He nodded.

"But—"

"Takes a few minutes, and no waiting."

"How can you know if—"

"I've got friends in high places. Also in low and bureaucratic offices. There's no blood test anymore, nothing except a few questions and proof you're who you say, and it's good for two months and it'll be proof of our sincerity. Next time any of them start in on you, tell them everything's taken care of already—and wave it around your head."

Perfect. A marriage license to be used like garlic for vampires.

Eighteen

THE afternoon also went relatively smoothly, though my seniors seemed agitated, as if a low-grade electrical current pulsed through the entire class. They did their work, participated in the discussion, and I couldn't put my finger on what was wrong enough to ask them about it coherently. So I asked incoherently by saying, inanely, "Everything all right?" They responded with that powerful blankness only a teenager who is hiding something can master. I deserved it.

We were having our final discussion about the book, talking about topics they'd suggested. We'd therefore once again gotten absorbed by nature versus nurture, and this time we included place, and how where we live and in what times might affect our lives. We touched on how much we all fulfill our parents' expectations and play our assigned roles in the family, and whether we have to continue doing so. We talked about the concept of fate, all in the context of the novel.

Somewhere during the discussion, I realized that Zachary, normally a voluble boy and an eager participant, had said nothing all period, and with a rising sense of dread, I understood that he was the still center of the hurricane that was crackling around the room.

They knew something I did not know.

I found out soon enough. He stayed behind when the day ended and stood in front of my desk, almost at attention.

"Yes?" I asked. "What is it? Sit down, please."

He considered that, then nodded and sat. "I tried to come tell you at lunch," he said.

"I was out of the building."

He nodded again, looking as if an enormous struggle was being waged inside him, something that needed airing; something that needed to be kept private.

"What did you try to tell me?" I prompted softly.

"I don't want to bother you."

"You're not. I'm sorry I missed you at lunchtime, but—what is it?"

His cast was on the desk, and he seemed to be engrossed in the messages written on it.

"Zach?"

He raised his head and looked at me with no expression, then he looked away, staring at the chalkboard while he spoke. "I'm ah . . . not going to be here tomorrow."

"Thanks for the heads-up. Is something wrong? Are you ill?"

He shook his head.

"Getting the cast off?"

He looked at his arm as if it were a completely new thing to him. "I . . . um . . . phoned the cops."

"Did you remember something?"

"Kind of. Yes."

I nodded, as if I actually understood what was going on.

"What did you . . . did you come in here to tell me what you remembered? Is that it?"

He nodded.

"Zach, you're a verbal kid. Could you use that skill now? What did you remember? What are you trying to tell me? I'm here. I'm listening. It's okay, whatever it is."

He looked almost angry with me before he took a deep breath, squared his shoulders and, watching me intently, spoke. "I remembered that I killed my father."

"Your fath—Tom Sev—you—?" That was most definitely not okay. That was not even true. "Killed him?"

He nodded.

"What kind of crazy—you just now *remembered*?"

"No, I just said that because you said that. I knew it last week. I hoped . . . I didn't think . . ." He shrugged both shoulders as if he were trying to throw a weight off himself. His expression said that he hadn't succeeded.

"But you came to me—you said you hadn't . . . I believed you."

"I'm sorry," he whispered. "I shouldn't have. You've always been straight with me. I was scared."

He still looked frightened. I leaned back in my chair, willing myself to think logically, not emotionally. My pulse rate was in the millions and I felt as terrified as if something tangible menaced me. "I don't see how you could have. You were in assembly."

He shook his head again. "Mr. Summers fell asleep. It was so boring. He has no idea when I left—maybe even wouldn't have known I left if I hadn't told him. It's not like he's going to tell you or anybody that he was out cold. So was half the class."

That was possible, even probable, given the sedative effect of Maurice Havermeyer's lectures. But still . . . "Tell me about it. Tell me what you told the police." This is not true, I heard inside of me. Don't even listen. Not. True. Not. Happening.

"I, ah, like I said, I was having a smoke out back of the school, and I saw him coming up the street, and I couldn't believe he was coming here because he never did. Never. I followed and saw he really was coming in, so I ran back around the building and in the back door and I came around, past the auditorium."

The same route I'd taken.

"But he wasn't there, so I went up the stairs and he was in your room—the door was open—standing there and sipping something like it was completely natural for him to be there. And I thought—this was stupid, because he wasn't like that, but we'd just had our blowup about college, and then he was here, in my school, so I thought maybe he'd come to tell me he'd changed his mind. That he realized he wasn't fair, that this one time he was going to treat me like . . ." His voice dropped to a whisper. "Like I was his son. Like he cared about me." He bit at his upper lip and shook his head. "I don't know why I had such dumb thoughts, but I went in and tried to keep it casual, and I said something like, 'Hey, welcome to my school. How come you're here?' And he wheeled around and looked confused and then angry. And he said, 'Leave me alone. Get out. This has nothing to do with you.' And I don't know—I was so angry. He had left his cup on the windowsill, so I dropped the stuff in it—"

"He didn't see you doing that?"

"My back was to him."

I stood up and walked to the window where I'd found the cup of tea. I backed away as Tomas supposedly had, which would have put me either smack into the chalkboard, the desk, or Zach, according to his scenario. "This is pretty difficult to envision," I said. "Where was he when you were doing this?"

"I don't know—my back was to him."

I walked back to my desk, and leaned against it. "Are you saying you always have roofies in your pocket, just in case? In case of what? I remember what you wrote about that kind of seduction. You called it rape. You called it all sorts of things, so was that all a lie to make the teacher feel good?"

He didn't answer.

"Besides, you were here, on a Monday school day. Carrying drugs? How about the truth this time?"

He looked straight ahead as if engrossed by the portrait of

Lord Byron on the side board. And he spoke as if I hadn't said a word. "And, like, I couldn't shut up. I wasn't shouting, but I couldn't stop saying things—everything bad he'd done to me, all along, and then this, about college. Lied to me. That's the worst. Lied like I was some kind of idiot, like it didn't matter what promises he made or how hard I worked to keep them. And then he came out of the room after me, and he didn't shout, either. That somehow made it worse. If he'd been angry back—if he'd *cared* enough to be angry back!"

That seemed too much for Zachary to contain. He stood up and paced the front of the room. To the windowsill and back toward the door. I was fairly certain he didn't even know he was in motion.

"He called me names, in that I-don't-give-a-damn-how-you-feel voice he has. All flat, slowing down like he didn't have the energy to talk to me, or like I was about as important as whatever he had for lunch, and I just—I don't know—I saw red, like they say. I really did, like things were exploding inside me, and I did shout that time, and he pushed me, pushed me away. Grabbed my arm, so I punched him with the other one. That was the only thing he'd ever taken time to teach me, how to punch somebody really hard. Except, see, the cast hit his face and I heard this noise—it was awful—something breaking, and he backed off from me, out the door, and he was shouting, and then I heard more shouting and I panicked. I turned around and ran down the back stairs and outside, and then I went back into the auditorium. Mr. Summers was awake then, but I said I'd only been gone a minute and he believed me."

"And then what? You came here later in the day insisting you were innocent?"

He stopped pacing, and looked at me with what seemed true regret. "I'm sorry. You deserved better."

My turn to stand up. "I'll tell you what I deserve—the truth and what you just told me was not it. That story is so full of holes I'm angry you'd think I'd believe it."

"The police must." He looked at his watch. "They'll be here

soon—I'm going outside. I thought that was decent of them, waiting till the day was over."

"No scene in the school?"

"No scene here. I just wanted to say I'm sorry. About the lying part."

What a waste. If any of this was true, what a waste. He'd finally recuperated from his father, gotten past whatever fury and despair had driven him for too long. He'd been able to let the true Zachary emerge and grow strong until, if this was true, his father reappeared in his life and now what? A prison sentence?

But it couldn't be true. Small details sounded possible—the punch on the cheek, perhaps—but as a whole, it did not make sense. Why would he lie this way? "You ran away while he was standing outside the room?"

He nodded.

"Alive, then. You forgot the falling down the stairs part. The fatal part."

He stared at me, visibly working to keep all emotion to himself. "He must have—he must have been falling, but I didn't see because I turned away and ran to the back, down the back stairs."

This was infuriating. "When did your father have a chance to drink the drugged tea?" I asked quietly.

His face first blanched, then turned scarlet. I had a sick sense that if he was hellbent on taking blame for something he hadn't done, I'd just shown him the raggedy patches he had to repair the next time he told his story.

"Has your mother gotten you a lawyer?" I asked. "You need one immediately."

He shrugged, and turned to go.

It wasn't hard to translate that gesture. "Wait a minute. Does your mother know what you've done? Does she know about your suddenly recovered memory? This bizarre confession? Did you tell her?"

He turned halfway around and looked at me briefly, his eyes wide and dead-looking. "I don't see why I'd have to ask permission to tell the truth. It's what she's always told me to do."

"Then why didn't you listen to her? It was good advice!"

But he was already out the door. He didn't hear me.

WHATEVER MY MASTER PLAN—or even my sketchy and improvised idea of a strategy—had been, it was now gone, trashed before I could recall it. I stared at the afterimage of Zachary, hurrying away to a doom he'd orchestrated, hoping for a revelation or insight that never arrived.

I finally roused myself. Mackenzie would be here in a half hour and in the meantime, Zachary needed a lawyer. He needed his mother and his mother needed to know about this.

I stopped at the bottom of the staircase. Students' home numbers were treated like state secrets. Staff was not given easy access to them, as if we were likely to abuse the privilege, to have pajama parties and phone the students in the middle of the night with silly jokes.

I entered the office ready to do battle with Mrs. Timidity who, in fact, greeted me with an expression so alarmed, I had to slow down and force out a smile.

She pointed toward the cubbies. "You didn't check."

Counting to ten to get calm would take too long. "I'm in a rush and—"

"You're supposed to."

"Mrs. Wiggins!"

"There's a message for you, that's why."

She might have been a painted backdrop with a movable mouth and a tape that would run until I clicked it off for all she looked likely to give up and listen to me. I nodded and went to the rows of open mailboxes.

"Your friend, she said."

I reached for the "while you were out" slip and saw "S. Berg" at the top of the pink square.

"Call me," it said in Mrs. Wiggins's careful but loopy hand. "I am asking her to put three exclamation marks because it's important. About the not so dear departed." Mrs. Wiggins had seen fit to write every word of that down, plus Sasha's number, which I knew by heart.

If I had had more time, I'd have been more annoyed. Here it was—another message that didn't include a message. Instead of making exclamation mark demands, couldn't she have said what was so important?

"I need to make a call," I told Mrs. Wiggins.

She nodded and reached out for the message slip. "No, not to her. I'll call her later, from the office, or she can reach me there," I said. "I need to call Zachary Wallenberg's mother. Could I have his home phone and emergency numbers?"

She tilted her head, chin up and to the side, as if posing for a coin. "Not allowed," she said. "Those numbers are confidential."

"They're for emergencies. This is one."

"Is he hurt?" She elevated, standing on tiptoe, to look out the door at the entryway as if expecting to see another paramedic crew in action.

"In trouble. It's important. It's an *emergency.*"

"I'll phone," she said, fumbling for and then nearly dropping the telephone.

"Please," I said, reaching for it. She was going to mess up the message—she didn't even know the message—and meanwhile Zachary was efficiently destroying his life.

She snatched the phone away from me and her eyes reminded me of photos I've seen of horses trapped near a fire. "I'll get in trouble," she said. "I—you've been nice to me, so I'm sorry, but—I'm in trouble already." She rolled her eyes toward the office door. "He—after what happened last week and I wasn't there. I mean here! He, Dr. H., he's very angry and he said he was giving me one more chance."

"That isn't fair. You didn't have anyone to cover for you. And by the way—did you hear somebody shout?"

"I wasn't here!"

"I mean on your way back, maybe?"

"No," she said. "No. Nobody shouted."

So that part of Zachary's tale was also a fabrication.

"Why? Did Dr. H. say I was here? He's pretty angry about the way I wasn't—"

"I'll talk to him, I promise. It'll be fine, but not now. Right now, I need to—"

She held the phone to her chest with both hands, protecting it from me. "I can't. I'm in trouble, and I need this job!"

She wasn't moving, and yet she was spinning, working herself into a frenzy about the phone and the danger it presented to her. I wondered if there was any validity to the old movie technique of a slap on the face.

"I don't have anybody in the world, and I need to work!" Her voice was high and close to keening.

So there was no Mr. Wiggins. I couldn't blame him for cutting out. Nor could I comprehend why he'd ever cut in.

"So let me, let me!"

And then instead of merely facing her, or worse, facing her down, I actually looked at her, saw her, a doughy woman of indeterminate age clutching a phone to her bosom, terrified that I was destroying her livelihood. I knew she had gotten this job because the term had already begun and all the superior secretaries were elsewhere. Nobody wanted the job, which was as underpaid as were all the positions at Philly Prep, except for Mrs. Wiggins, who desperately needed it.

I was ashamed of myself. Yes, Zachary was having an emergency, but I had the sense that Mrs. Wiggins's entire life was lived in a state of emergency—frightened, confused, and unfathomably desperate. That didn't make for a good school secretary, but it did suggest that a measure of compassion was called for.

"I'm sorry," I said. "You can dial. Please do. Hand me the phone when you reach her, if that's all right."

She stood frozen for a moment of thought. "I think it would be," she eventually whispered, and then she dialed. She listened. She frowned. "Oh, dear," she said. "An answering machine. She must not be home." She was halfway to hanging up when I reached for the receiver.

"Please," I said. "A message?"

Her mouth opened slightly, then she nodded, as if this were a new and amazing concept. I spoke quickly. "Zachary needs to be in touch with you, Mrs. Wallenberg. He's at police headquarters. He—he—he apparently has confessed to killing Tomas Severin. He needs a lawyer and probably more than that. Call me if you can." I left my cell phone number.

Mrs. Wiggins never looked robust or vigorous, but she now looked ashen, as if all her blood had sunk to her feet. She took back the receiver with her mouth half open and I feared she was having a stroke.

"Are you all right? Mrs. Wiggins?"

She took a sharp breath. "Yes," she said, "I'm—but that boy! He said he killed him?"

I nodded.

"How?"

"Pushed him down the stairs. You remember." Of course, Zachary had skipped over that part, but I was willing to bet he wouldn't when he talked to the police. In any case, she knew how Tom Severin had died, and surely she didn't have to be told that part of it. "Do you have a work number for his mother?"

She didn't seem able to focus on two things at once, and she still looked numb. "He—why would he?"

"Do such a thing? Or say he'd done such a thing? I don't know. I'm as baffled as you are, and as upset as you seem. Now, the emergency number, or her cell phone? I think she works and goes to school. There might be . . ." She still looked glazed. "What is it?" I asked quietly.

"Why would he lie? Say he'd done such a thing? He's a nice boy. He was sometimes the aide in here, and he had such good plans and was very polite to everyone."

"That's why we have to get him out of . . . Mrs. Wiggins, if you saw something that day, something that didn't seem important at first, or you didn't remember it for a while, it could matter, even if it doesn't make particular sense to us. I don't think

Zachary did it. His story is full of holes, but I'm afraid the police are going to believe him. It'd be easier than looking for somebody else because he's confessing. So if you saw something, anything—"

"No!" she said. "How could I? I was in the bathroom. I told you that! I told the police that! What are you saying?"

I put my hands up in a position of surrender. "Nothing—I only hoped that you said that about lying because you knew something, saw someone leave, had an idea that might help."

She held her head high, but she didn't meet my glance. "I would have said so if I had."

"You aren't afraid of anything, are you?"

"Me? Why would I be? Of what?" Her skin was putty colored so that she looked no more than half alive. How could I have asked that general a question? Mrs. Wiggins was afraid of everything. Including me.

"I meant—nobody's frightening you, are they? Telling you what you can say and what you can't?"

"Oh." She took a deep breath. "That. No. No. Who would? Why would anybody?"

"Right. Never mind. But about that alternate number, do you have one?" Every one of her responses was half a step off point, as if she were actually answering an entirely different set of questions, as if my words were translated into a new language before they reached her ears. I did not, however, have any idea what to do about that without frightening her still more.

"It's just that he wrote that lovely article in the paper—I saw it, even though I wasn't working here last month. And once, he was office aide and there wasn't much to do, and he told me about the book you were reading—*East of Eden,* isn't it, and about how the father liked one of his children more than the other, and—well, it was so sad I started to cry." She looked down and away and I was afraid she might be about to cry again. "And then he said he knew how that could be, and I cried even more. I felt like he was a friend. Do I sound silly? It was terrible, but he was nice to me. Kind. I mean . . . I must have looked pretty foolish, but he was . . ." She looked up at me again. "He isn't the type to lie, Miss Pepper."

"Amanda."

She blinked several times, then stared at me.

"Call me by my given name," I said. "We're colleagues, after all."

I had dumbfounded her, but she didn't respond in kind, and so Mrs. Wiggins she remained and, I, Miss Pepper. She obviously felt safer hiding behind the formality of surnames. Or simply basking in the memory of when there'd been a Mr. Wiggins.

She scuttled back to her desk, and opened a file drawer, but I saw her pause a second to put her hand on her heart and take a breath. I wished I had a way—a gentle, humane way—to find out why I was now terrifying her along with Dr. Havermeyer. He was holding her job over her head, but what was the weapon she envisioned me carrying?

She dialed another number and listened. "Her cell phone, I think. She's a student at Penn, did you know that? She told me." She listened, frowning, as it rang, then suddenly rushed to the divider and passed the phone to me. "She's answering!" The tinge of hysteria had returned to her voice.

I took the phone. Carole Wallenberg panicked immediately, and my first job was to reassure her that Zachary had not been hurt.

"Then—did he—are you calling because he did something?"

I knew she meant a minor offense: insulting a teacher, failing to hand in an assignment. She most assuredly did not mean that he'd announced he was a murderer. "He did something stupid, I'm afraid," I said. "He called the police and confessed to the murder of Tomas Severin."

I heard small and not so small explosions, staccato bundles of words that imploded one on the other and didn't make sense except for their emotional freight, which was clear enough. "How could he!" she said. "He's so—he's—I know why he did that—I know! He's so—" And then she was crying with small hiccupped sobs, so I waited again, watching Mrs. Wiggins's basset-hound eyes as she tried to comprehend what was going on.

"Do you have a lawyer? Know a good criminal lawyer?" I asked.

"He's doing this to spare *me*," she said in such a low, rushed voice I wasn't sure I'd heard correctly.

"Did you say to spare you?"

"To—to protect me. Yes. He's a kid, he has a code of gallantry, he—"

"Mrs. Wallenberg, do you have a lawyer? Because I'd suggest you call him right now."

More verbal explosions. "Oh, God, the only one I know was from my divorce, but no, she's not a—I'll find out—oh God."

"I think it would be good, if you can leave work—"

"School. I'm here at school, cleaning the lab. My grant hinges on my doing this."

"Can you leave?"

"I—yes. Of course. Soon. Why not? This stupid job—he's where?"

I told her again. "Would you like me to meet you there?"

"He—I . . . No, thank you. I need to, I want to talk with my son. I need to be with him. Do you think they'd believe him? No, never mind. I—he—thank you, but no. I'll—I'll—can we talk later?"

I thought we needed to talk right now, but my opinion wasn't going to carry the day. "Of course," I said. "I have some appointments first, but I'll be at the office later on—maybe five P.M.?"

"That detective place. Yes," she said. "I saw it in the paper. Zach told me, too."

"We're on Market Street, but you can reach me through my cell phone—"

"Fine," she said and hung up before I was able to tell her the address, the cell phone number, or even say that both were on her home answering machine. I'd been dismissed, except emotionally. I still felt very much entwined in whatever was going on. I handed the phone back to Mrs. Wiggins.

Not a piece of it made sense or, worse, it did make sense and I didn't because I was so prejudiced in Zachary's favor. I didn't want to believe, in fact felt nauseated by the thought that Zachary, no matter how understandably furious with his father, would push him to his death. And why would his mother think he was doing this for her benefit? To spare her what?

Was it possible I wasn't being any more rational than Carole Wallenberg, and that I couldn't bear to think of Zach as guilty because I believed he was my gold-star pupil, my vindication, my personal triumph?

How does a possibly irrational person establish whether or not she's rational?

Looking for Nina Severin's wayward brother seemed at best a detour at the moment, but at least it would allow time for talk with Mackenzie.

Mrs. Wiggins regarded me with a tight smile. I must have been standing there, inert, distracted, for too long. "Sorry," I said. "Sorry. I just . . . I was lost in thought."

"A lot to think about," she agreed, nodding.

"Are you sure he's lying?"

She nodded again.

"Would you be willing to say so to the police?"

She backed away from the center divider, her hands slightly raised, as if I'd trapped her. "Ohhh—no. I'd be too . . . I'm not good with words, I couldn't—"

"Not even to help him? A character witness? Something?"

"No. No. What would I say?"

"You'd say why you're sure he didn't push his father down the stairs."

"No," she said again. "I couldn't. Please, Miss Pepper, don't make me—don't—no."

I hadn't expected her to, but I'd been hoping that in the middle of her denials, she'd slip and say something more concrete about why she was sure Zachary hadn't pushed Tom Severin.

"It's a feeling, that's all." She said it while looking down at the floor. "It's just a—he's too nice," she continued, eyes still averted.

"He isn't the type, but a person can't say that to the police. They would laugh at me."

She was right, but I was convinced she was leaving other things unsaid. I had no choice but to thank her for the use of the phone and get ready to leave. I wrote down the phone number at Ozzie's, and the address. "In case Carole Wallenberg calls back, okay?"

She took the paper carefully, nodding, and then she read it and looked surprised and pleased. It was a weak form of joy, but still, it was the jolliest expression I remembered seeing on her. "I know just where this is," she said with such delight that I feared she usually didn't know where she was. "I could walk them there!"

"There's no need," I murmured.

She let out a sound that was close to a chuckle. Amazing.

"Is there—what's so—did I say—"

"I didn't—I wasn't making fun of you," she said, back to her worried expression. "It's just that I live right next door!"

I thought of the neighborhood, which was commercial, not residential, of the apartments above second-rate first-floor stores. I couldn't imagine where they found light, or air, but I could imagine how lonely they would be at night when the lights went out on all the first floors.

"I—I don't mean this badly," she said, "but I had no idea you were a dance instructor, too! Do you put on a ballgown when you get there, too, like the other lady?"

"Oh, no—I'm not there." I thought about the dance studio that never seemed populated, and the instructors in their sad worn tuxedo and ratty ballgown.

"But I live next door. Right next door. So I know there's a dance—" Then she did a double take, and I witnessed one of life's few actual jaw drops. "You're a detective? Miss Pepper—a detective?" Her habitual expression of fright had returned.

"I do clerical work to earn a little extra money. This school doesn't exactly pay well, and . . . you understand. I do the same things you do here."

"The detective agency." Her voice was dreamy, lazy. "I've wondered so much about what goes on in that place."

"Are you a fan of mysteries?"

She nodded. "I guess I shouldn't say that in front of an English teacher, should I?"

I couldn't tell if we were bantering, and this was all to be taken lightly, in the manner of normal people, or if she was now honestly nervous about having admitted her literary tastes. I took the safe and literal road. "I'm a fan myself. But my advice is to stick with the books, not real life. They're much more exciting."

She didn't look convinced.

"Stop by some time and see for yourself."

"Really? You'd . . . you'd show me?"

"Everything." I wondered what I meant by that—there was almost nothing to see. A large, drab room with desks, a wall, Ozzie's door, computers. But the idea made her happy. Maybe we'd bonded and she wouldn't be as afraid of me anymore. "I promise."

"Do I have to, should I phone you first, make an appointment?"

I shrugged. "If you want to check with me, that'd be good—only so you'll know if I'm planning to be there or not. But no appointment's necessary. Come whenever you have the time."

She was still beaming—actually beaming and dread-free—when I left the building.

Nineteen

was not as overjoyed. I was, instead, depressed about Zachary and confused about everything, including him. I stood in front of the school, waiting for Mackenzie, enveloped by the sensation that all of the people I'd been dealing with rejoiced in some way in Tom Severin's death, all of them chattering to their own purposes, and all of them lying.

I didn't know how they all lied, but I had the clear sense that not a one of them had told the complete truth, and that only the missing data was important.

Nothing was close to clear-cut, with Cornelius spying on Tomas, and Penelope spying on the both of them, and Zachary insisting he'd killed Severin and yet forgetting about getting the drug into Tomas's bloodstream or how he'd actually done it, and

Carole Wallenburg melting down over the phone and Georgeanne claiming no current relationship with Cornelius, but phoning him immediately after my visit—and what else? The mysterious person with whom Tom had had tea that day, and who'd slipped him the drug, if that's who did it. And where did the threatening phone calls fit in, and why did Tom Severin tell his son his visit to Philly Prep had nothing to do with him?

Worse—when any of these questions were answered, would they have any bearing on who killed Tomas Severin?

Mackenzie was on time, and we drove out to the southwestern part of the city, past Penn's ever-expanding campus into a neighborhood of run-down row homes, their porches tilted, and some vacant and boarded up.

I recited my list of questions. It felt good hearing them said out loud, but it didn't work any magic cure.

"The force of the blow," Mackenzie said. "That could have been what he meant—it pushed Severin down the stairs. He did fall backward, after all."

"It didn't sound that way, but I bet that's what he'll say to the police."

"Manslaughter, then."

"He said he heard a shout."

"I can't tell you how many people I've interviewed who said they heard shouting—and it turned out to be them. They were shouting and didn't realize it."

I didn't like any of these responses, so it was lucky that within a minute, we pulled up outside The Green House. That was its name, and that was its description as well, though the acid green of the clapboard didn't suggest anything that grew naturally. The building was ringed by plantings, and sat next to a property completely given over to a garden and display stands. I looked around. It was almost possible to see waves of the energy this area was putting into reclaiming itself. There were still sadly neglected houses, but they were in the minority. Tiny brick facades had window boxes and painted shutters, though there were still metal grills over most first-floor windows.

"This is actually a nice project," Mackenzie said. "I did some checking on it. Nobody has real gardens around here, but they have little backyards, and community gardens, and The Green House is greening the city, patch by patch."

"I hope in another shade, though."

"They have classes, too."

"Does it make sense to have a guy who was imprisoned for growing marijuana working in a nursery?" I whispered as we walked to the door. "I wouldn't call this the five-minute excursion Zach mentioned, but it isn't far from the school."

"You have to decide if you think he sold somebody the drug or he used the drug on Severin. Which one is our theory? I forget . . ."

And then we were inside The Green House, in a room filled with potted chrysanthemums and tiny poinsettias, and vases and pots for forcing amaryllis during the bleak months of winter. The space smelled of wet earth, almost as if it were spring.

"You Jay Kress?" Mackenzie asked a man in his twenties who'd been carefully watering a row of mums.

The young man froze, his arm still halfway out, the thin hose dribbling onto the floor. He looked from Mackenzie to me and back to Mackenzie and finally nodded and asked, very softly, "Why? Who are you?"

"We've been hired to help out with matters pertaining to the Severin estate," Mackenzie said, "and if you could give us a minute—"

His eyes had narrowed at the word "Severin." "A minute, okay," he said. "No more. I'm busy here."

"We'll be quick. You are, I believe, related by marriage to Tomas Severin?"

"So? I didn't have anything to do with what happened to him, if that's what you're asking. I barely had anything to do with him ever, in fact, and that day, I was here the whole day—ask my boss. I'm like a slave in this place."

His words were tough enough, but his voice was soft, and low. A gentle voice.

"I'm sure you know there were drugs involved in his death," Mackenzie said.

"That's what this is about?"

Mackenzie shook his head. "We aren't the police."

Jay pushed out his chin. He's used to this, I thought, or getting used to being questioned whenever the word "drug" applied to the situation. "Yeah. I read that. I heard that, too, from Nina. So? You're not thinking— I don't have anything to do with chemical garbage, man. Never did. Everything I did was natural and organic, no sprays even. Not the same at all." He shook his head with disdain, then looked sharply at us. "And I don't do that anymore, either, okay? I'm retraining, see? I'm into this now," and he gestured with his arms wide, embracing the room of growing things. Unfortunately, one of his hands still held the hose, and I was watered along with the potted plants. "Sorry," he said.

"No problem." I dried my cheek. "Were you . . . close? On good terms?"

He watered another pot, focusing on what his hand was doing, then he turned to us more directly. "Why lie? I hated him, he hated me. He treated my sister like . . . No, we weren't close and I wouldn't want to be close with such a jerk. Ask my sister." He shook his head and watered the next two pots and I noticed his hand trembled slightly, but that could be because we made him nervous. "People don't know."

"Sounds as if he treated you badly," I said.

He shrugged again. "Within his rights. My sister, she thought I could move in with them for a little bit when I—well, you probably know about it, right? When I got out. Our parents are out in Arizona. Nina and Tom had this huge house with lots of empty bedrooms, and it was just to get on my feet, get my bearings. Tom said no. Didn't want an ex-con around his kids. But . . . a man's home is his castle, like they say, it was his call, even if he moved out of the castle the next month and didn't seem to give a damn about his kids then.

"I actually respected him a little when he said I couldn't stay there. First time I ever saw him think about his kids, try to protect them, even if it was stupid. But hey, it was an honorable impulse."

"Must have been hard on you, all the same. Where could you go?" He looked barely older than my seniors, too young to be abandoned that way.

His shrug was a tic, trying to say that no matter what he had to say, no matter how sad it might sound, it didn't bother him at all. That's what it was supposed to convey. It didn't work. "A shelter, halfway house kind of place. It wasn't that bad. Nina gave me money for food and some clothes, and I stayed there maybe three weeks, and then Nina found a friend who let me have this job, and I rent a room from somebody in their house, but I'm still on a trial basis, so I can't talk to you forev—"

"What was it like, in the shelter?" I asked.

Mackenzie shot me a quick glance that asked me to get back on track, but I didn't know where the track was, so I let the question stand.

"Mostly it sucked. The people there—they were pretty hard, some were nuts, and old, but—" the shrug again, "some were okay. There was a girl around my age for a few days. She was okay. And this guy who'd really been around, seen the whole country, and this one lady who, like, provided refreshments . . . When she'd get hold of a bottle of wine we talked a lot, told each other our troubles."

"Everybody must have had lots of troubles," I said.

He nodded. "Some of the stories got interesting. Real interesting. People have been through some really bad stuff." He paused, watching us.

He was still a kid, and so obviously withholding something—and hoping, almost daring us to probe, make him tell.

I honored his unspoken request. "In what way interesting?" I asked.

"Very. Especially if you were interested in Tom Severin."

"This story, it was told by the guy who'd been around or the girl or the lady?" Mackenzie asked.

"The lady. Small world, huh? Turns out I didn't have to wait for Hallowe'en to find skeletons in Tom's closet. And ghosts, man." He shook his head as if still in wonderment.

"She knew Severin?"

"Better than his own wife did. Even Nina didn't know how much of a bastard he was till I told her."

"Like what?"

He held up his hand, like a traffic cop. "Guy's dead, so what does it matter? Nina knows, and I'm glad. Makes her not care so much about losing him."

"Could you tell us who the woman was who knew Tom Severin so well?" Mackenzie asked.

Jay shrugged, then shook his head. "I never knew her real name. She called me 'honey' and I called her 'ma'am,' and we both called the other guy 'Tex' even though he was from New Jersey, and that made us all laugh. We were a little . . . you know."

"Drunk? High?"

"It was wine. Only wine . . . and I never saw her around after that night. That's how that place is. People come in, then they go. Must have moved out, and I did, too, a few days later."

"Could you describe her?"

"Old."

"Like what?" Mackenzie said. "Like me?"

Jay looked at him appraisingly, then nodded. "Yeah, maybe."

Poor C.K. Thirty-six years old and Old, just like that. When teens see salt-and-pepper hair, that's it.

"Did she say where she was from? Where she'd been?"

He shrugged. "Not that I remember. The thing was, she told her little story and then Tex, he told how he'd messed up three marriages, and she didn't say much more."

"Any more you want to say about those ghosts and skeletons?" Mackenzie asked.

"Not really. Like I said, the guy's dead. None of it matters anymore. It wasn't like national news or anything." He busied himself straightening the row of bulbs and that seemed that. I tried to think whether there'd been any actual information in what he'd said.

I could hear the deep breath he took, and then he looked at us as if we were slow-witted students. "Here's the point," he finally said. "You look at me, and you see an ex-con."

I saw a plant-loving skinny kid, not yet twenty, who was toughing his way through life with little success. Nobody would picture Jay when they thought the term "ex-con," but I was afraid knowing that would hurt his feelings.

I hoped the nursery business worked for him.

"You think criminal, you think bad," he said. "But you looked at him, you saw big time. Mr. Made It. The ideal. Success. What a fake! What I learned is that people commit big crimes—crimes that really hurt people, ruin people, destroy people—and they don't go to jail for it." He turned and carefully examined a small plant, pulling the leaves apart, then almost unconsciously patting it back into shape while he spoke. "What they do is mean—evil, maybe—but there's no law against it."

"Like not letting you stay at his house?" I asked softly.

He shrugged. "Sure," he said after a pause.

"It would make me very angry."

"Yeah. Me, too." His eyes widened. "But that doesn't mean I hurt anybody."

Of course anybody is capable of anything, but I couldn't imagine him assaulting Severin, no matter how much he hated the man, and even if we could figure out how and why he'd have been inside the school.

We'd come here because he'd been involved with drugs, but I also couldn't see him selling that kind of drug out of this green spot. I'd double-check with Zachary about whether this nursery had been part of his research, but I was sure the answer would be a resounding "no." "Thanks for your time," we both said, almost in unison. "You were a big help."

"Really?" He shrugged. "How? I still don't get what you wanted in the first place."

* * *

I STILL DIDN'T GET what I wanted, either, when Mackenzie dropped me off at the office. He had work to do at Penn, and then he'd join me later before we headed home.

I hadn't wanted to meet another sad, messed-up young man. Or to hear vague intimations of stories that further confirmed that Tomas Severin had been a royal jerk.

I wanted to know who killed Tomas Severin—and I wanted it clear that it hadn't been Zachary Wallenberg. We hadn't come within shouting distance of getting that.

The weather had gotten wetter and colder, but even so, I pulled the hood of my raincoat up over my hair and stood in front of the office while Mackenzie's car pulled away. He'd agreed that Jay had been something of a dead end and that we'd work on the Zachary situation as soon as he finished up at school today.

And I? I kept feeling as if there was something to be done that would be more valuable than sending out bills and reports while I awaited Mackenzie's return.

I thought about Jay, and his gentle rage at his dead brother-in-law for cruelties that were within the law, and how he would probably have been in agreement with the woman at The Manse who'd felt something had been so wrong in the Severin household that the authorities should have been notified, and it had to do with a daughter, now presumed dead. Except that Ingrid had insisted "she" had somehow killed Tomas. Had she meant this daughter who would, then, be alive? Or had that been the ranting of a woman sinking into dementia?

I replayed everything I could remember of Meredith Arbusson's words at The Manse and remembered that she volunteered at the library—the main library—most afternoons, when the children came in after school.

I was only a few blocks away, and the rain was so gentle, it could have passed for heavy mist. I could walk to the library, talk with her, and be back well before Mackenzie was ready to work again. She'd at least know about that cryptic family, and she seemed eager to vent about it and if she was there today, her husband wouldn't be around to censor her.

Nor was my husband-to-be around to censor me, to remind me to stay on track. I headed across the street, toward the Parkway. It looked as much like the track as anything else did at this point.

Twenty

THE rain became more assertive with every step I took, so I hurried along, noting with sorrow the patches of bright dead leaves being washed down and away. And then I was there.

There are few more satisfying destinations than a library, particularly when the weather is less than perfect. To be out of the cold or heat or wet and into a world bordered with books is close to as good as it gets, and I felt that again as I stood there.

I wanted it to appear we'd met accidentally, and the problem was coming up with a reason to be in the Children's room. Then I realized she didn't know my occupation, only that I was about to be married and wasn't going to have the ceremony at The Manse, so I wandered around the room, remembering my father bringing me for my first visit here as a preschooler and how awed

I'd been by the enormity of the treasure house. I remembered it as the size of a football field or a castle, and now it was simply the size of a pleasant children's library collection. Cozy, actually. It had obviously shrunk while my back was turned.

Then I saw Meredith helping a child find a book, opening it and describing why this was a volume dear to her heart. No wonder the woman had raised such an exemplary daughter. I wandered close, waited till the little girl had padded off, clutching her treasure.

"Excuse me," I said. "But do you know where the fairy-tale collections are?" Forget the units I'd taught on using the Dewey decimal system.

She turned, her expression helpful and friendly. "I can surely . . ." She frowned slightly, either surprised to find an adult in search of fairy tales, or with a sense of familiarity. "Don't I . . . ?"

"It's Mrs. Arbusson!" I hoped my expression of surprise didn't look too false. "We met Sunday. I was just here on another errand, and I thought that a book of fairy tales might work into a unit on folklore and myths I'm teaching and—too lazy to look it up, I guess."

"Er . . . forgive me. I remember you, always remember a face," she said, "but your name?"

"Amanda Pepper."

"Ah, yes. I hope you aren't too furious with my daughter. She's an amazing woman, but getting her to make up her mind on serious things like where she'll be married . . ." She shook her head in despair. I could imagine my mother mouthing the same words—except, perhaps, for the "amazing" part, and I thought I'd therefore found a path into Meredith Arbusson's confidence.

"I'm so glad to have bumped into you," I said. "I wanted to talk to you ever since Sunday. I was hoping it wouldn't be an imposition, but I thought you'd know about other sites, that you'd have good ideas about putting on a December wedding. Given that you're also a little late in the planning, if you don't mind my saying so."

"Well, I'm not late, if you don't mind my saying so. My

daughter is. She is completely in charge of her wedding. Pretty much the way she's been about her entire life. I, on the other hand, tend to be compulsive. It's the way nature keeps the human race going, making the neurosis skip a generation. It also makes the generations always be on each others' case. It'll serve her right if she has a daughter who's a planner, the way I am."

"Ah," I said, looking down at my hands. "I thought . . . my mother's in Florida and so—communication and . . ."

"Oh, my dear. Of course. She's told me about other places— I've gone to look at some with her, so it's the least I could do, given that we snatched that place from under your nose." She checked her watch. "Would you consider standing in the rain— under cover—while I indulge my secret vice?"

"It won't be much of a secret then."

"Secret from Philip the Puritan."

And so we wound up huddled against the door, under the smallest of overhangs, along with five other people. I looked out through the drizzle, over the traffic moving around Logan Circle to where banners hung outside the Franklin Institute of Science, another warm and solid building filled with fond childhood memories.

I had no fond memories of standing in the rain shivering, but there I was. Needless to say, I was the only nonsmoker in the group, but I remembered times I would have been puffing through the raindrops, too. That didn't make it more pleasant to shiver and stamp my feet while Meredith Arbusson lit up and silently inhaled and exhaled a few times before she said, "How are your wedding plans coming along?"

"Not so well."

"Are you cold?" she asked, as if surprised.

"No," I lied. "I'm fine." I was on the verge of teeth-chattering. I hadn't expected the drop in temperature and wasn't dressed for it. But Meredith Arbusson's expression of incredulity suggested that she found the environment bracing and exhilarating as would any woman of character. I thought warm thoughts and tried to stop goose bumps from forming. "But I'm afraid that we—"

"You don't have a place, now that we've pulled the rug from under you, is that it?"

"Oh, no, I didn't mean—" But I did mean. I meant to prey on her sense of guilt. If I could have arranged for a trio of sobbing violins to stand behind us, I would have done that, too.

She blew a ragged smoke ring into wet air. "Philip isn't to know about this, right? This is between you and me."

"You make Philip out to be such a Puritan, but he seemed sweet."

"Philip? After the way he practically gagged me when we were talking?"

"Oh, he didn't, not really. He just seemed uncomfortable . . ." Tell me, I mentally signaled her. Finish the sentence he interrupted that day. Pathetic when you're relying on telepathy when for all I know, thought-beams might be water soluble and would fall to the cement without reaching her.

"Many things make Philip uncomfortable. He's an old dear," she said, "but he's peculiar when it comes to talking about people. He calls it gossip. Isn't that funny?" She snorted, cigarette smoke coming out of her nose. Then, with a final drag, she looked at me and smiled. "I call it talking." She dropped the cigarette and stepped on it, then carefully picked it up and put it in her pocket. "I do not litter."

I smiled back, hoping we'd now go find a warmer, drier spot.

No such luck. Meredith lit up again and took a lengthy drag, looking at the cigarette in her hand while she exhaled and then inhaled again. She apparently smoked packs too quickly to read the Surgeon General's warnings on them. But how could she believe her husband didn't know about this habit? Were there binge smokers? Did she only smoke when volunteering at the library? Was that in fact why she volunteered in the first place?

"The good news about Philip," she finally said, "is that he's a man of great honor. The bad news is that it means when someone else behaves without honor, it pains and distresses him." She glanced my way, and then looked at her cigarette—only half was left—with a wistful expression. I sensed that a third smoke was on the way. "I gave them up, you see," she said. "I promised my daughter and Philip, of course, that I would stop this. I know it's a bad habit, and . . ."

"When was that?" I asked.

"Sunday. We went out to lunch after we made the arrangements at The Manse, and . . . Philip would surely consider this a breach of honor. I promised, you see, and what makes him most uncomfortable is a betrayal of trust. Especially with people that you, well . . . trust." She seemed lost in contemplation of her own hand and the burning cylinder in it. "The bad news is, he considers talking about the breach of trust as gossip. It isn't the easiest thing on earth being married to an honorable man." She exhaled and laughed. "Not that I'm recommending a dishonorable one, you understand."

And right then, between puffs of smoke that must have muffled them, my intense telepathic messages hit their target. "What were we talking about when he went into his Grand Inquisitor mode?" she asked. "The wedding? The funeral?"

I tried to look as if I needed to think back. "About . . . I think—yes, we were talking about the missing—about Tomas's sister, and whether she was alive or dead, and you were upset about the way the family, well, not Mr. Severin senior, had treated—"

"See, that's precisely what I mean. Philip has never gotten over that disappointment. It had nothing to do with his working life, and in truth, we weren't all that close with the Severins, not even while Philip was his number two man, but even so, even so . . . He felt it was such a display of weakness on Tomas Senior's part, it was as if his friend had presented himself wearing one face, and then had revealed that it was only a mask. The reason he doesn't want me talking about it is because it still makes him uncomfortable. He doesn't want to think about it, but, my goodness, if more people would have spoken up, have dared to speak up to Her Highness—"

"Mrs. Severin?"

"Ingrid, yes. The czarina of fashion, of What Is Correct and

What Is Not. Nobody dared to say anything if they wanted to be a part of that world. And Tomas Senior doted on her. He was much older than she was, and he treated her like a pet, or a toy. Indulged her and turned away from evidence of how cruel she was to her daughter. I finally said something, but only after Philip had decided to leave the firm. It was time to go off on his own, which he did, and I didn't care if I ever was part of that world again." She seemed satisfied with that, and might have ended the conversation, though I knew she didn't mind staying outside in this miserable weather because the longer we stood, the greater the opportunity for yet another cigarette. This one was down to a burn-the-fingertips nub, and she sighed and tossed it to the ground, repeating her careful grinding of it, and then retrieving it and putting it in her pocket.

"Do I dare ask what it is you said?"

She glanced at me, her eyebrows slightly raised. "Philip's nowhere in sight, is he?" She smiled to herself, obviously still relishing the memory of telling off the social dictator half a century ago. "I told her that her cruel style of mothering had gone out with fairy tales and even then it had been stepmothers, not birth mothers, who behaved that way. To treat one child as if he's perfection and the other—well, it wasn't Cinderella because the girl didn't have to sweep fireplaces, but it was something akin to it. An inside-out Snow White, maybe, with the beautiful queen fearing a nonrival. Not that she actually poisoned Shippy."

"Her name was Shippy?"

"Sigrid, actually. Ingrid and Sigrid. Cute, yes? She was supposed to be a little Ingrid, a tiny clone. Her crime was that she wasn't. The story goes that Tomas called her by her monogram—S.S., which apparently was on just about everything she wore or touched. He called her the 'S.S. Sister,' and that was thought to be quite darling, because everything he did was overpraised. But 'S.S. Sister,' of course turned into 'steamship' first, and then ship and thus to Shippy, which stuck. And you're probably wondering what Ingrid said back to me, right?"

I hadn't been, but it seemed rude to admit, so I nodded.

"You've met her, so you know how imperious she is. So she straightened up and told me that I could raise my children however I chose to, and she would do the same, thank you. And that neither I nor my children were welcome in her house again. It was the very sound of freedom to me."

"What did Ingrid do that was so horrible, and why?" I asked.

She seemed to need to shake herself back into the present, and then she stood for a while, both hands in the pockets of her blazer, considering my question. "Why comes first," she finally said, "and you aren't going to believe this, but it's God's truth. Shippy's crime was being fat. And that is why she was treated like a prisoner. Shippy didn't fit Ingrid's image. She wasn't something adorable to trot out for visitors to see, which is to say, she wasn't a miniature Ingrid. She was, let's be honest, the worst you could be—unfashionable—at age two, and three, and five, and seven."

"That's it?"

"That was more than enough for Mrs. Chic, but the fact that her husband allowed it to be enough to exclude and punish makes it still worse. Philip, of course, is sure Tomas Senior didn't truly understand the extent Ingrid went to. Like starving the child, forbidding her to come to meals, firing servants if they gave Shippy food, except for the diet rations taken up to her room. And when nothing worked—the cook did sneak up food, or she somehow got it—they sent Shippy away. Now I know, I know—many children are sent to boarding school, and they grow up to be well-adjusted adults, but not that many children are banished, and that's what was done to Shippy, and she knew it. And she wasn't only sent to boarding school, but to fat farms, and fat-kid camps, and to psychiatric facilities. She ran away from just about every one of them, but she couldn't run home of course because they didn't want her, so she got into lots of trouble. Lived on the streets when she was a teen, selling herself in exchange for a place to stay."

"And her family?"

"Did nothing, except when notified of her whereabouts, they retrieved her and sent her away again." She looked at me, shrugged and said, "One more. And then I'll toss the rest of the pack and that will be it."

"Good luck," I said. "There are clinics if this doesn't work. Or those patches."

She nodded, rather impatiently, eager to get the next cigarette into her mouth. Once it was lit, and she'd had a major drag, she nodded again. "You're probably wondering why I know all this. I am not as much of a snoop as this sounds, but even though he was banned from the household, our son Benjamin is—make that was—a schoolmate of Tomas's, and so he'd come home with these stories about Shippy, all told from the official family point of view."

"Tomas went along with it all, I assume," I said, vaguely remembering something intimated along those lines on Sunday.

She nodded. "Why wouldn't he? He was the golden-haired darling. And then Tom Senior died, and we thought at least Shippy would be safe because we knew he'd set up a trust for the girl. He and Philip had talked about protecting the children, at least financially, so we knew about the trust. But it somehow got reinvested in stock that all but disappeared. Reinvested by son Tomas. Would have been worth millions. Many, many millions if the stock had stayed in the company."

My goose bumps were returning, and I still didn't know how the sad story of Shippy had any potential link with Tomas's death. "Do you think Shippy's dead?"

"I assume that. If for no other reason than that she wasn't at the funeral."

"But she was estranged—"

Meredith Arbusson nodded, almost impatiently. "Yes, yes," she said, "but I think she'd have come." She sighed and shook her head. "She'd have come, hoping that this time, her mother would speak to her, would acknowledge her. Might even accept her. She had this pathetic need that nothing seemed to squelch."

What huge amounts of pain Ingrid's self-centered worldview had created. "Had she tried before?" I asked.

"She sent letters and phoned. One day, when she was about

fifteen, she showed up at my house and asked to use the phone. I was in the room when she called. She was polite enough, but they were still quite annoyed and rude. Ingrid asked her if she was still fat. That was that, and Shippy disappeared again. There'd been a car, a friend, waiting outside. I didn't know what to do—to betray her trust by calling the police—and where would they take her? Her family wouldn't accept her. But I still feel guilty about doing nothing."

"What could you have done in that window of time?" I wondered whether the phone calls grew less polite as the years went by until they could have become the "you don't deserve to live" calls Tomas had described to Sasha. Maybe Shippy wasn't dead, simply elsewhere. A phone call could be made from anywhere.

I thought about Jay's reference to the skeleton in the Severins' closet. About legal cruelties. His ideas locked around this news of Skippy and felt a perfect fit.

"I assume she wouldn't exactly grieve at Tomas's death," Meredith said.

Would she rejoice? Would she actually cause it, and then finally receive a share of the family wealth?

Without my voicing it, Meredith tossed doubt on that tidy supposition. "Her father left her the obligatory one dollar, and nothing more, and Tomas accepted that situation when he took the helm. She reappeared once again that I know of. There were probably other times I didn't know about. But she phoned me that time, because she had remembered me as being kind, she said. Imagine! What a sad commentary on how few friendly voices there must have been in her life. I put her up for a few days and gave her some cash, nothing enormous, and she called her mother and—well, this is incredible, but all Ingrid said was, 'How much do you weigh?' And Shippy still weighed too much, so Ingrid hung up. I just wanted to shake that woman, shake her till her skinny bones rattled. Her daughter—by the time she came to see me that time, she'd been married twice, both times to wretched men—the kind of terrible men a girl who doesn't believe anyone could ever love her would accept. She had nothing, nobody, not even a decent education. You should have seen her. She looked awful. I'm not talking about her size, but about her skin, her hair. She looked unhealthy, which she probably was."

"Did she try to reach her brother?"

Meredith Arbusson nodded. "He refused to see her, too. And worse, refused to part with even a fraction of his fortune. I made her ask about the trust, and he informed her that the holdings were now virtually worthless. That the trustees had felt the company's stock was too 'risky' at the time, and converted the shares into investments in other stocks that, alas, didn't work out. I say he looted it, but she didn't have the wherewithal to take him to court, and you know that Philip wasn't going to let me get involved as some kind of third party. I did talk to her about getting counseling, and . . . she left. I never heard from her again."

"I take it that she isn't likely to be inheriting from Tomas," I said.

Meredith Arbusson twisted her mouth. "Miracles happen," she said, "and she probably could make a claim based on that looted trust fund—if she had it sufficiently together to think it through and hire a lawyer. Otherwise . . . seldom do selfish people miraculously give away their money, and I don't think he'd leave her any because he didn't have to."

An echo of Zachary saying in essence the same thing about the college tuition being withdrawn because the law didn't demand it. Apparently, Tom Severin didn't do anything generous unless the law compelled it. Which meant—he didn't do anything out of generosity.

"As odd as this sounds," Meredith said, "I always felt, at least on the few opportunities I had to be close to the situation, that Tomas was afraid of his sister." She glanced at me, as if to confirm how peculiar that was. "Guilt makes for strange relationships—and strange relatives, too!" She laughed at her joke more emphatically than I thought it deserved. "He knew what a rat he was, what a nightmare of a brother, what price his soul was paying for his mother's favor, and how grossly unfair it all was. It turns my stomach, but then I try to remember that I am grateful to the Severins for showing me how not to raise children." She looked at me. "I realized how easy it was to create a Tomas Severin, a boy who's handed everything, unjustly praised and adored, and taught that he can dump people like his sister when it's convenient. My children were also privileged, and I made it a point to help them have a focus in life that wasn't like Ingrid's, that wasn't shallow and self-centered."

"And you succeeded," I said, "judging by the daughter who's getting married."

"Yes," she said seriously. "She's a good soul, and so are her brothers. But we were supposed to be talking about your wedding, weren't we?"

"I meant to, but it's getting late. If I could phone you if I really get stuck, I'd appreciate it. I won't do it often, I promise!"

"Are you organizing your own wedding, the way my daughter is?" she asked.

I felt a whine begin in me. The lament of how I wanted to be in charge, how I did not want the overblown circus that was being forced on me, how I was barraged on a daily basis—

I stifled it. I was tired of feeling whiny and oppressed. "Yes," I said, and I knew that this time, I meant it. I felt calm about it all for the first time. "Yes, I am. We are. My fiancé and I. It's going to be precisely the way we want it."

"Good for you," she said. "Don't let anybody push you around. It's your wedding, not theirs."

"Thanks," I said. "It's been a treat talking with you."

She pulled another cigarette out of her pocket.

"Have a lovely time at your lovely daughter's wedding," I said.

"And you, at yours," she answered. I watched her inhale, exhale, smile, and nod. "After all," she said, "it's your—"

"Big day," we said in unison.

In the land of the bride, cliché is king.

Twenty-one

Ozzie's office—our office—was only a few blocks away, across the Parkway, and for the short walk, I mentally sorted and filed, and tried to organize everything I had ever heard from any source that might pertain to the Severin family, and more precisely, to the skeleton in their closet, the sister who didn't bark in the night. Shippy Severin.

She was nowhere and everywhere and too central to ignore, but I needed the advanced geometry that led to her and away from Zachary, and I needed some reason to believe it existed.

I walked in the rain, considering what this could mean. The one thing I knew about her habits was that she made phone calls and Tomas Severin had been upset about phone calls from someone whose voice he almost recognized.

And? And then?

I needed a whole lot more before I'd dare try to sell the idea of Shippy Severin to the police, or even to my one ex-cop himself. At the moment, everything about her was invisible, unknown—and omnipresent.

I walked upstairs to the office, glad to be out of the rain and looking forward to a respite of methodical clerical work that required minimal thought, routine actions.

And I would have done that. I'd settled in at the desk with a cup of hot water, and one of the tea bags I now kept in my desk, and I'd gotten as far as booting up the computer, when somebody knocked on the door.

Ozzie happened to be nearby, refilling his coffee cup with the house sludge. "What is this with you lately?" he growled. "This used to be a nice, quiet place."

Right, I thought. Two knocks in two weeks. A regular madhouse.

Ozzie returned to his pebble-glassed-in cubicle, not bothering to consider the possibility the person wanting entrée might also want him. After all, it wasn't pizza-delivery time yet.

I opened the door and beheld none other than Sasha Berg dressed in shaggy sheepskin against the elements—the Himalayan elements. Someone small and encased in a black hooded raincoat stood behind her. I must have stood there a beat too long, because Sasha, her Sherpa guide hood dripping onto her nose, raised her eyebrows. "Aren't you going to let us in?"

I opened the door wider. "Sure, but—what are you doing here?"

"The secretary at your school said this is where you'd be, and we spent all afternoon right around the corner, practically, at the Four Seasons, no less, m'dear, so I thought—"

By this point, she was inside, shaking her ankle-length sheepskin out. Turned right-side out, the way the sheep had worn it, would have kept more water off her. "This is Nina Severin," she said. The little woman pulled off her hood.

I recognized her from Ingrid Severin's house. That did not,

however, explain why Tomas Severin's final wife—the woman Sasha had told me screamed at her over the telephone—and the woman he'd been dating when he died would be socializing, let alone come a-calling on me together.

"Please t'meet you." Nina Severin's words seemed to swim more slowly than her lips moved. I had obviously been less memorable than she'd been that day at Ingrid's.

"I'm sorry there isn't a comfortable place to sit. Most people don't actually come here."

"I've seen detective movies," Sasha said. "Damsels in distress come in, state their problems, hire the shamus, and get him in trouble."

Nina nodded agreement. Her head seemed loose on the neck, and I wondered how much the two women had had to drink before deciding to drop in on me.

"When we're in reruns," I said, "and we return to the nineteen-forties, I'm sure foot traffic will increase. These days, most communication is done via phone or e-mail."

Sasha poked me. "Don't be such a stick. I wanted to see the place, and if I waited for a formal invitation . . ." She wandered, as much as one could, through the room, detouring around the empty, standard-issue desks and running a finger along the front of the steel file cabinets. She even paused to inspect the potted plant that in its shock at being in Philadelphia, and worse, in our negligent hands, had grown into a tough, straggly specimen, a sort of street-smart palm.

"Although," Sasha drawled, "now that I have seen this place, I can say with assurance that it ain't much. Goodwill discards plus computers. The new noir?"

The widow Severin giggled, then clapped her hand to her mouth.

"Is there some way I can help the two of you?" I asked.

"Didn't you get my phone message?" Sasha smoothed her blouse, a candy-striped semi-transparent number that looked as if it had last seen the light of day when Eisenhower was president.

The petite woman wandered off to the corner, to put her raincoat on the clothes tree. "I got word that you had phoned," I said.

"Aha!" she said, as if that sufficed.

"I wish you'd actually leave a message when you leave a message. I was in a terrible rush, and I had no idea what—"

"It was about her," she said, jerking her head in the direction of Nina Severin. "It wasn't like I wanted to blurt it out to some stranger. And that particular stranger, your secretary, didn't sound that bright a bulb in the first place."

"She isn't. What about her?"

"The secretary?"

"No—her." Sasha's "her" was now approaching my desk, smiling. She raised her eyebrows and pointed to a chair, Mackenzie's chair, actually, and I nodded and invited her to sit down. Sasha carried over a small bench that had been near the clothes tree.

"How can I help you?" I asked again.

"We're here to help *you*," Sasha said.

Nina Severin's smile was wide and joyous. Talk about a merry widow. But she had every reason to be jolly, given her estranged husband's abrupt demise. Instead of her plummeting into reduced circumstances, he'd plummeted into death and left her with all the money and no philandering husband. What could be better? No love lost—but he was.

If only Nina had been anywhere near the school last Monday. You didn't need to be large to push somebody down the stairs. Of course, there was the question of Severin's cracked cheek . . .

The widow Severin sighed expansively, then looked at Sasha, and giggled. A merry widow and a happy drunk.

"Nina was kind enough—or brave enough—to phone me," Sasha said. "She felt . . ."

"Bad," Nina said with an explosion of sound, as if "bad" were a rare, precise, and dangerous word. "I felt real *bad*."

I waited, nodding encouragement.

"She'd been understandably upset, as"—Sasha leaned over and touched the smaller woman's shoulder—"anybody would have been!"

They'd obviously bonded, but that didn't clear much up for me.

"I was rude," Nina Severin said. "Ruuu-ude!"

"To whom?"

"To Sasha! Just because she was dating my husband!" The sound waves she produced boomeranged back through the alcohol fumes and Nina exploded with laughter. "Hah!" she shouted. "That didn't sound right, did it, but he was *always* dating somebody else. The man was engaged to somebody else while he was still married to me, for God's sake. But when he was dating Sasha, he was cheating on the person he was cheating on me with and dumping me, too—that really made me mad."

"I can only imagine." If I wanted stories like this, there was always daytime TV. I could feel my smile hardening and becoming painful.

Sasha must have noticed. "That's why Nina called and suggested we have a drink at the Four Seasons."

"To apologize," Nina said. "I'd been rude on the phone." Then she smiled at me, and I could picture her in school, a good fifth-grader, handing in neatly written assignments, and beaming the same self-satisfied happiness upon her teacher. "I called her a bitch."

"An English bitch," Sasha said with great glee.

I did the teacher thing. "Thanks so much. I love hearing about people doing the right thing. Thanks for going out of your way to tell me about that. But now, I've really got a lot of—"

Nina frowned. "It wasn't out of our way. We were just over—"

"When Nina was apologizing," Sasha said, "she explained how she tended to make phone calls when she was upset, and she feels—"

"Bad," Nina said. "Real bad."

"—about several of the calls."

"He made me really angry," Nina said. "Grrrrrr! You understand that, don't you? He was not a good man, or a nice man. Sometimes I think about the twins, and I realize their father's dead, and that's scary and sad for them, kind of, but you know what? They barely ever saw him. It's going to take a long, long time before they notice that he hasn't been around."

"The phone calls, Nina?" Sasha prompted.

"Oh, yes. I called Ingrid and told her what a bad mother I thought she'd been, and how spoiled her son was. But she doesn't understand half of what's going on, so that might be why she listened so calmly. And one time, that pill Penelope—that's what I call her, Penelope the Pill—she picked up the extension and told me I was a disgrace." Nina giggled again. "I think she listened in a lot of times."

"You called a lot?"

"I did it . . . a few . . . I made—I don't know how many times I called."

"And?" Sasha prompted.

She could have filled in the gaps herself and moved this process along, but then, she was the person who left messages that said nothing. She probably loved the suspense. "Remember?" she now said. "We decided to come tell Amanda because she's trying to help figure out what happened to Tom."

"Oh. Tom. Right. Well, there was this bad week," Nina said. "I was upset. Tom had moved out, so I invited my brother to come over and he told me really bad things Tom and Ingrid had done. Things I hadn't known. And I guess we had too much wine with dinner."

We waited. "And?" Sasha and I finally said in unison.

"We got a little crazy and we both called him and said bad things and I'm ashamed of myself because now he's dead. And we . . . well, we did it more than one time."

"Tom? You phoned your husband—" She was the phoner? The one thing I was sure of—I'd thought—was that the mysterious Shippy had phoned her brother.

"My brother, really. He did the talking to my *estranged* husband who was cheating on the person he was cheating on me with, you remember. And in other ways, he had cheated other people, too."

"I remember. Did you—did he—say something you're sorry about?" I asked.

She nodded solemnly. "We phoned a couple of times. With Tom gone, Jay came over a lot." She shrugged, as if making crank calls followed coming over as the night did the day. "Mostly, Jay talked, but sometimes I'd do this—" She lowered her voice. "Do you hear me?" she asked in a deep tone that was obviously fake, but could confuse a listener. "It was—it was a prank," she said in her normal voice. "Just to scare him. Shake him up a little. He made everybody else miserable. Turnabout seemed fair."

The threatening calls were made by his brother-in-law and his wife? Wouldn't he recognize their voices? Or hadn't he spent much time with Jay at all and perhaps hadn't heard his wife's strange ability to sound like a bullfrog.

I felt too tired to revise my thinking, and instead had to squelch a rush of annoyance that this inebriated woman's confession messed up my only working theory. "What did you say to him, Nina?"

"Jay did the talking mostly," she reminded me.

"Fine. What did your brother say?"

"We lost our manners, I'm ashamed to say. That's part of why I feel so bad. That, and how I was with Sasha." Her turn to lean over and pat her new best friend's arm. "Anyway, it was prank stuff, nothing like a real threat."

Tom's final date, the other-other woman, sat near her, nodding support. Who had changed the rules of sisterhood? "You, Jay, whoever was talking, told him he didn't deserve to live," Sasha said quietly. "Right?"

Nina looked down at her hands, which were folded in her lap, and she sighed and nodded. "That was a terrible thing to say because then, he died. "But Jay told me such things about him. At first, we thought . . . but we didn't. We didn't . . . we didn't do what we could have."

"Which was what?"

"We didn't ask for anything. We could have. We could have promised not to tell people how he ripped off his own sister. How she deserved to inherit money but was homeless instead. Homeless!"

She was talking about blackmail. She and Jay hadn't blackmailed her husband, and that was her mark of pride.

"All we did was *tease* Tom about it. Make it clear we knew something about him, and that it was rotten."

"About what, Nina?"

"About the skeletons in his closet. About the ghosts of his past. About how we knew stuff, and he, well . . . he didn't deserve to live. And I think once we said that maybe we'd tell people what we knew. We didn't say anything specific. Just . . . once, I think, Jay said something like that the skeletons had come out of the closet before Hallowe'en."

I remembered his saying that at the nursery. He was obviously quite fond of that turn of phrase.

Sasha looked at her. "What's it mean?" Then she looked at me. "He didn't say anything about that part to me."

Maybe the specifics of some of the calls—the ghost and skeleton ideas—had been too frightening, too private, too specific and potentially dangerous for Severin to share with Sasha. Maybe he would have told me about it, had he lived. Maybe, in fact, that's what he needed to talk about with someone.

"You mustn't berate yourself because of what happened afterward," I said. "The important thing is to move on." I meant it literally—I had things to do—and I meant it emphatically, but once again, someone knocked on the office door.

"People obviously come here all the time!" Sasha said. "You weren't telling the truth."

"You were leaving, weren't you?"

"Are you kidding? This is as good as a late-night movie. I want to see who comes in next, and why."

I didn't bother to protest. It still wasn't pizza-delivery time, so I didn't even look in the direction of Ozzie's frosted door, but went to open the door.

"Good!" Carole Wallenberg said. "You're here. I was hoping—"

"What is this," Nina asked, "a Tom's old wives convention?" Then she looked at Sasha and said, "Sorry! I don't mean to leave you out or anything . . ."

With great relief, I saw Zachary behind Carole. He wasn't locked up. They hadn't believed him, at least not enough to charge him with the crime. Not yet. "Come in, please. Both of you."

"I'll phone you later," Carole said. "This is obviously a bad time. You're busy. Besides, it isn't urgent. Everything's okay for now. I only wanted to explain. I was a little over the top earlier."

"I told you that you don't have to explain anything." Zachary looked and sounded sullen. "You shouldn't."

"Don't go," I said.

"It isn't me, is it?" Nina asked from her chair. "Don't tell me you're leaving because of me? Be angry with Brooke, if you need to be angry with anybody, but not—"

"Who is Brooke?" I felt as if I was "it" in an obscure game, the object of which nobody had told me.

"Tom's wife after me," Carole said.

"Before me," Nina said. "So I never knew you or did you any harm, Carole, and you know it."

It was fascinating watching Nina wind herself up into a fury based on nothing, a petite tornado packing massive destructive power.

Carole's nostrils flared. "I never said—"

"Really," Nina said, "if you think about it, we're family. One big family. My twins are Zachary's half brother and sister. Think about it! Not that you've ever acknowledged that." Nina's whirlwind imploded, and she was almost visibly sliding down an alcohol slicked route into profound self-pity. "You never brought Zach over to meet them, you—"

"Who ever invited us, who ever remembered, I wasn't—"

"Mom!"

"Jeez." That from Sasha, who probably didn't have a clue as to what was going on, but who'd lost her buzz and glow. "Maybe we ought to—"

"As if I were a floozy, just because he'd been married before—"

"And married still when he met you, don't forget!" Carole shouted. "And why are you here, anyway? The police didn't haul you off!"

"Mom! They didn't haul me—I called them."

She wheeled to face her son. "As if I could forget that stupid fact!"

"I'm here because my new friend Sasha thought I should tell Amanda—"

"And I'm here to talk to her, too. This isn't all about you, Nina."

"Okay, everybody. Stop it! One person at a time and no—" I wasn't shouting, and I was proud of being able to control the urge to shout, but I needn't have been, because shouting might have been effective—I surely wasn't.

"What were you going to tell her?" Carole demanded.

Nina sat farther back in her chair. "I already told her, and I don't have to tell you anything. Certainly not if you use that tone of—"

Sasha stood up to her full six-foot-plus-heels glory, her arms in their see-through candy-stripes spread wide. "People," she said. "*People.* This isn't a war zone. Nina came here to clear something up."

"What?" Carole demanded. Each of her sentences was followed by a mournful, "*Mom.*" Zachary sounded as if he was in hell. He'd been rejected by the police, which I was sure he saw as humiliating, and now his mother was committing the mega-sin of the parent of an adolescent: making a scene in public. He looked touchingly pitiable, a big, good-looking teen with a plaster cast on one arm, an expression of exquisite agony on his face, and body posture suggesting a desire for invisibility.

"I'll explain," Sasha said. "I got Amanda involved in all

this—in Tom's death—because he told me he'd been getting threatening phone calls."

"*Calls?*" Carole said.

"*Mom!*" Zachary's "Mom's" were a metronome failing to regulate her flood of words.

The note had said "Calls. Amanda Pepper." Maybe it was grammatical, after all. He was seeing me about the calls. But why the Philly Prep part?

"What's this with the calls?" Carole said, once again ignoring her son. "My son does nothing—nothing!—and the police question him and—and you made calls?"

"If you'd listen for once . . ." Even with her arms now lowered, Sasha was sufficiently commanding to cut short Carole's tirade.

I told myself to be considerate, to understand how distraught Carole Wallenberg was, but understanding why something is happening doesn't necessarily make the event bearable.

"Everybody's upset," Sasha continued, "but nobody's blaming anybody else for anything." She turned to me. "Are there more chairs? It'll feel better if we're all sitting down."

She had a future in mediation. "I'll get them," I said. Every Tuesday evening, Ozzie had a poker game at the office and the table, chairs, and chips were kept always at the ready. My visitors fell oddly silent while I retrieved two chairs from the utility closet. Sasha had somehow convinced them that nothing would or could proceed until everyone was properly in place.

I unfolded the chairs, with Sasha directing, saying, "There. Put that one right there, so nobody trips over anybody else." Zachary and his mother sat down while I returned to my desk chair and realized that we'd formed a rough circle. I thought this was clever of Sasha except that I didn't feel so much part of a round table discussion group as part of a kindergarten class, and I had nothing to show-and-tell.

Carole cleared her throat. "I came here to explain, and now's as good a time as ever because I want to get this over with. Finished. Chapter closed."

"Mom!" Zachary said. "Not now. Not with other people—"

"I already told the police, so what difference does it make who else hears? I'm not ashamed about anything I did." She folded her hands across her chest and looked like somebody who was profoundly ashamed and badly braving it out.

"What?" I finally had to ask. "What is it you want to say? Feel free."

"Zachary wasn't telling the truth," she said. "About what he did to his father. But you knew that."

"I thought so and hoped so," I said. "And I certainly hope you have a way of proving that."

"I did. I do. I told the police, which is why they kicked Zach out." She paused, looking defensive and satisfied. And Zachary definitely looked as if the police had humiliated him by not believing he was a killer.

"And, ah, you told them . . . about . . . ?"

She might have responded, but at that moment, the door opened, this time without benefit of a warning knock. All heads swiveled to see Mackenzie. "I interrupt something?" he asked. "Group therapy? A séance?"

"This is C. K. Mackenzie," I said to the group. "I work for him, after school. He's the actual licensed PI."

"He's also her fiancé," Sasha murmured, though I wish she hadn't. The women, even warring Nina and Carole, called time out to consider Mackenzie for a moment, then toss me an appreciative look. I'd done well in the mate-hunting sweeps.

"This is Nina Severin, the late Tomas's widow," Sasha said, "and this is Carole Wallenburg, the late Tomas's first wife, and their son, Zachary. You know me, so that about does it."

Mackenzie's got a fine poker face, even when there's no game on. Not as much as a blink when Zachary was named, though here was the very problem he'd promised to "work on."

"Carole was explaining why Zachary's confession wasn't—"

"Confession! He didn't do it!" Carole Wallenburg was back to full-speed and full-volume. "You have to have something to confess—it was a fabrication. A well-intentioned dumb lie; he was protecting me, he thought, but a dumb lie all the same."

Mackenzie glanced my way. "Join us," I said. "I'll get you a chair."

He knew perfectly well where the chairs were, but I was sure he'd follow me over to the closet, where I could do a quick fill-in about Shippy Severin.

He did follow, but before I could whisper a word, he spoke softly and quickly. "They're here, Manda."

"Obviously." I tilted my head toward the group. "But they won't be long. As soon as—"

"Not them. The Mafiosas."

"No. Not for three more—"

"Nonetheless, they're here, waiting for us. At our home. It appears there is panic in the land, fear that you and I are not giving sufficient attention and gravitas to the issue of our future, to our life together, to—"

"The shower isn't till the end of this week. They said they weren't getting here till Thursday."

"They consider this an emergency. They consider their little convention an intervention. For your own good."

"Before they have me committed?"

"Think of it this way. It's a sign we won't have in-law problems. Our mothers are getting along famously. They colluded. They plotted. They planned this. All of that without a single sour note. Not many families can make that claim."

"Did you know? Were you in on—"

"Absolutely not. My mother phoned me when her plane landed an hour ago, and she'd already hooked up with Bea, and Beth was en route to the airport herself."

"Beth knew." Ambushed by my sister. "But not now—I can't possibly—"

He nodded again. The room wasn't all that large, and we'd been moving, slowly, back toward the circle as we spoke.

"And what do you have here?" Mackenzie whispered. "It's very Nero Wolfe-ish, isn't it? You've gathered the suspects—"

"They gathered themselves."

"Are you ready to point the finger yet?" Mackenzie beamed a

guileless smile at me and set up his folding chair, joining our circle. Actually, he had no choice. Our desks were out here, so the chances of his getting any work done while the show-and-tell circle carried on an arm's length away were nil.

"Should we bring you up to speed?" I asked.

"If you weren't doing that, then what were you whispering about back there?" Sasha demanded.

I smiled at her and didn't answer and hoped she interpreted that to mean something wild and sexy. I hoped even more that she didn't know the Marriage Mafiosas had descended because I hoped she hadn't been part of their conniving. "First," I said, "Nina came here with Sasha because she thought we should know she and her brother made the phone calls Tom found worrisome."

"You made them?" Mackenzie asked. "You could have saved a lot of legwork and time if you'd—"

Nina looked down at her hands again, a chastised little girl. Then she looked up and shrugged. "What does it matter? That's all we did. Stupid crank calls, like in junior high. Big deal, big deal . . ." Her eyelids were at half-mast, and she had the only semi-comfortable chair.

"We weren't talking about that anymore," Sasha said. "Carole was saying how Zachary—oh, you explain, Carole."

Her eyebrows rose in the center, and she looked under enormous strain, but Carole seemed determined. "You have to understand: I have never been as furious with Tom as I was a week ago," she said, "and I've been angry with him more times than I want to remember. But this time—his own son, his firstborn's college tuition, and he'd promised. He'd laid it down like a challenge, and it was so easy for him, petty cash for him, too. This was pure spite. Meanness. And right after he'd said all this, I saw a little notice in the paper about an award he was going to be given. For good works, and the article said something about his distinguished career, his patrician roots. It was like a slap in the face."

She looked as if she might orate on Tom's offense forever, she was so filled with its outrage, but to my relief, she stopped abruptly, and looked around as if seeing us for the first time, and when she spoke again, it was softly, with little inflection. "It made me want to do something—anything—to wipe the smug expression off his face. Not to kill him, for God's sake, but to make him feel the way he made Zachary feel—like dirt, like trash, like less than nothing. And right around then, Zach's piece about drugs had been published, and of course I'd seen it and read it as he wrote and rewrote it.

"I daydreamed about Tomas drugged, staggering down the street, vomiting, being incoherent and picked up or ignored as a drunk. I obsessed about it. It was the only revenge I could think of. And it seemed so easy to arrange. It's easy to make GHB in your own kitchen, and it was easy enough getting the makings, so I did it. I know it was wrong, and—"

"Really stupid to tell the police," Zachary said. "Now—"

"It's better than what you told them! At least mine was the truth. I've hired a lawyer. We'll see. I made it. I had it. I tried to meet him for lunch, because I knew he'd have a couple drinks and that would make the drug more powerful. But he had a date, couldn't. Didn't want to meet me anyway, to tell the truth, so I told him something. News that I didn't think he wanted to hear about . . . someone's whereabouts. Someone he was afraid of. He met me because he thought I knew more, but I didn't. Still, there he was. And that's all there was—I bought our teas and dropped the stuff in his, we talked awhile, and I went my way and he went his and I never saw him again. I knew he never drove into the city. Took the train, so he wasn't going to get behind the wheel and hurt someone else. Other than that, I had no idea where he'd go, but I hoped it would be embarrassingly public, that was all."

So much for the mystery of the drugged tea, and the whole cause and effect chain that was linked in my mind. There were no links, only an enraged mother out for a humiliating revenge.

And her son. "You knew?" I asked quietly of Zachary.

He swallowed and looked at his mother.

"I didn't think he possibly could," Carole said. "I never wanted him to. But he'd been looking for something—"

"The laptop," Zachary muttered. "I needed to use it."

"I'd taken it with me that day, and when he pulled it out of the backpack, he saw the chemicals. Never said anything."

"Until I heard—until afterward—I thought they were for some experiment in chemistry."

Which, in a way, they were.

"And then, when you put two and two together," Mackenzie said, "you—"

"Thought I'd killed his father!" Carole seemed astounded by this, although she'd quite blissfully admitted to drugging the man. "I would never—no matter what." Then she deflated somewhat. "I was careful with the dose, enough to humiliate, to disorient. I assumed he'd have had alcohol with lunch. I even figured that in. But I understand."

"And that's why the sudden confession," I said to Zach.

"I thought—once they knew about the drug, I thought—I'm a kid, I used to get in a lot of trouble, they'd go easier, they'd believe me. And if it didn't really make sense what I said, then they'd let me go and not look our way anymore. I mean, who was going to think of my mother?"

Deceitful, but clever, actually. He was a smart kid.

"Zachary, what actually happened?" I asked. "The absolutely true story this time."

"Like I said. I saw him go by, followed him in, found him in your room, thought—well, you know."

I wouldn't make him confess his hopes again, make him feel again the pain of his father telling him that his presence at Philly Prep had nothing to do with Zachary. Really, that nothing about his father had much to do with Zach.

But my mind did register the third part of Severin's message. Calls. Amanda Pepper. Philly Prep. And that Carole had told him somebody's whereabouts. The note started to make sense.

"He went out of the room," Zach said, "and I followed him,

and I kept trying to get him to talk to me, just talk to me, but he was acting strange—now I know why, but I didn't then. I thought he was drunk, and I guess that made me angrier. I said things, angry things, and he grabbed my arm and held it down while he lifted his other hand, like he was going to hit me, so I swung out—to protect myself, to push back his hand, but I used my free arm—and the cast, it smashed into his face, and he shouted and backed away and sat down, hard. I didn't know what to do—call an ambulance or what? But he shouted that I should get away from him, stay away from him, so I did. I left."

"Zach, I understand you said you heard shouting at the time. Did you mean your dad?"

Mackenzie astounded me. I was sure he'd dismissed and trashed that idea when I told him about it. I would love to be able to check out the filing cabinets in his brain.

Zachary shook his head. "Somebody else. Somebody downstairs shouting like 'What's going on? Who's up there?' You know, the regular stuff. That's why I took the back stairs, so they wouldn't see me." He was supporting the arm in the cast with his good hand, and he looked down at it, as if it had a life of its own.

"So Nina and Jay made calls," I said, trying to get a timeline.

"Do I have to tell the police?" Nina said.

"I will," I said. "And they'll probably get in touch with you, to verify it."

"That's *all* we did, though." She looked smaller and smaller with each word. "It was stupid saying things about skeletons, but we were angry. It was a bad time. He'd . . ."

"Dumped you. Everybody knows, Nina. And frankly, there's no shame in being dumped by Tomas Severin. But what do you mean by 'skeletons'?" Carole looked on alert. "What does that mean?"

"I don't know. It's only that I heard . . . my brother said . . ." She shook her head. "It doesn't matter."

"Maybe it does," Carole said. "Because on the phone, before we met, I told him I'd seen a ghost. A ghost he knew."

I thought about Carole's life, where she might have been. On campus, in the lab where she worked as part of her tuition grant. Carpooling. I thought about Tom Severin's note again.

"Ghosts and skeletons, oh my! Halloween's really in the air!" At least Sasha was having a good time.

I'd had it. "How about trying something new?" I asked. "How about if just this once, everybody told the truth? So far, not one person in this whole mess—not one!—has considered doing that."

"I never lied!" Carole said.

"I never even spoke to you before today!" Nina said, sitting back and hugging herself.

"Please! There are lies of omission, as everyone knows."

"That wasn't my fault," Sasha said. "Tom only talked about what I told you. No ghosts and skeletons, that's for sure."

"That figures. He was lying, too. He left out the part that really scared him. I thought you were telling the whole truth this time, Carole, but you left out the small detail of who—and where—your ghost was, didn't you?"

"I recognized her," she said. "Back when I was married to Tom, she tried to make contact. She recognized me, too."

"Who?" Nina sounded whiny, a cranky, sleepy child annoyed by the static around her. She yawned, and sighed, and closed her eyes.

"The skeleton in the closet, the ghost in the attic of Tom's mind," I said.

Twenty-two

"WHAT are you doing?" Mackenzie asked when I stood up.

"It's finally finger-pointing time." I nodded to him to come with me. "Call a taxi for Nina," I told Sasha. "She can't drive home in that condition."

"But you didn't—I—but who is—"

"What about us?" Carole demanded. "What's going on?"

"Beats me," Mackenzie said.

"If you'll give me ten minutes, you'll know. Everybody will. Even me."

We made our exit, ducking out while Carole said "Hey!" a few times, and Zachary did his "Mom" protest, but halfheartedly, as if he'd forgotten its purpose.

"What's going on?" Mackenzie asked as we descended the staircase.

"Mrs. Wiggins. She said she lived next door. That gives us two options—you take the left, I'll take the right."

"Who the hell is Mrs. Wiggins? What am I looking for? What do I do when I find her?" He stopped, and I nearly tripped over him. He put an arm on mine. "Tell me who she is and why I should care."

"She's the new secretary at school."

"What the—"

"No, wait. She's the reason Tom Severin came there, thought we'd be a good idea—not because of us, but because Sasha said where I worked. That's why the note said *Calls. Amanda Pepper. Philly Prep.* He thought I could verify what Carole had told him. I could do it for him, find out bad things about her, without his being directly involved. Who knows? He didn't want to face her."

"It's raining," Mackenzie said. "I'm standing out here in the rain because?"

"Mrs. Wiggins is—was—Sigrid—Shippy—Severin. His sister. Resurfaced. Ready, or so he thought, to make her claims again. Ready to tell the world about her rotten brother. That note they found on him—I thought the drawing was a doodle, a smile and a seven, but it wasn't. It was a little boat. A Shippy memo. Remember? Remember how everybody said he was afraid of her? Rightly so—he'd treated her so badly."

"She's here?"

"Next door. Whoever finds her, give a holler."

"And she's the killer," he said softly. "She was there, in the school. Lying about hearing nothing, seeing and knowing nothing—including not knowing the victim."

"I hope not." We both took off.

The building on the right was a sad yellow brick affair. The real estate agency on the first floor's windows were filled with cards listing homes, their edges curled, their photos faded and uninviting.

The entrance to the upstairs apartment was via an uncomfortably dark staircase, and I thought of Mrs. Wiggins trudging up these steps every afternoon. And yet it was better than the shelter had been. She'd found a job—the job nobody else wanted, perhaps, but still a meager living—and established a life of her own.

"It's got to be this one," Mackenzie said, taking the stairs double-time. "A cranky old man and woman live in the other one. In their eighties, I think, and they look as if they've been quarreling the last seventy-five of them."

I pushed the bell, but heard nothing.

"Broken?"

I knocked. We both took deep breaths. I smiled at the peephole, and the door opened. "Miss Pepper!" she said, her mouth agape. "What on earth? What are you doing here?" Then she saw Mackenzie and stepped back a pace.

"We're so sorry to bother you," I said. "But we have a few questions. They're important, or we wouldn't bother you. Do you think we could come in?"

"Oh." The blood drained from her face. "I don't think—it's such a—there really isn't—I don't even know this—no. No, I don't think so."

"You're right," Mackenzie said. "We're rude to barge in on you this way. We can talk out here, or right where we're standing."

Nice of him, particularly given the weather and the fact that her front door was not protected from the elements.

"Am I in trouble?" she asked in her rabbit-in-distress voice.

"Do you think you are?" he asked.

"I think maybe."

"Why would that be?"

She looked at me before answering. "Because Tomas died."

"Your brother," I said softly.

She nodded, then kept her gaze on her feet while she hugged herself.

"And you were there," I said even more softly.

This time, the nod was barely perceptible. Then she looked up. "I am in trouble, aren't I?"

"Not with me," Mackenzie said. "Not with anybody I know. Because you didn't do anything wrong, did you?"

"I tried not to."

"But you're afraid nobody will believe that it happened the way it did."

"I was in the—that was the truth, the way I said. I didn't see him come in. But when I came back to the office, I heard shouting. I was scared, but I called up and nobody answered and—I was still scared, but I went upstairs. He was there, all alone, but hurt. His face . . . he'd been hurt."

"He recognized you," I said.

She nodded, her expression bleak. "He got all crazy, no matter what I did. He was standing and kind of waving—I mean his body was waving, and he sounded different, but I hadn't heard Tommy in a long, long time. I thought he was drunk, to tell the truth. He said things about money, about how I shouldn't have come back because I wasn't getting any no matter what I said or who I told. I didn't know what he meant. I still don't."

I did. Ingrid's sanity and will were both still up in the air, up for grabs by Cornelius, so why not by Shippy. And Tomas was so guilt-ridden about his sister that he believed she was out to get him, as he'd "gotten" her. All that had been compounded by what he understood to be blackmail-like phone calls. Why not believe she was behind them?

"I wanted Tommy and my mother to talk to me again," she said. "I wanted them to see that I got myself straightened out. I had a good job again, and a place of my own, and I thought . . . even if I'm not . . ." She looked down at herself and said nothing for a moment. "We're all a lot older. People change, so I thought by now . . . I thought he'd be happy to see me. I'm his sister. But when I went toward him—he was crazy, talking crazy—I couldn't understand what he was saying, and he waved his arms like he could make me disappear and backed away. And then—and then—" She shook her head and inhaled.

"Try," I said. "It's important."

"He was too close to the stairs. They were right behind him, and he was going to fall and I shouted, and when I tried to grab him, to help him, he shouted 'Go away!' and took another step back and . . ." She shook her head. "I ran down after him, but then, I could tell. He wasn't moving. I got scared about what I'd done. I always have things come out wrong, and now—he wasn't moving. I went into the office and sat at my desk and put my head down. I didn't know what to do. And then I heard the scream. That was you."

"You didn't do anything," Mackenzie said softly. "You tried to help him."

I thought it through and it made sense. I remembered Liddy Moffat upset about scuff marks at the top of the stairs, wondering how they'd gotten there. Now I knew. If a man fell directly backward, his heels would leave those marks. But if pushed, he'd have been propelled away from that spot, wouldn't have left marks that close to the top.

"How about you put on a raincoat and come next door," I said. "You'll see our office and be warm."

"I guess I'm in big trouble."

I shook my head. "No," I said. "No, you're not." Apparently nobody was.

Nobody had killed Tomas Severin.

Nonetheless, everyone had played a part in his death.

Jay Kress did a bit by sharing the stories the "old" lady at the shelter, Shippy Severin Wiggins, had told him. He probably thought the stories were going to give Nina and him leverage against Tom during the divorce, insuring that it would be more generous than was Tom's wont. Nina did her bit by pouring the wine and deciding it would be fun to harass Tom with phone calls about skeletons from his past.

Carole played a double role by telling him outright that his sister was in town, at Philly Prep, and of course, by putting the drug in his system. She had no way of knowing how those two actions would interact and throw suspicion on her son.

Zachary himself did nothing except attempt détente, but in

the course of it, he'd walloped Tom's cheek in clumsy self-defense, further disorienting the man.

And finally, Sigrid Severin Wiggins, someone Tom had erased from his life—and bank account, and from what was legally and justifiably hers—tried to help him, tried to make contact.

Tomas got so twisted in his greed and guilt and anger—he hoisted himself on his own petard.

Tomas Severin had murdered himself.

And, worse, he had lived so that there were, if not outright pleasure, few regrets at his death.

Twenty-three

NERO Wolfe didn't have to face his perturbed mother after he'd solved a crime. Why then did I, did we?

We'd accomplished big things today—unraveled a tangled mess, sent Carole and Zachary home on a more even keel, and even talked to Shippy Wiggins about her future, which, apparently, might well contain some of the money that was rightly hers. And, I secretly hoped, a comfortable and speedy retirement from the secretarial desk at Philly Prep.

We deserved to bask. Instead, we had to face the music.

There are times I wish you really couldn't go home again, and this was one. But I had moved beyond whining and even beyond playing possum, and there was no turning back.

"We need a plan," I said. "A unified front. The definition of insanity is trying the same thing again and expecting different results. Let's try something completely new."

WE ENTERED HOLDING HANDS and smiling, and they smiled back. These were good women. Overenthusiastic, and overinvolved, but compared to mothers like Ingrid who saw her daughter as a fashion accessory, these mothers were perfection itself. They simply wanted us to be happy—wanted it a little too much.

And so we gave them a blueprint of how they could get their wish, to see us happily, blissfully married in the way that would delight us and presumably, therefore, fill them with joy as well.

"Friday?" they squawked, almost in unison. "This Friday?"

We nodded. "Friday. City Hall. There's time for the dads to fly in, too," I said. "Instead of a shower, we'll call it a wedding celebration party at Sasha's. She has the space, the food and wine, and the party spirit." I'd called her from the car. She thoroughly approved. So like that, my wedding color scheme was resolved: moss green, to go with the English gentleman's china.

"But—but—"

"It's what I've always dreamed of." I admit I was exaggerating. I'd dreamed of this—or dreamed it up—for twenty minutes at most, but in today's fast world, that's close enough to always. "We have three days to go crazy with whatever's left to plan. We can shop for my dress after work tomorrow. How's that?" I was ready to wear whatever their overdecorated hearts desired.

"And . . . your bouquet?" my mother asked softly.

"That, too. I'd love to know what you think would be best."

No lists, no haggling, no wedding consultant, no rented hall, no gown, no bridesmaids, no color scheme, no florist, no registry, no invitations. Just my beloved and our beloved—once they stopped organizing our wedding—family and friends. The people who mattered. The ceremony that mattered. The beginning of the rest of our lives.

Bliss.

"After all," I said, "we're only getting married once."

I took the words right out of their mouths. What else could they say except a variation of what we said that Friday: I do.

We did.

GILLIAN ROBERTS won the Anthony Award for Best First Mystery for *Caught Dead in Philadelphia*. She is also the author of *Philly Stakes, I'd Rather Be in Philadelphia, With Friends Like These . . . , How I Spent My Summer Vacation, In the Dead of Summer, The Mummers' Curse, The Bluest Blood, Adam and Evil, Helen Hath No Fury,* and *Claire and Present Danger.* Formerly an English teacher in Philadelphia, Gillian Roberts now lives in California.

Her website address is www.GillianRoberts.com—and she enjoys receiving fan e-mail at Judygilly@aol.com.